The
Kootenai
Lodge

Book Disclaimer

This book is a work of historical fiction. That means the story, characters, and events in it are mostly created from the author's imagination, although they are inspired by real places, people, and events from early 20th-century America. While some historical details and social conditions may be based on facts, they have been adapted to fit the story and may not be fully accurate.

Any characters, places, or events that might seem similar to real ones are purely coincidental and not intended to represent actual people or historical events. The author has made every effort to create an engaging and meaningful story while honoring the historical period.

This novel also deals with difficult topics, such as trauma, betrayal, and loneliness, which were common struggles for many orphans and immigrant children during this time. These elements are included to highlight the strength and resilience of individuals facing hardship and to help readers understand what life was like for vulnerable people during this era.

Finally, the views and ideas in this book are entirely those of the author, JK Worth. They are presented to support the story and should not be taken as factual accounts or representations of any real group or historical event.

Books by JK Worth

The Hungry Horse

Columbia Falls

The Kootenai Lodge

The Master of Counterpoint

Coming in 2025

Lying Awake in Whitefish, Montana

Kootenai: The Restoration

JK Can be reached at: jkworthauthor@gmail.com

On X: jk_worth

This book is dedicated to my "baby" sister PKW. She has more strength and courage than anyone I know. She is my hero and watching her fight her way through multiple cancers for fifteen years is an inspiration and a fight that I could never survive. She is cancer free and engaged to a wonderful man from England.

The Kootenai Lodge

By

JK WORTH

TWIN HAMMOCKS PUBLISHING, LLC

Miami, USA   2024

1

Some people seem to get all the breaks; most don't. Why is it that many of the things we want are bad for us, and many of the things we don't turn out to be exactly what we need? Everything in life is a choice. Yours or somebody else's made for you. This is the story of a young girl without options, without choices.

Carolina was born in 1905 in a small German town outside of Leipzig. She was orphaned the following year. She didn't know anything about her parents or family when she was put on a ship to New York by her "caretaker" in 1914. The name on her pinned tag was shortened to Carolina Augusta. The immigration authorities chopped it like so many other new arrival's names. Wilhelmine was erased from her records. Carolina never knew her full name, anyway; shortening it removed a mystery from her life. A Lutheran charity volunteer picked her up from immigration and took her to a church-run orphanage for the night. The next day, she was put to work in a large household in New York City. The lowest charwoman in the house, she was grateful to have a place to sleep and food to eat. She was only nine years old. War was on the horizon in Europe, so maybe her guardian in Germany had sent her away to protect her. She hoped it wasn't because he didn't want her.

The voyage to America was cold, wet and covered in a heavy veil of sea sickness and terrible odors. She was pretty for such a young girl. That made her a target for boys and even men much older than she was. Carolina was cautious when anyone tried to get too close. No one could be trusted since she was shipped off from her homeland. She already survived danger and betrayal more than any child at that age should.

Carolina was an enigma. The only thing she knew about herself was that she was born near Leipzig, Germany. There were no records of her birth or her family. Her caretaker had never claimed her as a relative. She was his servant girl. Her only possessions were her few clothes and an old violin.

Carolina was even more alone in America than in Europe. Vanquished to a foreign country and not sure what she did to deserve it.

She didn't make friends with the other nine servants. In the hierarchy or caste system of servitude, she was considered illegitimate. She was an orphan with no memory of her earliest years. She couldn't argue against it. She wondered if she was illegitimate. She had no family to lay claim. Not even a distant relative.

She loved music and would often sing quietly to herself to help survive her loneliness. She had an amazing ear and had been taught to read German, English, and music. She didn't remember having any teachers. Many things were blocked from her memory. Way too many. One thing she would never forget was her love of gingham fabric. She had one dress; it was dark blue and white. It was too large, but she didn't mind that. She would outgrow it, but not as quickly. Her hair was straight, dark brown, almost black-looking in the evening light. Her eyes were a brilliant blue color. Her face was perfectly shaped and gave her the air of someone from a much higher station. She carried herself differently than most grown women and the other servants noticed. There was an aristocratic sense to her natural and unrehearsed movements and grace. This had to be taught, or at least on display, for her to see and mimic. She would grow up to be a sophisticated and elegant woman, or so she dreamed. She was a Cinderella now; she thought about the tale that was old as time. This would just be a passing situation, and she was willing to wait patiently until her prince arrived and find respite in her private dream. Her "*liebestraum,*" as she called it.

Nine long years passed with barely an increase in her stipend. The "war effort" was a repeated excuse instead of a reason. The only significant increases were in her job description. She was constantly "offered" more responsibilities. The family knew she would be a senior staff member soon enough. They didn't allow her to leave on her one day off that was given every two weeks. They told her it was for her safety, but the reality was she was trapped by her low standing in life. Her low pay also kept her from saving enough money to escape and find work somewhere else. She was trapped in an economic prison. Now eighteen, Carolina was a beautiful young woman. She still wore the dark blue and white gingham dresses. The meager salary she earned was used to buy her some sort of happiness. An Edison Gramophone gave her joy. It was in the main salon, but she was not allowed near it. Her favorites were the violin concertos, symphonies and the grand organ fugues. She also was moved by the Irish tenor, McCormack. She could only hear fragments as she walked by during her workday.

One afternoon, while the family was away, a 24-year-old ice delivery boy named Friedrich Schmidt lured her to the basement ice storage bins with a plea for help with the doors. He claimed he didn't want to set the ice blocks on the floor in order to open the ice bins. She agreed. She had known him for a few years and saw him delivering ice often. He always smiled at her. They usually talked about Germany and Leipzig. He seemed like a nice young man, but this time would be different.

He came up behind her after dropping the block of ice on the floor. She turned around as he put his hand over her mouth to stop her screaming. Carolina was assaulted in the basement of her home by a man she trusted. Her uniform was ripped by her attacker. When he was finished with her, he warned her not to talk about it or he would come back and hurt her again.

2

Carolina fixed herself as best she could. She wasn't crying anymore; she was angry and in pain. The other women in the house were no help and treated her like she invited his advances. She put on a clean dress and headed to the door.

"Where do you think you're going? You're not allowed to leave."

"To report this to the police." She shot back. They couldn't stop her, and they knew it. This would bring shame to the house, and they would be stained by it too. She could care less. She was going to hurt her attacker by seeing him jailed.

The leers she received from the policemen frightened her all over again. When she told them her attacker's name, they asked her to give him a pass. "He served in the war. Give him a break. A short, little cop who knew him said while coming to his defense."

"I want him in jail!" she screamed.

The cops told her to go back home and think about it before doing anything rash. Carolina didn't need to think about it; she wanted him behind bars. Suddenly, she started to bleed, and now her blood was on the precinct floor. She needed to be in a hospital. The cops now seemed worried about her. They took her themselves. Two officers carried her the three blocks to the entrance and helped her onto a gurney. A nurse rushed her into an exam room. Carolina told her the whole story. This nurse would take care of Carolina and the useless cops. "My name's Clara, what's your name?"

"Carolina, Carolina Augusta."

Carolina thought of Clara Barton. She was the most famous nurse in the world. Founder of the American Red Cross and European nursing charities. To her, this Clara "Barton" was better.

They next day, she learned from Clara that her attacker had fled the city. She knew some of the cops and liked most of them. They gave her the information they had. He fled to Connecticut, where he had an uncle that lived in Hamden. The cops were shamed by Clara and by their own consciences. Schmidt would be on a ship to Europe before they could get him. He spoke fluent German and disembarked in Bremerhaven ten days later. The same port Carolina embarked from on her voyage to America. She hoped he would never return to New York. She was glad she moved to a different home. He wouldn't be able to find her.

Carolina couldn't stay in the hospital. She had little money. Clara decided to help her, and when her shift was over, she took Carolina home with her to recover. They stopped on the way to collect some of her things. The staff had set her possessions on the steps outside servant's entrance with a note that told her to never return. She didn't and never looked back. She stayed with Clara to recover and look for a new job. Clara would be helpful. She knew most of the women in the area from her hospital work and their volunteer work. They all had very large homes and always had staffing problems.

Carolina was bored with sitting in the small apartment all day. She felt better. It had been almost a week. She couldn't stay still any longer. She got dressed to leave and look for work and a way out of her predicament.   As she was leaving, Clara came in. "I have an appointment lined up for you tomorrow morning!" Carolina showed a smile on her face again.

"Who is it?"

"Mrs. Cornelius Kelley. I know her from the hospital charities. She is a smart and tough woman, but she is also very kind. She needs help with some of the bedrooms. They have quarters for you in the house."

"Thank you so much Clara; you are the best thing to happen to me in a very long time. I won't let you down. I promise."

Morning couldn't come fast enough for Carolina. Her appointment was at 10:00 and Carolina was ready by eight. She arrived early and loitered outside until one of the children saw her through the window and asked her who she was. "Are you our new nanny?"

"No, but I am here to meet Mrs. Kelley for a job in your beautiful home." She closed the window, went to the front door and let her in.

"You might as well wait inside; follow me."

Just as she came in, the butler stopped them both.

"What's going on here? Who are you?"

"I am here a little early for an interview with Mrs. Kelley and this young lady invited me in. I can wait outside; I didn't mean to barge in."

"Francis, you know better. It's my job to see who comes in and who goes out. Next time, I'll tell your father."

"Please, no. I'll be careful not to again." She meant it.

"My name is Johnson."

"My name is Carolina Augusta. I'm sorry for the commotion." She was worried that she sabotaged her interview.

"It's quite alright; please wait over here in the library." He escorted her in. "Mrs. Kelley will be down shortly."

Carolina followed Johnson into a beautiful wood paneled room. Its walls were adorned with thousands of books. It looked familiar to her, almost like she had been in a room like this before. The home she worked in until a week ago was large, but nothing of this magnitude. It did have a library, but after seeing this room, it looked like an imposter. Carolina was looking at all the interesting things in the room when she quickly stopped. She didn't want to do anything inappropriate, especially after her run-in with Johnson. She sat down, look straight ahead and mentally prepared for her interview.

Mrs. Kelley was a full-figured woman and mother. The Kelleys had five daughters. That was enough for Mr. Kelley. They both gave up on the boy he always wanted. He loved his daughters very much and Mrs. Kelley even more. They were a happy couple and a wealthy family. They were both hardworking and the payout was visible all around them.

Johnson opened the door and showed her in to meet Carolina. "Good morning, my darling; my name is Mrs. Kelley." She spoke very calmly but with command and kindness. Clara's description was spot on. "Thank you for meeting with me on such a short notice. One of my girls left unexpectedly to be with her sick mother." Louise left early yesterday morning to travel back to England. Mrs. Kelley bought her ship's passage, gave her $200, and had her driver deliver her to the pier. She also gave her a proper suitcase instead of the canvas shoulder bag she had stuffed with everything she owned. A few dresses were rustled up from the back of the girls' closets. They would give her a lift in status. Nobody knew about this generosity except for her secretary and Geoffrey, her driver. They understood the rules of the wealthy. No talking about the family's affairs and no gossiping, ever!

"Oh, I'm sorry to hear that. I understand if this is a temporary situation." Carolina said with a little letdown in her voice. She stopped her negative thoughts and decided to be the best upstairs housekeeper Mrs. Kelley every had. She would make this temporary job permanent.

"It's not temporary unless you're not capable. We'll both know soon enough." This made Carolina happy. She liked Mrs. Kelley and felt safe and secure in her home. Although she couldn't put the assault behind her, it carried less fear for the future and she hoped, maybe fewer nightmares.

"Tell me about yourself, Carolina Augusta."

She loved the way her name rolled off Mrs. Kelley's tongue.

"That's a very regal name, you know. Princess Carolina Augusta was a well-known beauty among the royals. Austrian, I think. Were you named after her?"

"I don't know. When I arrived in New York, they shortened my name. They removed Wilhemine. I know that wasn't my last name. I never knew my mother or father."

"I'm so sorry." Mrs. Kelley thought back to her own wonderful childhood and her parents' love for her. She knew she was more fortunate than most, even at a young age.

"Where were you born, honey?"

"Leipzig." She didn't tell her it was in a small farm village outside of Leipzig. She didn't want to be thought of as provincial, especially inside a home of this grandeur.

"You're German?"

"Yes, Ma'am, I am."

"Your English is perfect. Do you speak German well?"

"Yes, I do. A little French, too."

"Clara told me you worked for Mrs. Bradbury. I don't know the family. Why did you leave?"

"It wasn't because of the quality of my work. I, I, I'd rather not tell you right now. It was a personal matter with one of the male workers."

"I understand; we can leave it at that."

Mrs. Kelley was relieved that she didn't have to talk with Carolina about her problematic "love life." She didn't want that sort of thing introduced into her household or for her daughters' consumption.

Carolina was relieved that she didn't have to relive her tragedy. She was still suffering some physical and also immense emotional pain. She knew she was tough, but was surprised at how her life had been broken to pieces by this assault so easily. She knew that she would survive. She also knew that someday, her attacker would be judged and convicted. She believed that eventually, your deeds catch up with you. The thought of him facing the consequences gave her a little solace.

"I've heard enough. You come highly recommended by Clara and sitting here talking with you, I can tell you are intelligent and not afraid of hard work. Adversity always creates a grateful and hard-working person. Can you start right away?"

"I would like to start today, Ma'am. I don't want to overstay Miss Clara's hospitality."

"Consider it done. Johnson will meet with you to discuss your compensation and the rules of the house. He will show you to your room and introduce you to the staff when they dine this evening. I will introduce my daughters to you tomorrow. I think they will like you. My oldest is studying German and music." She leaned in and whispered. "Between you and me, she could use your help with her German."

"I can help with her music, too. I studied music in Leipzig." She didn't remember any lessons, but assumed she must have.

"Aren't you just full of surprises?"

"Johnson."

"Yes, Mrs. Kelley." He was standing outside the door.

"We have a new staff member. Could you find time this afternoon to orient her to the things she needs to know? She will stay tonight and start in the morning. We will need someone to gather her things from Clara's home."

"Clara?"

"You know Clara from the hospital. Carolina comes highly recommended by her." Mrs. Kelley turned to Carolina and winked."

"Very well, then. If you two are finished…"

"We are. It was very nice to meet you, Carolina. Johnson will get you settled in."

"Follow me, Miss Carolina."

"Thank you, Mrs. Kelley. I will make you happy you hired me."

"I'm easily fooled, darling; you'll have to convince Johnson." She gave her another wink. As another woman, she knew that meant to stay on Johnson's good side, but that she was the boss of this house.

3

Carolina's orientation with Johnson went well. He seemed fair but firm. He would not stand for gossip or drama, vulgar language, lying or drinking of alcohol. Mrs. Kelley hated alcohol. Mr. Phillips had a liking for Scotch. It was an expensive habit. Not the cost of the Scotch. It was the cost of the deal he made. They had reached a truce by supplying her love of expensive art with the money it devoured. He later recalled that he gave his wife an unlimited budget to pay for her artwork. He also quipped that she found a way to exceed that budget. He didn't care about the money; they had way too much. He thought it was funny that his wife didn't drink but she loved to gamble. They even had a Roulette Wheel in the game room. During parties, she was known to run the games of chance.

She met most of the staff at dinner. She liked them a lot more than Mrs. Bradbury's brood. She also liked that none of them knew what happened to her last week. She didn't know that Johnson was friends with Mrs. Bradbury's "man." He knew all about it and now Johnson did. Johnson picked up Carolina's last remaining belongings from the Bradbury house. Nothing much, just toiletries. He wouldn't normally handle such a lowly task, but this trip had two purposes. The second was to do a sort of background check on Carolina. He didn't do it because of anything Carolina did or said. He did it because of his loyalty and concern for his employer. He was glad Carolina didn't tell Mrs. Kelley about her rape. That fell under the drama category to Johnson.

Carolina received a very good recommendation. Johnson was glad he checked her out. He would keep her secret and welcome her. His next stop was at Clara's apartment to gather her things. He wondered if she could play the violin he was juggling together with the large suitcase that was missing a handle.

She was quite happy with her wages. She would make more than two times as before and have more time off. Carolina felt rejuvenated.

Mrs. Kelley saw her in the morning and asked Johnson if she could steal her for a moment to meet her five daughters. "Of course."

Mrs. Kelley saw something in Carolina that she wanted to replicate in her offspring. The way she carried herself. Her confidence and intelligence. She wanted her daughters to be influenced by her. It would serve them well to be around a strong, smart, well-schooled and independent young lady. Maybe they would want that; maybe they would see the value of hard work and surviving a rough start in life. They needed a dose of reality to interrupt their gilded life, and Carolina would be a good example. She didn't want to throw a bomb into their protected world. She just wanted them to know how lucky they were and to see how a woman could overcome any obstacle that stood in her way. Mrs. Kelley was more than a loving mother. She was not their "friend," she was their mentor, and they were her disciples. Discipleship can be easily misunderstood. The root is discipline. That word conjures up harsh, punishment-like consequences for some people. It is a misnomer. Discipline is caring. It is not harsh, unless the discipliner is sadistic. It is love and caring for their future. Jesus' twelve were called Disciples. He taught them with love and compassion and so did Mrs. Kelley with her daughters. She was happy to embed this example into her daughters' lives.

Carolina met them all at once. Mary, Constance, Francis, Erin and Nicole. Mary was the oldest at eighteen and Nicole was the baby. She was seven. They were fine young ladies for the most part. Mary was not a beauty by any means. At least compared to the other girls. She had the softest heart, as is common with the less attractive. It was her heart that made her beautiful and Carolina saw that inner softness immediately. She wanted to show her another way. She wanted her to not fear the world that was stacked against her. She wanted her to thrive, and she wanted to show her how! They soon became best friends, to the chagrin of Johnson. He mentioned this to Mrs. Kelley and was quickly and firmly shut down. Carolina had a hall pass and that irritated Johnson. He did appreciate that Mary had a mentor and friend. He liked Mary the most and that was good for everyone involved.

Carolina's first day and first test were the three third-floor guest rooms facing north. The third floor was solely for visitors. It had seven guest bedrooms and bathrooms and slept fourteen in absolute luxury. No one was staying in residence, so the floor was empty and quiet. She was told to get those three north rooms ready for guests and wait until Johnson came up to inspect.

Carolina began to prepare the room and make the beds. She entered the first bedroom, took one look at the linens folded on the mattress and rejected them because they were not properly clean and ironed. They were put there by Johnson intentionally. When she brought them to the laundry room to be redone, Johnson was surprised and impressed. Carolina passed her first test at the Kelley house orientation.

She obtained a proper set and made up the three rooms that she was directed to do. The other two rooms passed her linen inspection. She quickly made the beds with perfect military-style corners at the foot and cleaned the bathrooms. She dusted every place that could foster dirt and dander and opened the windows after she cleaned them to allow fresh air to circulate. The three rooms were now perfect. She swept and mopped the hallways and rolled the carpet back down. Checking all the lights, she made a note to replace the two burnt bulbs.

While waiting for Johnson, she finished the other four bedrooms and then waited outside the north bedrooms for his arrival and critique. After a few minutes, she began to polish the brass doorknobs and hinges. Another thirty minutes passed, and she found a ladder in the hall closet and used it to clean the dead insects in the ceiling lights. Johnson finally came up to inspect the three rooms she was responsible for. After noticing the bugs were gone from the light fixtures, he nodded his approval and entered the first room to inspect Carolina's work. He was amazed at her attention to detail. The room was perfect, and the bathrooms and closets were spotless. He noticed the windows were cleaned and the floors were flawless. They moved to the next room. Same. The third room was as good as the first two.

Johnson was impressed with her speed and attention to detail. He ran his hand across the top of the door trim and saw it was without any trace of dust. Carolina didn't miss a thing. Since she had cleaned the three rooms so quickly and so thoroughly, he asked her to clean the other four rooms that were left.

"I already did while I was waiting for you to come up."

Johnson was stunned. "Carolina, I would like you to train the other girls." It came off as a joke, but there was more truth to it than not. "They can't make a corner on the bed like you can." He said after lifting the bed cover off to look. "I'm also going to increase your salary. Please don't say anything to the others."

He checked the other four rooms even though he knew he didn't need to. That's when he noticed the polished doorknobs and hinges. He shook his head ever so slightly and rolled his eyes out of respect.

"What's next, sir." She asked as she handed him a note about the two light bulbs that needed renewing.

"What's this?" I always check the lights to make sure none are burnt out. Johnson folded the note and put it in his inside breast pocket, but not before noticing the perfect and almost calligraphic Spencerian-style handwriting. "Who is this person?" He silently wondered. "Is she testing **me**?" He thought to himself.

He hadn't planned anything additional. He figured she would be up there all-day redoing things and responding to and correcting the mistakes that every new hire experiences. She outran her coverage, as they say in college football.

"Let me show you how to properly serve lunch. Follow me." He said with pride to his star pupil. She already knew the proper way. She was curious about what new things she could learn.

Nothing new was gleaned from her teacher when it came to lunch service. She did notice the fish fork was improperly placed but was smart enough to not point out the mistake. Instead, she carefully mentioned how they did it slightly differently in Europe. Johnson immediately noticed his error and tried to recover it by calling it another test. "Well done, Carolina Augusta, it's hard to fool you!"

Mrs. Kelley could be heard with her daughters in the library. She came over to the day dining room and saw them working on the table settings.

"How is she doing, Johnson?"

"Just fine. I think she will work out." Johnson would have a private conversation with Mrs. Kelley later that afternoon to go over the dinner menu. At that time, he will tell her how incredible her skills and mannerisms were. He came to realize that his fish fork mistake was not unnoticed by his student. Her people skills were perfect. He always was nervous when staff interacted with visitors or houseguests. That would be of no concern with Carolina. The way she treated his obvious error with the fork whilst leaving his dignity fully intact was so brilliant, he thought. Although her skills made him happy, it also made him realize that she probably wouldn't make this home a career. A person like this could not be confined to such a rote job.

4

As the days and weeks passed, Carolina felt comfortable and appreciated for the first time in her life. She would wake up with a smile on her face and was a blessing to the house. Mr. Kelley was so thankful she was having an influence on his daughters. Her role was shifting to teacher and confidant to his five precious girls. She was, in essence, juggling two jobs. Juggling is not really the right word. Mastering them was a better description. Mr. and Mrs. Kelley were seeing changes in their daughters' attitudes—significant changes. They always loved their children; now they really, really liked them.

Carolina was rewarded with the full-time job of "finishing" their children. Johnson was the highest-paid employee, and Carolina was now the second. Johnson hated to see her leave her position as Head Housekeeper. After all, she just got the promotion two weeks prior. He knew it was best. What would anyone prefer for their family? Polished doorknobs or polished children?

Mary was now learning German at a surprising speed. She was learning music theory from Carolina, too. Carolina had an uncanny innate, almost instinctual command of music. She was surprised and had no explanation. It just came to her somehow. Her piano playing was self-taught. She was able to pick up just about any instrument and play it after a few hours. Her favorites were the violin and the Bach

Flute. That old style Baroque flute was not seen very often, replaced by the more modern French style. She was excited to find it in the music room. She recognized it from the musicians she watched at the Thomaskirk church back in Germany as a little girl. She had never played one, but in one month, she played well enough to be seated in any ensemble.

The girls were a joy to teach and be with. That was not always the case, even two months ago. A real change was overtaking these girls.

As summer was approaching, Carolina saw another mood captivating them. She asked Mary what was going on. She learned that they were saddened by the fact that they would be leaving for their annual trip to their summer home on Swan Lake outside Bigfork, Montana. They didn't want to leave Carolina for ten weeks. They all loved her too much.

The Kelleys hired twenty local people to care for them during their stay. It worked out well for the New York City staff as it allowed them to visit their families for an extended time during the summer months.

Carolina saw the wonderful photographs of their summer cabins. It was a stunning setting. The family stumbled on it when one of Mr. Kelley's accountants traveled to Montana to see the land that was to be purchased for shoring timbers intended to be used at Mr. Kelley's mining company. It was a virgin forest, and the massive trees would be used to support the tunnels used to reach the valuable ores. They would also hold back the excavated walls of the open pit mines. Mr. Kelley owned the Anaconda Mining Company in Butte, Montana. It was the largest copper mine on earth and was the perfect metal for a country and world that was electrifying. Copper wire was the best conductor of electricity and as a bonus, copper water pipes were replacing the poisonous lead ones worldwide.

Mr. Kelley received a telegram in 1906 from his employee that he sent to inspect the land before the company purchased it. The telegram was "terse."

Mr. Kelley STOP

I visited the property yesterday STOP

You need to see this place for yourself STOP

I think I found the recreational land you've been looking for STOP

I will quit my job if you don't love it STOP

R. Baines

Mr. Kelley had planned a visit to the Butte mines in thirty days. He would continue on to Swan Lake to view the land at that time. As soon as he saw it, he instructed Mr. Baines to change the purchase agreement from the Anaconda Mining Company to the Cornelius Kelley Family Trust. He would buy it for his family and friends. His minor partner, Orvis Evans, would build his own cabin on the lake. His wife Mary designed the huge timber and stone Cabin and started construction immediately.

Mrs. Kelley, like so many wives that don't have the same love of the mountains and lakes as their husbands, was intent on Newport, Rhode Island. She was slowly converted with the photographs that Mr. Kelley commissioned to make his job easier. They hired a man named Kirtland Cutter to design the centerpiece of their new Montana playground. Mr. Cutter was a famous designer well known for his Pasadena, California home designs and more complicated projects such as the USA pavilion at the Chicago World's Fair as well as the stunning Davenport Hotel in Spokane, Washington. His home designs were Arts & Craft in style and made him famous. The home that Mr. Kelley would build was quickly dubbed the most perfect example of lodge-style log construction in the United States. They called it The Kootenai Lodge. Pronounced koot-nee. Respectfully named for the Idaho Indian tribe that would come through the area to hunt and fish a hundred years ago.

The girls explained to Carolina that the New York staff never came with them. The only exception was Johnson. They needed him to train the staff, and run the summer operation and the diesel generator to power the 600-acre site that was set aside from the timbered land. The trees you couldn't see from their property were logged and sent on to Butte.

Carolina was saddened now. She didn't want to leave the girls for ten weeks, either. She also didn't have anywhere to go. She had no family or friends outside the home. She didn't want to leave the house, but she certainly didn't want to stay in it alone. She had so many questions. Would she still be paid? She thought not. Who would pay someone for not working? Could she find a rooming house or take on work in another home for the summer? She started to panic a bit but closed those thoughts down as any strong and intelligent woman would do. She knew she would figure things out and be just fine.

5

After moping around the previous week, Carolina decided she needed to start looking for a place to stay for the summer. She walked over to the hospital to see Clara to talk about a temporary summer job and a place to stay. Everybody with money left the city during the hot, humid and smelly summer months. Clara might be able to help with finding employment again.

She waited outside for her shift to end and waved to her as she walked down the entrance stairway. "Carolina Augusta, how have you been?"

"Really well, Clara, really well."

They hugged and held hands as they walked down the street together. Clara kept a watchful eye over Carolina. She felt her healing was progressing well. She checked in on her once a week.

"I need your help, and I need to find a summer job and a place to stay while the Kelley's are in Montana for the summer."

"You can stay with me."

"You are too kind and generous, but I couldn't do that."

"Yes, you could, and I could use you this Summer to help the hospital as we plan for the annual fall fund raiser. It's a paying job, and Mrs. Kelley would approve. She's in charge this year."

"I overheard her talking with the girls about "getting in shape" for the ball," Carolina remembered.

"She told me she wants them involved and that you have really been working hard and turning them into very special young ladies."

"They really are special. Kind and sweet and very intelligent." Carolina gushed about *her* children. She wished she had a photograph of them all together. It was too expensive for now.

"You should talk with Mrs. Kelley right away about this before they hire someone." Clara didn't want her to wait. She wanted to work together with Carolina.

"Okay. I'll go ask her before dinner. Is that soon enough?" Carolina smiled, hugged her and ran back home yelling. "Goodbye!"

She was so excited that she almost ran into the house through the front door. She stopped before her foot hit the second step and, backed away and headed around the side to the servant's entrance. She waltzed in, singing and dancing. Johnson just shook his head.

Carolina went up to see the girls and check on their studies. They were pretty good about working when no one was watching and today was no different. "Okay, girls, we must start planning for the Hospital Fall Fund Raiser. Your mother is in charge this year and you all are going to make her the proudest mother in the city. Oh, and your dad, too."

A few murmurs were heard but immediately squelched after Carolina turned her head toward them.

"I am going to teach you to dance!" Carolina was caught off guard as soon as she said it. "I don't know how to dance!" She shouted out to herself without making a sound.

"You know how to dance?" Mary was very interested in learning to dance. Carolina showed her how to look more attractive and how to move with elegance. She wore clothes that didn't detract anymore. That was a change for her. She thought she would be better off not drawing attention to herself. She felt that she was homely, and she just wanted to blend in with the furniture so no one would pay attention. That just would not work for Carolina. Bright dresses that showed just a little bit of her figure were added to her closet. No white lace socks anymore, either. She was growing up now and had to leave a lot of those childish things behind.

Carolina had Mary's hairstyle changed to shorten the look of her face. She wore hats to church and now on outings with her mother. The hats reduced the size of her forehead and showcased her beautiful green eyes because people weren't focusing on her weaknesses anymore. She would no longer be treated as an ugly duckling, especially by herself. She was coming into her own and she felt it. That bit of confidence propelled her to a different level. It's amazing how the way someone carries themself changes observer's opinions. They went to the park one Saturday morning and two different young men looked at her a little too long. The first one surprised her and she turned back to see who he was looking at.

"He's looking at you silly!" That morning changed her life and marked the day that ended her childhood. The second young man caught her off guard and caused her to laugh a little too loud. She didn't laugh to be mean; she laughed because she was so excited. He heard it and it made him mad. It didn't stop him from turning around for another look, though. She was learning how to flirt, no matter how crudely, on her first attempt. Carolina suddenly noticed a little swish to her hips as she walked along the park's stone sidewalks. "Where did that come from?" She thought. It came from watching Carolina.

As they walked home together, Mary gave her a big hug and kissed her cheek. "At the rate you've been changing me, maybe my next kiss will be from a boy?"

"Keep it up and I'm going to tell your dad!" Carolina giggled.

That was last Saturday. Now, she wanted to walk in the park a lot more.

Carolina saw Mary out front talking to a neighbor and waved as she approached the house. "Time for lunch." That gave her a reason to go inside. The neighbor lady was what you would call a "buttonholer." Mary was glad to getaway gracefully.

"She walked up the stairs, came into the house and went to the dining room. Carolina went to the basement dining room, where the staff ate their meals. Not to eat yet, but to assist in the family lunch. The staff would eat later.

Mrs. Kelley rang the bell in the kitchen. Johnson quickly ran up to see what was needed.

"Ah, Johnson. Could you ask Carolina to join us for lunch? We must talk to her about Montana. We'll need another place setting."

"Certainly Madam. I'll send her right up."

Johnson was surprised she was invited to lunch. He was never invited to dine with the Kelleys.

Carolina was just as shocked as Johnson when he told her to join them for lunch. "Hurry up, we will be serving soon."

Carolina washed her hands, combed her hair a bit and straightened out her dress. She looked down at her shoes and wiped a little soot from the street off. She walked up the stairs and entered the dining room like she was walking into a ballroom. It was a natural walk to her.

She didn't know what Mrs. Kelley wanted. She wasn't scared, but she was a little concerned.

Mr. Kelley stood up and sat her between himself and Mrs. Kelley. He helped her with her chair and then sat down only after she was settled.

Now, she was scared. "What is going on here?" She thought. The room was silent. Mr. Kelley always changed the dynamics of any room he was in. The family dining room was no different.

Mr. Kelley asked if she would like a little wine with lunch. She declined. That made Mrs. Kelley smile as Mr. Kelley spoke to Carolina.

"Carolina. I want to take a moment to thank you for all you are doing for my family. My daughters are not the same as when you arrived. They are growing up to be quite an impressive and happy group of young ladies. You are an amazing young woman yourself. I have never seen Mary so happy and confident and pretty."

Mr. Kelley looked at Mary and smiled a contented and proud fatherly smile.

"Just look at her." He bragged. "Whenever a father's children or wife are not happy it's a problem, and a man does not usually hold the key to unlocking the mystery of a female problem. Let alone setting the proper course of action when the seas are unforgiving."

He looked at his wife and then his five daughters, and for a minute, he didn't mind not having a boy.

Johnson came in with the other girls to serve lunch.

"We'll continue our talk during lunch."

Mrs. Kelley was served first and then Carolina.

"That means I am a guest, not a servant. At least for this meal." She thought to herself. She was thankful for this family.

The five girls were served next and finally, Mr. Kelley. Carolina saw Nicole reaching for her fork before Mr. Kelley picked up his and gave her a look. She quickly put it down and straightened her lace napkin. Mrs. Kelley saw the look and saw her youngest daughter respond. "So, you taught them that." She silently deducted.

Mr. Kelley started to reach for his fork but quickly stopped and asked about the charity event. The girls were fooled by his quick move and went for their own. They all stopped before laying a hand on them when they saw he balked. Mrs. Kelley giggled and reminded him that it was in the fall. "Oh." He said.

He reached for his fork again and stopped to ask what month. The girls almost fell for that "trick" again. Little Nicole wouldn't be fooled this time. Mrs. Kelley was almost bursting at the seams. Mr. Kelley had no idea what was so funny. He rethought about having a boy again and wished for another man in the room.

"The children are waiting for you to pick up your fork so they can begin to eat. You're torturing them."

Carolina couldn't hold back her own laughter. Mrs. Kelley joined her, as did the girls. The whole room was howling with laughter. Mr. Kelley couldn't resist any longer and joined the pack of hyenas surrounding the dinner table. Johnson came up because of all the noise and had a look of fear.

"It's ok, Johnson. We're laughing at our manners. Could you bring me another fork, please?"

The laughter began all over again as Johnson started to leave the room to bring another fork.

"I'm sorry, Johnson. Bring my fork back. You deserve an explanation."

"Yes, sir?"

"Evidently, Carolina taught the children not to begin eating until I picked up my fork. I went for it the first time and the girls were fooled when I didn't pick it up. They all stopped before touching their forks. I did it again as I asked another question. The second time, they weren't fooled and one by one, we all broke out laughing."

Johnson began to laugh, and everybody started up all over again.

The girls were staring at their father's left hand. He faked it once more and then picked up his fork. They all looked at each other and the laughter resumed all over again.

"Ok, enough. We have things to talk about and the food is getting cold."

Mrs. Kelley looked over at Carolina and told her that Clara called. She had talked with her about another job this summer.

Mr. Kelley and I were hoping you would join us and the girls for the "Summer in Montana."

Carolina almost choked on her fish when she heard that.

"I should have talked with you about it earlier. I hope you will consider it."

"Yes, yes, yes, yes, yes!" She said while pointing at each girl. Nicole reminded her that pointing is very rude. Carolina was holding back a giggle again and so were the girls.

"Oh, Mrs. Kelley, I wanted to go so badly but I was told only Johnson accompanied you to Montana."

"That was before you came along, Carolina. We want you with us. I know we've only known you for two or three months, but we consider you family. Right Girls?"

They all chimed in agreement, as did Mr. Kelley.

"I'll take you shopping for proper Montana clothing. We can all go. Except Mr. Kelley, he hates to shop."

They finished their meal. Mr. And Mrs. Kelley had never dined with the staff. They thought that would be awkward for everyone. She did go down one time to eat with them after one of the younger girls was killed in a fire while visiting her mother. That was the last time. Nicole was just a baby.

"Thank you for inviting me to dine with you. It means a lot to me."

Mr. Kelley arose from his chair to help Mrs. Kelley with her chair. The girls started to rise as he walked behind Carolina. She shot the girls another look. They all sat back down and waited for their mother to stand. Mr. Kelley was facing the girls. They knew they made a mistake. Their father winked at them and smiled at their quick recovery. He would fondly remember this meal for the rest of his life. He often told the story at his club. Starting with the fork incident. After telling it, he would take a slow, deep breath and then let it out all at once. He was savoring the little snippet of his family life. That precious memory was retold at his funeral in 1955. Instead of laughing, the girls all began to cry. When they looked at each other, they all erupted in laughter, to the chagrin of the pastor. Nicole said later that the pastor's glance reminded them of Carolina, except this man held no sway over the Kelley girls on any subject that was not spiritual.

6

June arrived quickly. It was like in the month of December, waiting for Christmas Eve. It felt like the clock had a mind of its own and started running ahead of time now as it ticked off the beginning of the long trip to Montana. The Kelleys, Carolina and Johnson were in the new car. First one they ever bought for the city. Mr. Kelley knew Henry Ford personally. His first car was not a Ford. It was a beautiful, deep green-painted Bentley. He loved that car and kept it for over thirty years.

"Everybody ready for the train ride?" Mr. Kelley asked. Eight yeses were heard.

Carolina asked where all the bags and train cases were. They had over thirty items to load on the train. Johnson told her that they were loaded yesterday.

"That's why a small bag with the items you need for the trip was needed. The bags are stacked up in the storage room on the train. You can't get to them."

"They let you do that?" Asked Carolina.

"They do when you own the train car."

Mr. Kelley had the plush Pullman train car made even more elegant. Mrs. Kelley help to design the interior and select the artwork. They had a private bedroom with a large bed. The bathroom held a tub and shower. The girls had bunks, and Johnson had a very small but private room in the front. Carolina had the sixth bunk. It was designed with a separate entrance so that a boy could occupy it. The boy they never had was replaced by Carolina.

The Bentley dropped them at the train car located at the very end of the train. This would be home for three days. Their meals were prepared by the train staff and delivered on rolling carts from the forward cars.

The Pennsylvania Railroad line's locomotive started to move the wheels. It was so slow at first that Carolina never thought they would make it in a week. As the steam and smoke increased, so did the speed.

"That's more like it." This was her first train ride.

As the train started gaining speed, Carolina started to feel like she did on the boat from Germany. She went into the bathroom and vomited. She was very disappointed that she was sick. She wanted to have a perfect time with the girls and family in Montana. It started out as a fairy tale. Chauffeur driven Bentley to Penn Station. Private train car with sleeping quarters for all. And now this. She wanted to enjoy every second of this dream and it was interrupted by the contents of her stomach. She laid down in her bed and pulled the curtain. She told the girls that she needed a few minutes.

The vibration of the train and the sound of the tracks beneath the steel wheels lulled her to sleep. She slept for over an hour and felt refreshed. She prayed she wouldn't get sick again. As she walked to the sitting room, she was greeted by Mr. Kelley.

"There she is! Did you have a nice rest?"

"I did; sorry, I felt a little queazy."

Mr. Kelley appreciated Carolina's dichotomy. She grew up with nothing really and was now a teacher to his children. She knew more about etiquette than the whole family. Johnson included. He couldn't reconcile it. She spoke three languages, studied music and now taught both subjects like a scholar to his "sophisticated" girls. Just like at her first household, he didn't want to lose her either. He would never let her go if he could help it. He thought about talking to Johnson about offering her more money to sort of lock her down. He approached everything like a business deal. This was different. A successful businessman separates emotions from making decisions. He couldn't with Carolina. He would tell her his motives when he offered her a huge year-end bonus. Johnson would not be involved. It would cause hard feelings and cause friction. It would be their secret.

He felt better now. He asked Mrs. Kelley to bring him a glass of scotch before dinner.

"I will not!"

How about we draw cards to see who gets it?

"You're on daddy. I'll get the cards."

She could never turn down a bet and Mr. Kelley knew he couldn't outplay her in any card game requiring skill. That's why he chose to draw cards.

"I won. Put a little ice in it for me, please. Oh, and a lemon peel dragged across the rim would be a nice touch."

Then came the dreaded words.

"Two out of three?"

He had to say yes. It's usually best to let your wife win on the little things. He looked at it like a business investment. After all, he was in the marriage for the long haul.

They both pulled cards. He laid down his King and she laid down her Ace. This went back and forth for a few minutes before Johnson came up from behind and put a napkin down next to him to hold the Scotch on ice with a lemon twist rubbed along the rim to bring out the flavor.

"I didn't want you to die of thirst! What may I bring you, Mrs. Kelley?"

"Nothing yet, Johnson; I have to beat this carpet bagger!"

Johnson really loved this family, too. Before running the household for the Kelleys, he headed two different ones in England. The staff was never allowed to interact with the employers. They would be sent packing—literally sent to their rooms to pack and get out.

The first time Mrs. Kelley kidded Johnson about his "stiff upper lip," He was frightened to show any emotion. He needed his job. She immediately knew his fear was about keeping his job.

"Johnson, are you comfortable here with us?"

"Oh yes, ma'am, I certainly am."

"You seem to obey orders."

"Yes, of course, Ma'am."

"You need to know something about Americans. We don't have a monarchy, we don't have titles, although some try to buy them. We don't own castles, although some try to copy them, and we are not as spoiled as our former countrymen in England."

Johnson thought he was about to get a dressing down.

"You are allowed to laugh while around us. Not at us, please, with us. Understood?"

"Yes, ma'am, I will."

"Johnson. Why are your shoes so dirty?"

He quickly looked down as he was exiting the room and saw his shoes were spotless.

"Gotcha!"

Johnson laughed a little. He wasn't that amused as much as relieved that his shoes were clean.

"I can see I'm going to need to work on you a little more."

"Yes, ma'am, thank you, ma'am."

Nowadays, Johnson could laugh a little louder around the Kelleys. Carolina lowered the bar, and he saw things as less serious and less to be fearful. Johnson's way of joining in on this kidding was to prepare and bring the scotch over to him during the wagering. This is how a British butler could safely join in on the fun. Carolina was bringing joy to everyone in the family, Johnson included.

They changed locomotives in Chicago. Up to Minneapolis, through North Dakota and onto the flat land of eastern Montana. They were now riding on J. J. Hill's Great Northern Railroad, and this route was known as "The Empire Builder." He, of course, was a friend of Mr. Kelley. He seemed to know everybody.

Carolina looked out at the vast, flat landscape and wondered where all the mountains were that she saw in the photos. She didn't like Montana as much as she was hoping.

The train tracks turned south for a few miles to navigate around a lake and Mary was the first to see the soaring, snow-covered majesties.

Carolina looked in awe. Her mouth was open for so long that Mrs. Kelley snuck up from behind and put her hand under her chin and gently closed her mouth. That's all the Kelley girls needed to start laughing out loud. Carolina started to laugh, too. Every time they made fun of Carolina, she felt even closer to her "family." She felt closer because it was genuinely born out of love for her. It was like they were taking a child to the zoo for the first time. When that child sees their first lion, the chaperon enjoys their excitement more than their own first time seeing a lion. And now, for the first time in her life, she had a family, and they were showing her the world outside of the city. She was showing them how family life should be. Even though she had no family, she showed them the way. This was a family that she knew would look out for her, protect her and love her. She thought about them every night while going to sleep. It gave her such peace and contentment. Her prayers began with the Kelleys and ended with the Kelleys. She felt like a daughter more than an employee and she certainly was truly now an informally adopted member of the Kelley family.

As their train approached the mountains and the climb up the Rockies, Carolina felt sick again. The trip would end soon in Whitefish, Montana. This was the closest train depot to the Kootenai Lodge. Carolina was glad she could step on land soon and begin her "vacation" on a lake in Northwest Montana without the queasiness and vomiting.

At noon, the train pulled slowly into the yard and depot in Whitefish. It was a quaint little railroad town. Most of the homes were "catalogue" homes. These were mail-order homes bought from Sears Roebuck and Company and Montgomery Ward. Hundreds of designs were available. Each home package contained everything needed to build a home, down to the last nail. The prices were quite inexpensive, especially if you were near a railroad spur. They even had furniture packages. Whitefish was a new town, and the main street was a dirt road. A few tree stumps were still in the streets. Whitefish's nickname was "Stumptown."

Three black Continental limousines were waiting for them at the European-styled station. It resembled a Swiss hotel. After greeting the family back to Montana, the staff quickly got to work to unload everything from the train.

Mr. Kelley went to inspect the new Continentals. The Continental Company would later merge with Lincoln Car Company and become Lincoln Continentals. He liked them. They were housed in a three-car garage near the station. Only to be used to travel from the train to Swan Lake. They didn't actually navigate the entire 46 miles to the Kootenai Lodge. They had to stop about three miles before and the passengers would climb into Model T Fords and the luggage was put into Model A Ford trucks. The roads were dicey and filled with ruts, and sometimes, a fallen Larch tree would block the way. They always had saws in the trunk in case they had to clear the road. They needed to ford the Swan River in their Fords to reach the eastern side of Swan Lake. The Continentals were ill-equipped to travel over the 18" rocky stream bed that led to the property. They were dispatched back to Whitefish to be washed and waxed to await their summer visitors.

The Swan River ran North through the property. Every river ran South or West on this side of the Rockies. The Swan River was magical and its disregard for topography gave it a special and even mystical legend.

As the entourage traveled South to the Kootenai, Carolina was stunned by the beauty of it all.

"Big Sky." Mr. Kelley said. "That's what it's called."

Carolina instantly understood what he was talking about. She was astounded by the huge white and puffy clouds set into a beautiful blue canvas. The palette had only two colors. The clouds were painted first and then the blue was added so that the artist wouldn't diminish the brightness of the white. You could see clouds that were a hundred miles away. It was like the heaven's ceiling that she imagined when she prayed. Everything else was so green and healthy; everything was so pristine, pure, and clean. She wondered how she could return to the city and the dirt and smells after living in this paradise for ten weeks.

They transferred to the Fords and drove the last three miles to the iron and stone gates that were opened and waiting for them. They heard a gunshot nearby. It was Johnny. He fired his pistol to alert the staff. They were all waiting in the main home until they heard that call. They moved out in front and lined up in a straight file. Each one had on a name tag. That was Johnson's idea after too many mistakes were made by Mr. Kelley. They would come off in a week as he dusted off last summer's memories.

Twenty workers were standing at attention. Mostly all from Bigfork. This job paid more than most of their wages for the year. It was cherished by the locals. Mr. Kelley always had one or two "scholarship" workers from Butte. They were children of the mine workers that had the toughest jobs. It was a reward to the worker's family. Johnny was one of two this year. He was 15 years old. Their pay was standard for a hired hand; the only difference was the bonus as they said their goodbyes for the year. Last year, it was a $200 bonus. Almost as much as the father's annual pay at the mines. The children understood that the money was not intended for them, and they gave it all to their parents. Elsie was the second. Elsie was 13 years old. Her father was injured last year while saving one of the foremen from certain death. When a train hauling out ore ran off the tracks, he pushed the man away from the tracks and he fell back against the drive wheel. The wheel cut off most of his left foot. The foreman was so grateful that he gave him a job that allowed him to sit and work. After a year of healing, he returned to his new job. He would keep track of every train car that passed by his chair. Elsie would keep track of the silver, crystal, and china place settings that passed through the kitchen doors this summer.

The Kelleys liked to entertain big. The Kootenai Lodge had full breakfast, lunch and dinner table settings for 150 guests. The new bar that Mr. Kelley built for the gentleman had seating for 80 people, with a huge stone fireplace as the centerpiece of the room. The bar was fully stocked. The bar top was made of rolled copper and always perfectly polished. An electric engraving tool allowed special guests to sign their names on the bar top. Many famous people had autographed the bar top. The back bar was stocked better than a private club in the city. When Mrs. Kelley saw it, she sent Johnson to make arrangements to bring the roulette wheel from the house in the city and to buy two poker tables and chips. She laughed about it later. It was around the time she exceeded her unlimited art budget.

Carolina looked at the virgin trees scattered throughout the property. Trees so big that the girls would put their arms around the trunks to measure. It would take all five children's arms to circumnavigate. Mr. Kelley told her about one they felled because it had been hit by lightning two hundred years ago. The top was missing 150 feet above the burned-out stub that was over 200 feet off the ground.

"How do you know when that happened?" That's easy; you just count the rings. The tree was nine hundred years old and the rings on the old fallen top were 700. That tells us it happened 200 years ago. It was a giant lodgepole. On this side of the lake and river were the Larch, aspen, lodgepole, and many deciduous trees, including apple, cherry, and pear trees. On the other side of the lake were the Ponderosa Pines.

The cars and trucks pulled up in front of the main home and the Kelley family got out and ran inside to the grand living room. They grabbed Carolina to come with them. She looked at Mrs. Kelley and she gave her a nod.

When Carolina saw the magnificent room, she couldn't believe it was logs and stone. The peak of the wood ceiling was over 35 feet tall. On the walls were two giant grizzly bear hides stretched across the upper log walls. Next to them was a massive Polar Bear. If you squinted your eyes to only see the huge grizzly and then opened them to look at the polar bear, the difference in size was shocking. A world-record elk stood guard over the massive stone fireplace that could burn four-foot-long logs. The fireplace was a Ben Franklin design from a hundred years ago. It was still the gold standard. Something about the hearth at floor level, side walls at the perfect angle to reflect heat and the air intakes that let in outside air to fuel the fire. The girls all knew the story. They heard Daddy tell it a hundred times.

The thing Carolina liked the best was the wrap-around covered porch looking onto the lake and river. The furniture was cleaned and set in the correct place for viewing the lake and the sunset. Trout were catching flies off the lake and leaving behind beautiful rings of softly rippled water on the dead-still surface. This was even better than the paradise that the family had tried to describe numerous times. At dinner, Carolina would tease them about their lack of any descriptive skills. It was that much better than any words could describe!

"Alright, smarty, you describe it." Mr. Kelley leaned back at dinner and waited for her description.

Carolina thought for a minute and, in defeat, conceded and said, "Touché."

Walking back into the main room, she immediately noticed how much natural light flowed into the dark log room. Windows around the three main walls were tall and barely interrupted by the engineered supports. Those supports were designed to withstand an earthquake. They were the same on the outside and strengthened by bolts that pulled them together. The four square-inch openings cut into the support logs to hide the bolt and nut was covered with the original cutout and was not detectable. The Rock Maple floors were perfect and showcased inlayed designs. These wood floor slats were over an inch thick. It truly was the most beautiful log structure in the country. The local craftsmen were not as impressed as the visitors from the city. They were as fine a woodworking crew to be found anywhere.

Carolina noticed the large Steinway piano in the corner of the room the moment she first entered. It was nine feet long and made from Cuban Mahogany. Cuban mahogany is different from all other mahoganies. It has dark streaks throughout the brown wood caused by the Caribbean winds that continually caress and rock the trees. The piano also had an Ampico Piano Roll player installed under the keyboard. The original composers would "cut" them while they played their own compositions. Piano students love them because they can hear the music exactly how it was played by its creator. If you followed along with the sheet music, it was easy to tell who was better at transcribing the notes. The Romantic Period composers definitely had more latitude in the disparity between the playing and the written notes. While those of a more structured background were synced perfectly. The more romantically played, the less "accurate" in paper hard copy.

"Okay, girls, enough for now. I have work to do."

Carolina walked back through the entrance under the covered walkways in front of the bedroom doors. The beautiful fountain attracted colorful little birds. The planted geraniums surrounding the stone-walled patio attracted hummingbirds by the dozens. Virginia Creeper vines or "Western Ivy," surrounded the log posts that supported the extended roof that fronted the bedrooms. It looked like very big ivy leaves. This was a favorite patio for lunch.

Mrs. Kelley went to her bedroom. Mr. Kelley went to the office just up the hill from the Lodge. In it was a telephone, stock ticker, telegraph key, typewriter and office supplies. Business couldn't stop because he was "out West." He was a captain of industry and couldn't turn over the helm of his ship to anyone. Not even Orvis Evans. Mr. Kelley had a personal assistant that lived in the bedroom next to the communication room of the log and stone office. Coincidentally, his name was Kelly, John Kelly. Mr. Cornelius Kelley was called Mr. Kelley at the Kootenai. Mr. John Kelly was known as Number 2. Johnson didn't like that. The Anaconda Mining Company office at the Kootenai had the first telephone in Lake County. First power plant for electricity generation, too.

Carolina found Mrs. Kelley and entered the bedroom. It was so beautiful. Huge Stone fireplace and dark green painted wooden ceiling supported by log beams and stringers. Large windows that let in the sunlight. The upholstered furniture, window valences, and the drapery that were so heavy, they always fell straight and wrinkle-free. The wooden pine floors were lacquered and reflected the sunlight throughout the room. Mrs. Kelley seemed to have tamed the wilderness of old Montana.

"Hi, Carolina. Have you seen your quarters?"

"Not yet, the girls were showing me around. I am so happy you brought me here. I have never even dreamed of a place like this. It is heaven. I mean it."

"Have the girls take you to your room. We can all meet up on the lake deck in an hour. I'm so glad you came with us. I really mean it, darling; I really mean it."

Mary and the girls led Carolina to her room, that was in a separate cabin with five other workers. It was one of three dormitories for the staff. It had beautiful lake views from the front picture window. It wasn't extravagant, but it wasn't basic either. It had a big cast iron tub on four legs. The white porcelain was kept clean and shiny as well as the plumbing fixtures. Carolina had a private room, and the other girls had bunk beds in an open area that had a couch and chairs and served as the living room.

"This will work just fine." Carolina liked her small but private room. She noticed her suitcases were on a stand at the foot of the bed. That's when she noticed the sloppy sheet corners.

"I'll show them how to do this the right way in the morning."

7

The family was to meet up on the lake deck to make plans for the next few days. Carolina was, of course, invited. Nowadays, she seemed to be a part of everything the family did. She wished she could call Mr. and Mrs. Kelley "Mom and Dad." When she thought of them and when she prayed, she called them that. The girls didn't call her Carolina as much. "Big Sister" was heard a lot instead. Carolina didn't mind that at all. She felt like they were her sisters. She would do anything to protect them, and she truly loved them.

Boating, sailing, swimming, fishing, croquet, horseback riding, bocci ball, bicycling, horseshoes, archery, shooting and playing in the barn with the chickens and Hereford cows. They moved the large animals and chickens in at night to avoid tempting coyotes and mountain lions. Grizzly bears were already moving up to the higher ground, so they weren't a real threat.

Play clothes and western wear were checked in the mirror before doing a "walkabout," as the girls called it.

"Let's go to the barn first and we can visit Johnson Creek." Another coincidence and no relation to their man, Johnson.

On their way, Carolina noticed an opening in the ground with a bank vault door at the foot of the concrete stairway. She assumed it was to lock up all the valuable silver, crystal and china when they were not in residence. She asked Mary about it and found out the real reason for an underground vault.

"Daddy keeps his liquor in there."

"No."

"Yes."

"To hide it?"

"To keep it from being pilfered when we are in the city."

"It's not for other valuables?"

"No, just daddy's 'hooch'." They all laughed at that word.

"The silver and crystal stay in the lodge. They don't even lock the doors when we leave. Nobody steals anything in Montana, except for a bottle or two of liquor."

"Is there a lot inside?"

"I'll show you."

Mary told the girls to wait at the top of the stairs as she led Carolina down the concrete stairway. She opened the vault door and turned on the light. It didn't work.

"The generator must be down."

Just as she said that, Johnson was seen running to the generator cabin on the creek, just passed the vault.

The two of them walked in and even in the darkness, they could see racks and racks of shelving loaded with wooden cases of liquor.

The lights came on. Now, they could see the vastness of his collection. Hundreds of cases. Not just liquor, red wine, white wine,

French wine, Italian wine and hundreds of bottles of French Champagne. Mr. Kelley joked to his friends that he had enough to last his lifetime.

Mary closed the door as they went up the stairs. The underground concrete structure kept the temperature inside at 55 degrees year-round. No need to lock it. A clipboard and pencil recorded who took what and when. They never did anything with the list. It just was there to keep people honest and thinking that someone was paying attention.

All six sisters walked together to the barn. It was just completed the year before and besides the livestock, it housed Mr. Kelley's prized horse, named Copper. They went in to visit Copper, and Carolina noticed that the name over the stall door was CU. Mary saw her looking at it and said. "It's the scientific symbol for copper."

Copper was even a sort of orange-red like the copper that was mined. He was newly shorn and ready for Mr. Kelley to ride around the property in style. It was a large stallion. Mr. Kelley was the perfect size for his horse.

"Let's go swimming!" yelled little Nicole. Everyone agreed.

As they walked back over the stone bridge that spanned Johnson Creek, Mary had a strange feeling. It wasn't her stomach; it wasn't a dark feeling, it just gave her goosebumps.

Carolina changed into her "swimming costume" and came out of her room wearing it for the first time to go swimming. It had a little short skirt dropping from the waste with abbreviated pantaloons under it. The top was respectable enough but showed a little too much skin if she was going to a church outing. She had never gone swimming before. The girls promised to teach her.

They all met up at the docks and dared each other to jump in.

"How cold is it?" Carolina asked.

"Put your foot in the water, sister."

She did and was surprised that it was fairly warm. What she didn't know was the top ten or twelve inches was not a true indication of the temperature. When you went below that, it quickly got to fifty degrees.

"Go ahead, jump in, standing up. Over here, it's only three feet or so." Said Nicole.

And so she did. A blood-curdling scream soon followed and then the laughter as Carolina ran out of the lake.

"You tricked me! I'll get you back, you know."

Francis dove in off the end of the wide dock and swam around for a couple of minutes before climbing up the ladder hanging over the dock. She planned on swimming to the diving board platform floating a hundred feet from the dock but changed her mind and direction. She was freezing.

"It will get warmer by the Fourth."

July fourth was always a big barbeque for friends and staff. It was a time for everyone to enjoy the day and celebrate our Independence. Mr. Kelley had an enormous flagpole installed between the covered porch and the docks. It was surround by lavender plants that somehow were resistant to deer. The flag was huge and when a storm came you had to get it down quickly. Lighted from below it was beautiful at night.

Mr. Kelley had a StanCraft boat custom made for him. The builder lived six miles down the lake and would become well known for his designs. They were made of lacquered wood and brass. The upholstered seats were as comfortable as any furniture in the lodge. The engine was inboard and when you got her going, she would settle in with a smooth purr. Long and slim, it held eight people in comfort. Touring the lake was an after dinner sunset cruise from heaven. In Montana, the summer sun doesn't set until after ten. Eleven or so in the first week of July. If they stayed out past sunset, it didn't matter. Jim, the captain knew that Jackie would take a small fishing boat and lay out dozens of floating and tethered kerosene lamps so they could navigate the shallows without bending the prop on the rocky bottom. Staying past sunset was a common happening. Everyone, except Jackie, loved the beautiful lights on the still lake leading you home to safety.

Carolina couldn't decide which she loved more. Sunrise or sunset. They both had their advantages and differences. One thing that was constant was the stillness at both times. The breezes would just disappear for an hour or so and calm the lake.

There were no bugs in the summer at the Kootenai. Bat houses were located around the property to keep them from gaining entrance to the cabins. The first time Carolina heard the bats, it frightened her. She couldn't see them, but she sure could hear them sweeping in close to her head as she walked on the lush lawns.

Mary told her they were bats and the famiy loved them because they ate every bug and mosquito on the property during the night. Carolina kept her little cross on her bedstand and now she checked to make sure it was there every night to ward off Dracula. After all, her German homeland was close to Transylvania.

Carolina would play her old violin while sitting cross leg on the dock at night. It was so still; she could hear animal sounds coming from miles down the lake. Nothing intimidating, just muffled sounds of life skipping over the still waters.

Mrs. Kelley promised to buy her sheet music. They didn't have time to pick up the order before they left. For now, she would play the music that she found tucked under the felt lining in the old black violin case that looked like a baby coffin. It was squared off and big for the instrument, but it protected it and the bow. The violin showed a lot of wear, but the sound was better than most. The top had a small crack and part of the fingerboard was lifting up and proud. The close grain of the top wood was very unusual. The tree rings were so close together and tight. It must have been a very cold place where this wood was born.

She didn't know who the composer was. The only clues were the initials SDG on the top of the last pages. There were over twenty compositions, and she memorized them all. They were from a time long ago. She surmised the late 1600s or early 1700s. Definitely German in style, tempo and vibrance.

She heard the generator shut down. Johnson turned it off at night. Not so much to conserve the diesel fuel, but to keep things quiet. When it was on you could faintly hear it in the distance.

This was the time Carolina liked the most. Still and dead quiet. The bats were flying around, but as soon as she played her violin they would not be noticed. It seemed to her that her playing drove them away. She was frequently sick in the morning now and nighttime gave her a break from her nausea. She was warned about drinking the river water, but the warning was ignored. It looked so clear and clean and refreshing. She "caught" the river bug caused by upstream animals.

She opened her case and took out her violin and tightened the bow before checking and adjusting the tuning. She was ready to begin. When she played, she could see the notes. She had memorized the compositions, like any good musician would do. She would close her eyes and play without the distraction of reading the music. On the dark dock of the Kootenai, she could leave her eyes open and see the distinctive colors that each note possessed. The louder she played, the more intense the colors would be. She could identify notes by their hue. She thought everyone experienced the same thing.

She began to play a violin concerto from memory. It started out so slow and quiet and calm before delicately building speed and volume through various crescendos. Her tone and vibrato was understated during these concerts. The perfection of each note danced across the still lake and certainly had the energy to glide over the water to the foot of the mountain that was miles away. You could sometimes hear the whistle from the Great Northern locomotives as they pulled into Whitefish. That was more than forty miles over land.

Carolina felt like she was floating across the lake as she played. It was so dark she couldn't see her hands on the fingerboard. It allowed her a deeper access to the music and that was the drug that kept her under its spell. She played for over two hours before putting her violin and bow away in their resting place. Before leaving her little heaven on earth, she said her prayers quietly out loud. The way it delicately echoed over the water gave them a feeling of special importance, she thought. "Maybe God can appreciate my prayer more." She prayed for the people that she worked with. She prayed for Clara. She prayed for the Kelley family and as usual, referred to them as her family. She prayed for her new sisters and her new mom and dad. She ended by thanking God for the love he at last lavashed upon her.

She gathered herself and stood up to walk back to her cabin. She lit the kerosene lamp and walked down toward the lodge.

She heard someone crying. Not a child's cry. That relieved her. It was Mr. Kelley. He was sitting in his big chair on the deck, listening to the concert that she provided. It moved him so much, that he just started crying.

"Don't tell the girls you saw me crying. They will tease me for years over that one."

"Oh Mr. Kelley, I won't. Is everything all right?

"Everything is perfect. I'm crying from my happiness. I'm crying because I don't deserve any of this. I'm crying for my wonderful family. I'm crying because your music was so beautiful and I'm crying because when you prayed you called me Dad. Thank you. I hope you don't mind, that I was listening. You are my new oldest daughter. Come over here and give me hug."

He composed himself and as she walked away, he said "I love you, Carolina." Not loud enough to be heard. She heard it and started to cry. "I love you too Dad." Echoed off the lake.

Carolina felt special as she walked toward her cabin. She couldn't believe how perfect her life was now. It was worth the wait for her Cinderella life to change for the good. Her feelings of happiness were smothered in love.

There is something about Montana that brings out the best in people. Everybody sleeps better. Everybody has an improved attitude. Everybody smiles and means it. There is no place on earth better. Carolina was sold on it and felt like she never wanted to leave. Of course, she hadn't spent time in the Winter there.

8

Those long and lazy days brought out the best of everyone. The best word to describe it is contentment. The family and staff started the Fourth of July plans, and the Kelley private train car was delivering guests from the city to Montana. Five guest cabins were built on the property intended to be wedding presents for each of the daughters. It was a sneaky way to make sure they would visit every Summer, as they grew older and married. Until then they would be used by friends and family.

The girls teased Carolina about not having her own cabin yet. "You better start designing yours," Mary said. Each of the girls was consulted on designs and just enough of their ideas were incorporated into the plans that it seemed they were more involved in the predetermined outcome that Mr. Kelley desired.

"We'll see about that. We'll see about that alright." Carolina chuckled.

Actually, Mr. Kelley had staked out a location for his sixth daughter's new cabin. "Cabins" is a nice euphemism for these homes. They may have a rustic look on the outside and be made of logs and stone, but they are all modern and very elegant. They lacked cooking areas intentionally. Mr. and Mrs. Kelley wanted to dine with their family every night. Breakfast and lunch too.

The interior designers were chosen by Warren Sheets. Their designs where of the San Francisco style, that featured rich upholstery, glamorous draperies, and beautiful handmade carpets over solid wood floors. It was a whole different feel and look than what they had in New York City, and that was intentional. Most of the furniture was heavy, colorful, and fun-looking. It wasn't in the Adirondack style; it was in a new western mountain log home style. Mr. Sheets wanted his interiors to compliment and contrast the wilderness just outside the door. The interior ceilings and various wooden walls were finished with the finest enamels and lacquers. Seven coats, each hand sanded in between the next layer of paint, rendered a perfectly smooth glass-like surface.

It was the day, before the fourth of July celebrations and everyone was trying to complete the last-minute preparations. The pig would be on the spit at midnight. The Chinese lanterns would be strung everywhere. The fireworks were set up on the diving platform on the lake and covered with tarps. The red, white, and blue bunting was hanging from every place you could imagine. The fire pit was loaded with large logs covering kindling and paper. The kegs of beer were on blocks of ice. The lawn was cut low and was perfect. The diesel generator's fuel tank was full. Chairs and tables were placed perfectly on the lawn. One of the Herefords was butchered into steaks and ribs. The servers and cooks were hired from Bigfork so the staff could enjoy the day and evening events. It was to be a grand celebration, as usual.

That night came early for the Kelley family and the workers. The party would start at noon, but a lot of work was still to be done. Early to bed tonight. The weather was always a concern. Last night was not the "red sky at night" scenario that Montanans hope for before outdoor celebrations, especially early in the summer season. Backup plans and workarounds were always prudent and planned. The morning broke with blue skies though, and that was a relief.

Thirty friends from out east where there. The top of the Steinway was lifted and propped open. The piano player's paper rolls were laid out to be loaded beneath the keyboard. The original piano rolls were actually "cut" by the composers. It was as if the pianists themselves were privately playing their own compositions for the Kelleys.

Mr. Kelley had a surprise guest. The famous Irish tenor, John McCormack. He had just become a US citizen, and this would be his first Fourth of July in America. He was to sing "Keep the Home Fires Burning." A popular song that would certainly thrill the ladies. He was a favorite of Mrs. Kelley and Carolina. His records were often played on the RCA Victrola in the main hall of the lodge. He would also sing "The Star Spangled-Banner" before lunch. It wasn't technically the national anthem yet, but it was played at the beginning of most every baseball game, and at military parades. The difficult song was no match for the voice of McCormack.

11:00 chimed on the clock, and the girls all went to their rooms to get dressed, and ready for the festivities. Carolina would make the final check, inspection, and adjustments for the sisters. The weather was holding. It would be a glorious day, and evening to remember.

Smoke was streaming off the huge outdoor grills. Red, White, and Blue were everywhere. Table clothes, napkins, streamers, and bunting all were adorned for the party. Even the Buffalo head over the main entrance from the lake was draped in patriotic colors. The flag was inspected the night before and proudly raised high above the celebrants.

Carolina had the girls standing in line with their parents to announce and usher in the partygoers. Making sure the stage had been properly set, Carolina smiled and started to walk away.

"And where do you think you are off to young lady?" As Carolina turned around, Mr. Kelley whispered "Your place is here next to Mary."

Carolina stepped between Mary and Constance, raising her chin and with gratitude and graciousness she took her place with her new family. She wished Clara could see her here. She owed Clara everything.

After a splendid job of greeting their guests, the girls were finished with their responsibilities. Carolina had shown them how to perform their duties and welcome their friends and new acquaintances to their home in the mountains. The girls made perfect curtsies, that were noticed by their parents. Mary, Carolina, and now Constance were also noticed by the young men. Mary was much better at flirting since her first attempt back in Central Park. Constance tried her best, but Mary and Carolina would need to make helpful suggestions before any hooks could be set. Carolina had no interest in men. She didn't know if she ever would. Friedrich the ice boy, had destroyed the joy of discovering the opposite sex, and the playful coquetry that any young woman would remember and cherish as they grew older. It saddened and angered her very much that she was robbed of that part of her life by a violent selfish coward.

Even little Nicole had a polished look that afternoon. She had to temporarily put down her Teddy Bear and go it "alone" with her sisters. She was getting very precocious and was always the one to watch out for. She was impulsive to say the least. It wasn't born from a disobedient heart; it was her natural and pure spirit. "Everybody loves the baby," Mr. Kelley would always say. "Even baby snakes and crocodiles are cute!" Nicole was much cuter and sweeter than any baby snake or crocodile could ever be. Nicole would sit her Teddy Bear on the bench next to her as if she were on a lunch date.

The guests gathered around the covered deck, looking out on the flat lawn. Mr. Kelley thanked all for coming and wished them all a happy Fourth of July. He then introduced John McCormack to the surprise of his guests. Mr. McCormack told everyone how proud he was to be a new American citizen in words and song. His words were inspiring as well as his song.

He stood up on the covered deck and sang the Star-Spangled Banner. The private concert in the mountains of Montana was stunning and even raised a lot of tears from the audience as his voice wafted over Swan Lake. The clouds even seemed to move closer to the ground as if to hear better. Soon those clouds would be crying too.

Grace was said and the food was ready to be served to the patriotic partiers. Everyone sat down at one of the long tables, that Johnson laid out in the morning. Mary and Constance were surrounded by four young men, who were waiting for them to find a seat before they would commit to their own. Carolina quickly joined in as a sort of chaperone. She was not as popular as the two Kelley girls were today. Carolina was so stunningly beautiful that it intimidated young men. She did not mind. Mrs. Kelley thought that she didn't know her own beauty. That made her even more attractive in her eyes.

Mr. and Mrs. Kelley sat down with the three younger daughters next to the huge flagpole displaying the Stars and Stripes. Nicole even laid Teddy down on his back so he could look up to see the huge flag.

The band played marches and ballads and even a few dance tunes. No one danced. Nobody looks good trying to dance on the grass. Besides, Carolina had not yet begun the lessons for the girls.

As lunch was finishing, the lawn games and reclining chairs awaited. Horseshoes, croquet, badminton, and bocci ball were quickly started. The wind was picking up, and that played havoc with the badminton. The usually still lake was getting a bit churned up, and you could see the floating dock bobbing. Nicole and Francis went into the lodge to start up the piano rolls. The two large French doors next to the piano were open wide to let the music be heard on the lawn.

The storm came from the East. It surprised Johnson the most. The weather aways came from the west. That was about the only weather rule you could count on. It came with a fury. The wind was wild and destroyed much of the decorations. It came in the French doors by the piano and blew the fragile Ampico Piano Rolls to the floor. Francis closed and locked the two doors to protect them from further damage.

You could hear the lightening now approaching from the east and north. Johnson and Carolina gathered all the children and got them in the house. Mary and Constance came in followed by the four boy puppies that were sitting with them. The adults stayed on the covered porch to watch the display of Montana nature. The temperature dropped by 10 degrees in under ten minutes. That meant rain. A lot of wind and a lot of rain would be coming soon.

The workers managed to get the important things tied down and squared away. Everyone was ready for the show. Mr. McCormack said it reminded him of the pastoral settings in Ireland that would be interrupted by nature's violence born in the Atlantic Ocean.

It didn't take long for everyone to come off the deck and retreat to the safety of the Kootenai Lodge. A fire was started in the huge stone fireplace and attracted a crowd. Especially those who lingered too long and got wet.

Carolina left the two girls and their worshippers with the adults to watch over them and went into the girls' rooms to close the windows. The lightening was fierce, and quickly approaching the property. A bolt hit a tree on the croquet lawn and dropped a large pine branch onto the playground. Carolina looked out the window and saw Nicole running to the dock. She ran through the lodge out to the lawn screaming at Nicole to get in the house. When she got to her the lightening was crackling all around. Carolina grabbed her a started running back to the house. She was screaming for Teddy and tried to get away and go back for him.

"Where is he?"

"On the bench by the flagpole!"

Before anyone could stop Carolina, she ran back down the stairs onto the lawn and found Teddy on the bench. She turned to run to safety.

That's when the lightning struck the flagpole, and knocked Carolina onto her back. She was not breathing. The rain was pounding so hard, and it was so dark that it was only because of Nicole's shrieking her father heard her. Mr. Kelley ran to the sound. He rushed out to the deck and grabbed Nicole from running back out. "What is it?" She pointed to Carolina.

"Don't Move!"

Mr. Kelley ran out to bring Carolina back into the house. She was unconscious and not breathing. He laid her on the long couch just inside the door as Dr. Garber rushed over. He started to massage her heart. That was the state-of-the-art medical treatment in those days and was less than successful in the majority of the cases.

Because of the quick response, Dr. Garber was able to get her to shallow breathe. He kept up with the heart massaging for five minutes, as he noticed that her breathing, although very weak, was returning. He stopped massaging and saw she was breathing on her own. She was badly burnt on the top of her head, but still alive. She had Teddy in her grip. Dr. Garber pried him out as Nicole ran over to see her. She wasn't interested in Teddy anymore. Her sister needed her help. Teddy would have to wait.

The four young men carried her into Mary's bedroom, and gently placed her on the bed. She was alive. The doctor bandaged her head wound and stopped the bleeding. It looked like her scalp had been ripped off her skull. Her sisters were all hysterical as well as Mrs. Kelley. Dr. Garber sent them out of the room after he had them close tight all the drapery. They all waited outside the bedroom door.

Johnson brought him smelling salts. He wasn't ready to snap her awake until her breathing improved. Almost an hour had passed before he decided to try. He carefully and slowly brought the salts to her nose. She responded a little. He moved it just below her nostrils and she came to and started to breathe robustly. She opened her eyes as Mrs. Kelley came into the room. She rushed over to her bedside and told her how grateful she was that she survived. Carolina raised her right arm to her ears and pointed. She weakly said that she couldn't hear anything and that her head hurt. Her eyesight was clouded with colors and shapes, but at least she could see.

9

All the Kelley clan could think about was Carolina's bravery. They were very careful around Nicole. They didn't want to make her feel worse than she already did. Carolina had saved the youngest daughter and sister. Nicole knew it was her fault. She left Teddy on the bench. Carolina went out to save him, and she was still recuperating in Mary's bedroom. Mary would have to sleep with Nicole to help her get through her nightmares.

It had been a week now and finally, Carolina was able to come out of her room. She walked into the living room nook by the fireplace and curled up on the deeply upholstered chair. Her headaches were less and the headwound, although massively scabbed, wasn't hurting as much. Her eyesight was back to normal. She was vomiting more and more, though. She was often dizzy and confused. Her life had changed so terribly in less than a second during that storm. She worried that her new family wouldn't want to have a damaged daughter. The Kelleys and her music were her joys.

Carolina was deaf, and she knew it was permanent. The doctor said it would come back. She just needed more time to rest. She could tell it was not coming back. They moved the Victrola next to what was now her favorite chair. They played records, but she couldn't hear. Sometimes, she could see colors and recognize the notes, but it was very faint and confusing. Not like before. The colors in her mind were very subtle and dim now. Mrs. Kelley promised her that the best doctors in New York City were awaiting Carolina and appointments were already arranged. It didn't help to lift her dead spirit.

The girls were lethargic and completely uninterested in the usual activities that made them happy. They were all so sad, angry and depressed about their big sister's suffering.

Just when it seemed things couldn't get worse, they did. Carolina noticed that her pants were too tight, and she couldn't button them anymore. She stood in front of the dressing mirror in Nicole's room and, after gazing at her horrible scalp, looked at her big stomach. She turned sideways and suddenly realized what it was. She was pregnant.

She broke down in tears. "How can I tell Mrs. Kelley about this? What would the girls think of me? What would Mr. Kelley do." She thought silently. If she had a way, she would kill herself. She cried for days. She hid in her room under covers and vomited every morning.

Mrs. Kelley was really getting worried about Carolina. She was deteriorating and they all felt helpless. Local doctors had no potions to stop this downward slide. She wasn't eating and all she wanted to do was sleep. The girls were mystified and had no ideas or solutions to cheer her up. They decided that Mary had to stay with her and talk to her. That brought its own challenges. Written words were all she could "hear." Carolina could still speak with clearness and clarity; but the input slowed down the "conversation" by the transcription process of paper and pencil. The girls needed to break out of their depression and helping their sister, the sister who saved Nicole's life, would take center stage in their lives and pull them out of their own downward spiral. They had a mission and purpose now.

Mary decided to move in with Carolina. She had Johnson set up a twin bed in the large bedroom. Mary was going to get her out of her room by taking away her privacy. She was going to pull her out of this somehow and she was not one to give up.

Carolina hated the idea. She wanted to keep the secret about her baby. In the early 1900s, there was only one other option for an unmarried pregnant woman. She prayed for a miscarriage.

Mary's plan was working. The two girls started repairing their broken bond that each missed more than anything. After two days of living together and reconnecting, Carolina felt she had to tell Mary the truth. Mary was the best friend she ever had. She owed it to her, to be honest. She would tell her after dinner. A meal she couldn't eat.

Carolina stayed in her room again during dinner. The staff brought her a bowl of soup and a glass of milk from the dairy cow in the barn. She couldn't eat. She was too nervous, and she was starting to lose her courage.

Mary checked in with her after dinner. She had to spend some time with their houseguests before they left in the morning.

Carolina felt better. She would pretend to be sleeping when she came to bed to avoid her confession. It would have to wait until she was ready.

10

Mary came to bed early. It was still bright outside. The drapery took care of the lingering sunlight. She saw Carolina was sleeping. She bent down and gave her a kiss on her cheek and held her hand. Carolina sat up, hugged her, and kissed her. She couldn't lie about sleeping and she couldn't lie anymore about her situation. It was time to talk. The love Mary just showed gave her courage.

She waited until she changed into her nightgown. As Mary started to get in bed, she asked her to come over and sit with her on her bed. This "conversation" would require closeness to get through it. She needed Mary next to her.

"What is it, Carolina? Are you okay? Are you ill again?" Carolina understood her.

"No. I have something to tell you." Carolina took in a deep breath and slowly let it out. It was time to confess.

"Mary," she started as she wrote out her words. "I have something to tell you, and I am terrified that you won't like me anymore. That you won't respect me anymore. That your Mom and Dad and sisters will disown me."

Mary sat up straight and held onto Carolina's hand. She thought it would give her strength. She could tell this was serious. As serious as you could get.

Carolina started to cry. She wasn't able to speak yet. Mary's brain ran through a dozen ideas and scenarios of what it could be. Whilst she was trying to process it, Carolina started to speak.

"Do you remember when I first came to work in your house?" She nodded yes. "I interviewed with your mother in the library. She asked me why I left the Bradbury household, and I told her it was because of a problem with a male worker. I told her I didn't want to talk about it. She didn't pressure me at all. I told her I would rather tell her later."

"What happened?" Mary had never had such a grown woman discussion with anyone before now. "Do you want to talk about it?" Carolina could understand her lips and took away her pencil and paper.

"Yes, I have to." She paused and looked into her eyes. She dreaded the next sentence that would come from her mouth. "I was raped in the basement of their house."

There it was; she said it and then lost control of her tears and emotions.

Mary quickly hugged her tight and mouthed that everything was all right. Carolina read her lips and hugged her back and whispered that she loved her and that she hoped Mary wouldn't hate her.

That peeved her a bit. She picked up the pencil and paper and wrote: "Why would you even think that? It wasn't your fault that a man raped you. It wasn't anything you did!"

Carolina hugged her again, took her hand, and moved it to her stomach.

Mary wondered why. After a few seconds, she quickly moved both her hands to cover her open mouth, started crying for her, and then hugged her again.

After she composed herself, she mouthed, "I love you." And picked up the pencil to write.

"I will be with you until we are old ladies. I will never abandon you. I will never forsake you."

Mary had a hundred questions for her, but they would wait for another time. She didn't want to sully their evening by asking anything about the animal who raped her. She didn't want to hear his name, as if it would elevate him and diminish the horror he caused her.

After a long time had passed, Mary got up to turn off the light and crawled into bed with Carolina. She needed her sister now and her sister needed her. They cried together for a long time. They would figure out a way to tell the family in the morning. Carolina fell asleep first and Mary was glad that she did.

An hour later, Nicole quietly opened the door, crawled between her older sisters, and fell asleep. Mr. and Mrs. Kelley looked in on them before bed. They both felt better and smiled when they noticed little Nicole snuggled in. They hadn't smiled since the party on the fourth.

The group of 12 visitors would be leaving before 5 am in the morning. Mr. Kelley had his train car waiting in Whitefish and ready to be linked together with the Great Northern locomotive in the morning. The Ford cars and the Continentals were fueled. Tomorrow would be a family-only day for the Kelley Clan. Carolina would join them for breakfast for the first time since the accident.

The sun rose at 5:00 am. The guests woke up Carolina as they left the lodge and loaded up the three Model T cars for the ride to the

Continentals and the station. She opened her eyes and saw that Nicole was wrapped around her neck and drooling. Mary had a contented smile on her face, and she decided to close her eyes and try to go back to sleep. She didn't want to disturb her sisters or the safety and love she was enjoying.

Mr. Kelley was confused about Carolina. He didn't understand why she was all of a sudden so fragile. It didn't line up with what he knew about her. He couldn't reconcile it. He wondered if she was taking on a spoiled rich-girl attitude since she joined the family. It was so unlike her to lie around and not do anything. He was grateful for what she did on the Fourth. He really was; she saved Nicole's life, as she exhibited total disregard for her own. That was loyalty, family quality loyalty. Something was wrong, something was off.

Johnson was back from the quick trip to the drop of the quests at the limousines. The girls had already stripped the beds and towels from the guest rooms. Breakfast this morning would be at 9:00 to allow the Mrs. to sleep in a little longer after their late night.

One of the games they played at night was one of Mrs. Kelley's favorites. The morning before the games, she would direct the guests to the library to select a subject for their "talk." "They should be non-fiction and a subject with which you have no educational background. It should be new to you so that you can learn, and we can learn. It can be about knitting or rebuilding an engine or delivering calves. It can be about anything, but please don't put us to sleep."

Last night's subjects included Lafayette, Albert Einstein's new theory, Rachmaninov and Tesla. Mrs. Kelley's secretary always transcribed the talks and at the end, they voted on whose was the best. Mrs. Kelley's award-winning presentation was about the exciting subject of properly growing orchids.

According to the notes from last night, Mrs. Kelley won hands down. The transcription noted that it was "unanimous" and followed by a very rousing round of applause. Whether or not it was true or just being polite to your host, it seemed to be a pattern. She never lost. It didn't cheer her up. The notes would be typed up in the morning with carbon paper. Three copies were made: one was circulated at lunch, and one was filed with the hundreds that were in a book. The third one was kept by her secretary.

The morning was a typical Montana perfection. After midnight, the temperature could drop to 50 degrees. That, with the help of the bats, decimated the flying insect population and made sleeping during the summer with the windows open for a few hours and then closed after midnight *de rigueur.*

Sometimes, the coyotes were howling so loudly that it seemed they were just outside your bedroom window. Mary thought they sounded like hundreds of witches dancing around a fire and screaming. Whatever the girls thought of those packs of animals, it kept them safely inside the lodge until the morning sun gave them the "all clear" signal and dispersed the varmints to their lairs.

High noon in Northwest Montana was around 5:00 pm. Since dawn arrived around 4:00 am and dusk at 10:30 pm, the hottest temperature of the day was achieved around an hour before dinner. Dressing for dinner was usually a sleeveless dress for the females or a light tweed jacket and tie for the gentlemen. The ladies needed to bring a shawl of some sort to be put on after dessert. The men were good to go.

Some evenings, the gentlemen would get into the StanCraft and go to the "Rock House." This was a stone structure made for the gentlemen. It was a mile or so down Swan Lake from the boat docks.

Numerous stories surrounded this mysterious bastion of maleness. One very large poker table was in the center of the room. Jim, the boat captain, was the dealer whenever a game of poker or blackjack was enjoyed.

On the west wall was the bar. Well-appointed and well-stocked with the finest libations of the day. Cocktails weren't popular yet since the alcohol was genuine and didn't need to be masked. Prohibition was on the horizon, though.

Stories always circulated about the Rock House. Some said it was staffed with ladies brought up from Missoula or another class of women from the mining towns. That was not true. Mr. Kelley loved his wife very much and was never unfaithful. The first time he heard the story, he laughed out loud. "That's preposterous!"

One night, when the men were there drinking and gambling, Mrs. Kelley arranged for the female spouses to be taken there to "surprise the debauchers." They sent the staff to bed and then dressed up in short and scanty dresses. Certainly, risqué by the standards of the day. Mrs. Kelley forewarned them of her plan in the spring. It gave her female guests plenty of time to "shop." The shopping was usually carried out by one or two of the more immodest ladies' staff. They had lunches in the city to try on their naughty outfits. For some, it was the best lunch they ever had. Way too much laughing and maybe even a bit of Champagne. They secretly hid their costumes in their suitcases.

Meanwhile, Johnson overheard talking about the plan. Dutifully, he let Mr. Kelley know. Johnson was always at the Rock House when the men were there. He never saw a woman there, ever.

Mr. Kelley devised a plan with the men who would be there that night. He made arrangements with the oldest staff members to dress up as even older-looking and sneak in before the wives showed up.

They were dressed like Queen Victoria. All in black, and the only skin showing was their heads. Since there were many overweight ladies in the group, it was quite a sight for sore eyes.

Mr. Kelley even had a photographer there to memorialize the epic "double-crossing."

As the girls were heading to the docks to board their women-only cruise, Mary and Constance caught them and laughed so hard that they thought the men could hear it down the lake. Mary said they would think it was the coyotes.

"I'll explain in the morning." Mrs. Kelley laughed.

"Don't worry, you can do it tonight. We won't be going to bed for a long, long while."

A large flat-bottomed boat was borrowed from Stan. It wasn't a typical StanCraft beautiful vessel. It was used to deliver building materials to the other side of the lake. The Rock House was the first customer.

The ladies embarked with care. The night was dead quiet and still. A perfect evening for the attack. The victims would have no idea they were targeted. There would be no survivors or prisoners this evening. Or so they thought.

When the boat reached the stone stairway that reached up to the rock "cabin," the ladies all carefully made their way. Luckily, the men had illuminated the stairs, they thought. That should have been their first indication that something was up. Too easy and too safe of an attack. They all made it safely to the main door and gathered for the massacre. Taking off their shawls and outerwear, they were a sight to see. Eight, not quite, but pretty close to being floozies, were ready for their floor show.

The men were waiting around the poker table facing the door in their oversized robes that Mr. Kelley had especially provided for the counterattack. The robes covered their tweed jackets and ties. Mr. Kelley had his burgundy velvet smoking jacket on under his robe. Behind them were standing four Queen Victorias. Not quite as "good looking" as the world's oldest queen monarch, they were perfect.

The door slowly opened, as much for the surprise as for an abundance of caution that they might see something "untoward."

In they swarmed. They saw the men in robes and the four "grandmas" in black behind them and stopped in their tracks.

The men took off their robes and the four queens took off their hats and veils. With the door still wide open to the lake, they all roared with laughter. The girls told them they could hear the laughter all the way to the docks that night.

The four queens served everyone Champagne, strawberries and chocolates. These society ladies had turned into ladies of the night and each one seduced their customers/husbands. It was an evening to remember.

According to Mrs. Kelley, some of the floozies got a little frisky when they got back to their cabins. She would have to warn them about open windows at nighttime.

That was last year. No one forgot that night.

Unlike last summer, this was the summer everyone wanted to forget.

11

Breakfast was right on time at 9:00. Mrs. Kelley arrived first, followed by Mr. Kelley. The girls were already in the breakfast room located just off the kitchen. Mary and Carolina would have a sit-down with their parents right after breakfast.

Carolina was nauseas earlier, but now she felt better. Maybe it was because she would soon be relieved of her secret. Whatever the reason, she ate more than one serving. Everyone noticed and was glad she had her appetite back.

No fork jokes this morning. Those wonderful meals with the family were behind them, and meals were no longer for having fun. Nothing was fun anymore. There was a cloud of worry and concern for Carolina.

The girls finished and Mary asked if they could leave her and Carolina alone with their parents. Constance felt she was old enough for an adult woman discussion. Mary begged her and Mrs. Kelley and Carolina gave her a glance that ended that. The four girls left the room slowly and dejected.

Carolina started. "I have something I have to tell you. I should have the day you interviewed me, but I was ashamed and humiliated by it." She struggled to hold back tears.

"What, my dear, you can tell us. You can trust us. It can't be that bad. We're all family here."

Mr. Kelley nodded.

"It is that bad. It's worse than bad." Carolina gathered up the little courage she corralled and blurted it out. "I was raped at the Bradbury House!"

Nobody moved or said a word. Then, suddenly, after processing it, Mr. and Mrs. Kelley jumped from their chairs and went to console her.

"Oh, you poor thing," Mrs. Kelley cried out.

"Is he in jail?" Mr. Kelley said in the voice of a man wanting revenge.

They both had feelings for the torment she was suffering. They just showed them differently. Neither was incorrect, just emanating from different genders and different formulas of caring.

"No. He ran away to Connecticut and boarded at ship on the Long Island Sound." Clara found out from the police. "He fled to Germany."

"Are you okay, dear? At least health-wise."

Mary looked toward the only mom she had ever known and, holding back tears again, said.

"No. I'm pregnant!"

Mr. Kelley was thinking about ways to have this creep killed. He knew better than to talk right now. He looked down at her and noticed her horrific head wound again. He wondered if she had the fortitude to take what was thrown at her. He just gave her a hug and then a kiss on her cheek and spoke quietly. "I'll protect you; I promise you. I will protect you."

Carolina burst into tears again. She was surprised she had any left.

"Don't be sad, my darling. We are here for you, and we love you." Mrs. Kelley added.

"I'm not as sad as I am happy that you still love me, mom and dad." She had called them that enough times before, but it never seemed quite right. They weren't really her mom and dad. This time marked the very first time she truly believed it. It was natural; mom and dad were the perfect nouns, finally. The Kelleys had already reached that conclusion a while back.

"I think we should leave Montana early this season. We need to get Carolina to the city doctors. I'll sleep better knowing she's in the city. She'll sleep better in her own bedroom." When Mr. Kelley spoke, it was usually not up for debate. Mrs. Kelley would wash and mend her emotional pain. The doctors would tend to her medical pains and Mr. Kelley would protect her from any more trauma. That's the difference between a mom and a dad. Dads protect and a mother cures. Along with Mary, she had the best team any woman could hope for, and she now knew it. She was going to make it through this. She would be happy again somehow and she would get her hearing back.

12

Plans were made to return to the city in a week. The staff was not happy because they would lose work time and to them, that meant pay time.

A few late summer visitors were given the option to come out even if the Kelley family was not there. No takers. The fun of Montana for them was the Kelleys and their family. They wouldn't know what to do without them there.

Carolina wasn't as nauseas as she had been. She was four months pregnant now.

Before she left the Kootenai Lodge, Carolina wanted to go out to the dock alone after everyone retired for the evening. She wanted to try and recapture the happiness she felt playing her violin without anyone listening, without any breeze and in complete darkness except for the Milky Way. It was almost total sensory deprivation until the sweet sound of the old beat-up violin came to life and vibrated through the water and wilderness.

She snuck out the last night in Montana to draw her bow across the old strings for the last time at the Kootenai. She didn't know if she would ever return. She hoped so, but she wasn't sure.

Carolina slowly opened her old coffin-style case and carefully removed the bow and then her violin. It was intentionally slow to not interfere with the quiet as much as it was to remember everything about this night. Her memory of this night would have to carry her through the tumultuous months that were ahead.

She was sitting cross-leg on the end of the dock that protruded thirty feet into the calm lake. After the bow resin was applied and horsehair tightened, she tucked the violin between her chin and near her left ear and pushed it to her shoulder to hold it tight. Clouds moved in and were blocking the stars above. It was totally dark now.

Her violin was tuned by Mary earlier that evening. She didn't want to make a sound on the dock until she was ready to play. She put her middle finger on fret board and pushed down on the third string. She carefully laid her bow across the string and pulled the bow toward her. She saw a bright red color in her mind. She could "hear" the color red. It was a high C. She changed strings and dropped down an octave to middle C. Brilliant orange. As she let up on the bow pressure, the orange became very subtle, but still in her mind. As the sound became quieter, the color did the same. Dropping down to low C, she saw a warm green color when she pulled the bow. It reacted the same way to the volume. She noticed if the violin was not pressed down on her chin and shoulder and touching her ear, she couldn't see any colors. The vibrations of the violin gave her mind the colors and in turn the notes and then the imagined sound in her head.

Carolina could hear music again!

She immediately played her favorite concerto. The flashing lights were making her dizzy. The noise in her head was awful. She had to slow down and play a simple and slow tune. She stripped out most of the notes and played a "one note at a time" melody very slowly. She could hear the sounds again by interpreting the colors. That last evening on the dock, she simplified every composition she had memorized and "heard" every note, albeit slow and elementary. She continued for two hours before she was exhausted. She lay back on the dock and stared at the stars that were now revealed by the clear sky above. As she laid her head back to look upside down at the flagpole that almost killed her, she noticed the group of coyotes.

She jumped up and so did they. They didn't move. They were not howling. She picked up her violin and the bow accidentally slid across a string. The coyotes sat back down and looked at her. She played a few notes, and they laid down on the lawn. Carolina sat back down and started to play a lullaby to her new friends. She swears to this day that they fell asleep to her playing.

She had to go to bed. She stood up and bowed to thank her audience and they stood up to compliment her fine playing. Carolina put her violin back and laid the bow in after loosening the tension. She closed the lid and carefully walked towards the lodge. The coyotes backed away in unison and in a show of respect, they let her pass. "This was certainly an unusual evening." She thought.

She felt like she had been playing to no one and, at the same time, playing to the universe. It was her way of praying and repenting. It wreaked havoc on her emotions, and she liked that. It was the high to her lows. It made her feel alive again, not just surviving. She fell asleep smiling on her last night in Montana.

The crew got everything ready for the return to New York. Mr. Kelley paid all of the workers their Total pay for the season, including bonuses, in full. They left on a Friday and got to the house on Monday.

Doctor's appointments had been setup a week before, and they would begin on Tuesday.

Things were triaged in order of importance. First was a visit with the maternity doctor. Next, the head wound care specialist. Third was the ear, nose and throat doctor. Carolina thought the hearing doctor should have been higher in the standings, but after her late-night Montana concert, she wasn't as fearful.

Mrs. Kelley called Clara at the hospital to tell her about Carolina and to talk about the charity fund raising event that she would chair this year.

Clara asked if she could come and visit Carolina.

"Of course. I'll let her know. She has appointments all day tomorrow, so Wednesday is the first opportunity."

"That's my day off. I'll see you after lunch on Wednesday, if that is all right."

"I'll let Carolina know. She really loves you, Clara."

"You must know that she really loves *you*, Mrs. Kelley."

"I know. She's our new daughter. Mr. Kelley and I love her very much. She saved Nicole's life. I'm certain."

The doctor visits all went well except for the hearing. Same thing the Montana doctor said was repeated by the Manhattan doctor. "These things take time. Healing such a traumatic injury is a slow process."

When Carolina explained what she saw and "heard" while playing the violin on the dock in Montana, she backed away. The doctor had this look on his face like she should be in an asylum. She would keep it to herself from that moment forward.

Clara visited on Wednesday. They were both so glad to see each other. Carolina had a small clipboard with paper and a pencil to make things easier for her conversations. Clara was startled by her bandaged headwound. Carolina could tell and explained to her the entire story. She found that if she just told the whole story, it could be tucked away and ignored because there were no loose ends to ask about.

She told her about her pregnancy and how her attacker was still hurting her. Clara closed her eyes and slowly nodded. She thought there was always a chance she would become pregnant.

Clara told her that Mrs. Kelley wanted to hire me to take care of you, at least until the baby was born. I said yes. She will speak to you later about that to make sure it's okay with you. Clara put down the pencil and gave the clipboard to Carolina.

She read it and smiled. "Would you do that?"

Clara nodded yes.

"We must include Mary in this. She's my best friend and sister now. I don't want her to feel cast aside. I need her very much to get me through this."

She didn't know Mary was just outside the door and heard everything. She felt relieved that she was so important to Carolina. She was there because her mother told her about hiring Clara. She was jealous. Now, she was relieved with the plan.

"I can't wait to see her again." Clara scribbled on the paper. Clara refused to accept any money for taking care of her friend.

13

A tutor needed to be hired for the girls until Carolina could hear again. There had been no improvement, although she was learning to read lips. She made sure the family was looking at her when speaking and not covering their mouth. She was drastically improving and now, at dinner only needed a couple of times with the clipboard.

Life was trying to return to normal for the family and it was a little. Hour by hour was becoming day by day. Carolina was due just before Thanksgiving. 120 days if all went well. Carolina didn't want her baby. It would be a continuation of her attack. How could she love her baby and hate its father? Could she put it up for adoption? Just have them take the baby away before she even could see and hold it. Just as one crisis ends, another begins. It seemed to her as if she was under relentless attack with no time to regain her strength. Reinforcements from dark places were standing by, awaiting to take their shot at Carolina. She thought her prayers were not relative. She thought no one heard them. She thought they weren't enough for her battles.

They were enough. God wouldn't let her lose.

Carolina should have learned by now that keeping things wound up tight inside her wasn't good. She didn't want to involve others in her problems because she didn't want to make them feel bad and she didn't want to be the center of attention. She didn't realize she was taking away an opportunity for people to love and care for her. She was taking away people's instinctual desire to help by committing this coverup fraud. Deceit never worked for Carolina. Her German blood couldn't be overcome by logic; it was a noose that couldn't be loosened. The stoicism that allowed the survival of her cultural predecessors was slowly killing her. The stoicism that allowed a civilization to flourish didn't work anymore. This stoicism was not the hard work ethic kind; it was the mental kind. This was a new type of problem born from civilization's success. It evolved from a previous era of slavery to people and work that left no time for personal thoughts or improvements. It was a new type of slavery that caused you to turn away from thinking about other things that weren't for surviving. It gave you enough free time to let dark things slither into your life and crawl up to your mind. It's the old "idle hands" adage.

Carolina shut her eyes to try and make it all go away. Almost like a kid covering her eyes to make herself believe you couldn't see her.

She jumped up and ran to the toilet. She didn't make it in time.

A new tutor was found for the girls. They didn't like her much. She was too serious, and kidding, laughter and joking were not on her class syllabus. They would do their best until Carolina was reinstated.

September brought cooler weather and shorter days. Carolina was doing better and feeling better. She still had pregnancy discomfort, but her head wound was not the horror show she remembered. The scab was gone, and her hair was starting to grow back. It looked like at least her hair would return. Her hearing was not.

November came and caused the last leaves to drop from the trees. Carolina was healthy and so was the baby. She had a very big belly that really intrigued Nicole. She would constantly ask to feel the baby kick. Carolina enjoyed that, too. She wasn't nauseas anymore, but her back hurt from the weight she was carrying on her small frame. She was ready to give birth. She was not going to give up her baby for adoption. Those thoughts and feelings started to dry up as the baby became more real. When her doctor let her hear the heartbeat a few months ago, she liked that a living thing was inside her. She felt the baby was a part of her more than a part of "him." She never said his name, not even in her head. She didn't want any part of him connected to her baby.

Mary helped her to separate the rape from her baby. Mary wanted her to keep the baby. All the girls did. It would be their baby, too.

Finally, one night, the contractions began and intensified. Mary stayed with her to help settle her. Then, around midnight, she went into labor. The doctor was summoned to the house, and Clara was by his side, holding Carolina's hand. Mary was on the other side, holding her other hand. The girls were all up and excited. Mr. and Mrs. Kelley were in the bedroom, too.

"Okay, clear out everyone. We need some room in here." Mr. Kelley was the first one to leave. He wasn't going to stay anyway. A birthing room was no place for a man. The girls slowly left Carolina and went to the library with their parents to wait. Mary was allowed to stay and comfort Carolina. Clara would soon be "working" and deserting her post, holding her hand.

Carolina was frightened by the unknown. She wanted a baby girl. She wanted a healthy baby. She wanted to hear her first cry. She wanted to forget things, too.

The contractions were constant now and the doctor and Clara prepared the end of the bed. The head came first, and the shoulders slowed things a bit; after a few seconds, out popped the shoulders with the body next.

It was a boy. A healthy boy. She couldn't hear his loud crying, but she could see he sure was big. He was weighed the next day at eight pounds, 10 ounces. Mary worried that she would be let down by having a boy.

After cleaning up the baby a bit, he was laid on her breast. The moment she felt his breathing and his warmth on her body, she was so glad that she didn't give him up. She was his mother, and she would be there for him. He would not be an orphan like her. Never.

She looked at Mary and Clara and smiled. A big smile, they were smiling too. Carolina started to cry and the whole room stopped and looked at her with some concern. She was sobbing, but with the happiest grin on her face. She loved her new baby boy.

She didn't have any names for him. She had two girl's names she was considering. Certain it would be a girl; she didn't even consider a boy's name.

The rest of the family was invited in. Mr. Kelley hung outside the door for a minute to make sure Carolina was properly covered. He carefully looked and came in to see his first granddaughter, and he said so.

"Daddy, it's a boy!" Yelled little Nicole.

Mrs. Kelley leaned into his ear to whisper, "you finally got the boy you always wanted."

"My grandson it is then." That little sentence made Carolina realize that her family was her real family, and her baby was part of this family.

He had backups if problems arose. She was relieved the delivery was ended and that her baby was healthy. She hoped that this milestone in her life would usher in sustained happiness and contentment.

They left her alone with her new baby and gathered in the library. It was time for breakfast, and everyone was hungry. Johnson came in and was surprised to see the family all in pajamas and robes.

"Did the baby arrive?"

"Yes, Johnson. We have another man in the house." Mr. Kelley responded with a big, proud, grandfatherly grin while putting a cigar in his vest pocket.

Carolina had to get to work to come up with a name for her little baby boy. It would not be easy. She had no idea. She would keep his last name as Augusta.

She settled on Stephen David Gabriel Augusta. The first three initials; SDG, were on the music that she found in the old violin case. She didn't know what they stood for or meant, but she wanted to acknowledge them. The music gave her such strength and peace when she really needed it. Whoever composed those pieces was a musical genius and they needed to live on. She tried to come up with a name from her new family, but they were all girls, except for Dad and his name was Cornelius. So, baby Stephen, it was. It meant *crowned one* and she agreed. David meant *beloved* and Gabriel means *God is my strength*.

She told Mrs. Kelley her choices and she wrote them down so Carla could have a "Certificate of Live Birth" created at the hospital records room. Mrs. Kelley liked the names. She liked the new baby and she liked having a boy in the family.

The months passed by with only a slight improvement in her hearing. She was able to read lips really well now and resumed her position as the girls' tutor. The girls were happy to lose her replacement. She loved her new baby and so did the family. She never thought about his father. She didn't have a single nightmare after Stephen was born.

They all delighted watching him crawl, then walk, and then talk. He was using complete sentences at eighteen months. He knew the names of forty zoo animals and spoke of them in English and also with its proper Latin derivative. Mary made flash cards on cardboard and drew the animals above the names.

When Stephen was two, he had an ear infection. Carolina woke to his crying and would place a warm washcloth over his ear to soothe the pain and reduce the redness. After a week passed, the ear was healed, but Stephen still wanted his *mummy* to come back and put another warm washcloth on his ear and hold him.

When Carolina figured out his ploy, she stayed in her bed and feigned sleeping. Stephen would cry for a minute and then stop and listen for his mummy. After another minute, he would start to cry again and then stop and listen again. This went on for seven times until he stood up in his crib and yelled: "Hey, there's a crying baby in here." Carolina pushed the pillow over her face and burst out laughing. "He certainly is a smart one." She mumbled.

He loved music as much as Carolina. He was given a child's recorder and mastered it in a day. He composed musical arrangements of his lullabies that astonished his mother. "Mother." That's what he called her now. Stephen turned three.

The family returned to Montana the next year after the lightening strike. Carolina was happiest there. Her hair length on the top of her head almost matched the rest of her hair. She didn't need to wear hats now if she didn't want to. She didn't want to in Montana.

Mr. Kelley loved to play with Stephen now. Mrs. Kelley did from his birth. She even asked her husband to spend more time with his grandson. He said he would when he wasn't such a needy blob anymore. When he first started to talk and called him *Bumpa* he gave in. That was it. When he heard his funny new name, he was in love with Stephen all over again.

Thanksgivings and Christmases were so beautiful in the house. The two oldest Kelley girls were best of friends. They couldn't have been closer if they were twins. Carolina learned early on to let Mary take care of little Stephen a bit more than her protective instincts allowed at first. Mary was jealous, and that really helped tamp that emotion down.

The next summer in Montana saw a big change in Stephen. Mrs. Kelley purchased a clarinet, a coronet and a flute for him. He was already playing songs on Carolina's violin. It would someday be Stephens. Mr. Kelley wanted to buy a fancy Italian-made violin to replace the old and seemingly worn-out one she played. She politely declined because it was the only connection she had to her old family in Germany. A family she never knew. He understood. He had an old pocketknife that was given to him by his grandfather. It was his great-grandfather's knife, and he placed on it a great deal of importance. He was not the beneficiary of family wealth. He didn't inherit real estate, artworks or money. America didn't have that many generations under its belt yet. This wasn't Europe. He asked if he could have a violin maker "go over it" and fix the fingerboard and the cracks on the lower bout above the waist.

Carolina happily agreed, but she didn't want anything replaced. She wanted all the original parts and pieces. "Done!" Mr. Kelley said. He took it the next day to his office and asked his secretary, Mr. Gross, to find a repair shop in the city.

The secretary's brother played in the New York Philharmonic as a percussionist. He would start with him. He asked the Concert Master, and he suggested a man that worked on his violin and provided the address. He was six months behind in his work. He did recommend a young man who was good, but not as experienced because of his youth. That meant he was less expensive, too.

It was dropped off to be "refreshed," as they called it. Careful written instructions were left along with the violin to not replace any part. Repair only and refresh. Carolina didn't want it relacquered because she loved the patina. In reality, she was worried it might change it and the way it vibrated and the way she heard music from those vibrations. She wanted to please her dad, though, and so she handed it off.

The young man did a good job. He glued and clamped the fingerboard wood. He replaced the old strings with new and carefully tucked the old ones into the small storage under the neck. He did not refinish the wood on the lower bout where the hairline crack was. He left it alone. He saw that it was made from Alpine Spruce. He noticed that right away. The growth rings gave up that secret. They were so tight that he wondered what high mountain forest they came from. It was the finest he had ever seen and he felt he wasn't qualified to work on it. There were no markings that he could tell that would identify the maker. He had suspicions. The tail piece was repaired, and the bow was gone over and re-stretched with new horsehair. The original hair was placed next to the strings in the case. The bow had no markings, but the curve meant it was very old. Maybe from the 1700s. This was a special bow. It was made for a standard violin size and was correct for Carolina's instrument.

He took photographs with his new Kodak Camera. This was a special violin and he wanted to add his work on it to expand his thin resumé.

The case was an enigma. It was Italian-made; the markings and hardware were the evidence. It was in fairly rough shape and needed its own refurbishing. It was heavy, intended as safe storage during long trips in coaches. The top was curved and made from a single piece of wood. It would have been expensive when it was made.

He played it with the new bow hair. The highs were brilliant, helped by the bow curvature. The lows carried a deep and sensual vibration usually found only in the longer style bodies. He wished he knew who made it. He had suspicions about who the maker was, but nothing solid. He could use that information in his repair resumé.

Mr. Kelley returned it to Carolina a week after it was brought to the shop. She immediately opened the case to see it and play it. "The strings were replaced." She wanted the original ones.

"The old ones are in the case with the old bow horsehair."

That made her happy. She wanted every part of the old instrument. She was glad the crack was still there. It was so small and stable. The body and neck were cleaned but otherwise, the finish was just like she left it. She put it up to her ear and plucked each of the four strings as she tuned them. She was relieved that she could still see the notes. The next step was to play it. The neck fingerboard was correctly curved now, and she didn't have to offset her fingering to conquer the old and proud mid-fingerboard defect. The cracked neck was glued and clamped back, and the repair was not noticeable. It was smooth and tight.

She raised it to her chin and began to play a concerto. She stopped to thank Mr. Kelley. "It is perfect!" As she played, her worries vanished. She could hear the notes in her special way. It was a great relief.

Stephen came into the room, saw the violin and asked to play. Carolina handed it to him, and he noticed the fingerboard was smooth over the entire range of notes. He would have to adjust the mid-range fingering to not play flat. No problem. He began to play a simplified version of one of the old concertos that came with the violin. He noticed the bow and new strings. He nodded his approval while playing. It sounded beautiful.

14

Summer was approaching, and the household was preparing to return to Montana in the second week of June. Carolina and the girls couldn't wait to get back to the mountains. Either could Stephen. He loved it there.

As the day approached, Johnson had everything arranged to take to the train the day before. He would also inspect the Pullman Car to make sure it was ready for its owners' three-day trip.

Stephen's instruments and the violin would be carried in the passenger area and not the storage room. Not that he was worried about them on the trip, but because he wanted to play them while on the train.

Everyone said their goodbyes the day before and tidied up their loose ends before boarding the private train car. The trip was uneventful. They disembarked in Whitefish to the awaiting limousines. The road trip to the gates of the Kootenai was more pleasant this year. Some road projects greatly reduced the time and the bumps. The staff was waiting and lined up in front of the Lodge. Mrs. Kelley told the kids that dinner was set for 7:30 and to show up on time. Stephen would make sure of it. He was a rule follower. That kind of riled Nicole. She wasn't one of those types. She loved Stephen, though, sometimes a little too much for his liking. He felt his older sister was trying to boss him. They got dressed and met up at the barn to visit Copper, the Herefords and the chickens.

After getting reacquainted with the animals, the girls headed back to the dock. The walk to the bridge that crossed Johnson Creek caused Carolina's arm hair to stand on end. She had this feeling before. Like all the other times, it was strange, but not frightening.

They passed the underground liquor vault. It was stocked full for the season and beyond. Prohibition was the law of the land and Mr. Kelley was not concerned; he had a plan to deal with the new Amendment and he executed it.

They all went into the lodge bedrooms and started to get ready for dinner. Carolina helped with the younger ones. Stephen dressed himself.

Chef Caleen Hood prepared a trout dinner with capers and garlic. The four trout were caught off the dock that morning. Potatoes and wild asparagus complemented the fish. Huckleberry pie was not on the menu yet. Too early in the season. Early rhubarb would have to suffice for the pie. Johnson made sure the fish forks were well placed. They finished the evening with Cognac on the deck, looking out at the sunset. The lake was still; Stephen was not. He was bored. He asked his grandfather, if he could get his clarinet. He called him grandfather now. Bumpa preferred Bumpa. He nodded yes.

The concert was a surprise. He had been learning a Handel piece from the sheet music Mrs. Kelley bought for him. Stephen was four and played like he was many years older.

He loved to play on the dock with his mother. He attempted to learn some Paganini violin pieces that were insanely difficult. He would have them down in a few more years. His fingers were too short and he couldn't manage the fingerboard yet.

Nobody really knew how advanced he was. They didn't have any comparisons to help them. He would think back to the days on Swan Lake and how the music, the scenery and the solitude were a perfect combination for any musician. These were the days that set his sails with perfect jibing.

The Kelley's had to find an instructor for their suspected little genius. New York City was the right place for this young boy.

The Summer was a good time for the family. Not too many guests stayed with them. They girls were all growing up and tennis courts were added to keep up with the friends in Newport and the city.

The Eighteenth Amendment was passed by Congress. Mr. Kelley worked around the pesky law in an ingenious way.

He hired six men to fan out across the state to buy up all of the stock from every bar they could find. They paid retail prices, which was lucrative for the saloon owners. He had one requirement: a signed receipt witnessed by the mayor or sheriff of each town. He didn't want any questions of authenticity to be raised. The new amendment did allow owners of liquor or beer in possession before January 17th, 1920, to keep it for personal use only. Now, Mr. Kelley really would have a lifetime supply stored in Montana. Packed with cash, the booze brokers cleaned out every bar they could find and brought it back to the Kootenai Lodge. Open and empty bottles were bought at the same time. The open bottles were listed on the receipts.

Three years into prohibition Mr. Kelley realized his plan had a fatal flaw. None of his friends had the same plan. Soon, he was loading cases on his train when they departed the lodge to restock his New York City friends' homes. He foresaw this possibility and had a backup plan.

As stocks got low, he started to have liquor brought down from Canada through the Eureka, Montana border. The Sheriff was paid handsomely to leave the border gate open on certain nights. The truck rolled through after midnight without stopping on its way to the lodge. No muss, no fuss.

He even made sure the staff kept every empty bottle in separate containers to keep them from breaking. He would have his girls pour the illegal liquor into the US Tax Stamped bottles and destroy the Canadian-stamped ones. He was running a family corruption operation with his own daughters. They laughed about serving time in the "slammer for bringing in the "hootch!"

Having legitimate receipts for over six hundred open bottles of liquor meant he could fill six hundred empty bottles with the Canadian booze whenever his supplies were running low. It was brilliant.

Mrs. Kelley didn't find out about it until the 1950s. One of the girls, who were all sworn to secrecy, let it out one New Year's Eve party in New York. Luckily, she had just purchased an Auguste Renoir painting the week before. She smiled and kept her mouth closed. Mrs. Kelley was a very intelligent woman.

Their stay was coming to a close, and the girls and Stephen tried to do as many fun activities as possible before they had to leave. Mr. and Mrs. did the opposite. They enjoyed the peace and quiet that wouldn't carryover to the city.

Stephen and Carolina played the violin most of the time. It was his favorite, along with the piano. His playing improved dramatically from week to week. He was a natural. It gave his mother great happiness and pride. Stephen was now giving the nightly dock concerts under the watch of his mother. It had turned into a family tradition now as everyone came out to listen and enjoy the stars.

The intensity of the night sky and the Milky Way is what strikes people about the evenings. Mr. Kelley said he would bring a nice telescope on the train next year. He already had the concrete base poured and ready for it.

The last night at the lodge this Summer ended with a Paganini Concerto on the dock. The coyotes even stopped by to listen but kept their distance.

15

The years passed and the girls were now grown. Nicole was trailing the pack, not by much, though. The young men were swarming around them at dances and balls. Mary was an enigma. She was a homebody and seemed to have no interest in dating or even participating in the simplest rituals of young ladies. She thought they were stupid. Once she had mastered flirting, she had no interest in exploring "the next steps." She had a reputation as a tease. That was not accurate. It was spoken by young men that were insecure and childish and surprised that she hadn't fawned over them.

Her family's immense fortune seemed to emasculate quite a few of them, too. The complications weren't worth the possibilities for her. She still preferred her sisters' company.

Stephen was now a violin virtuoso. Like his mother, he could "see" music. The colors and intensities were identical. Carolina liked that the most. They were so much alike. The fact that her son was almost her twin meant to her that he wasn't like his father. Father? What a strange thing to call him. She quickly stopped that course of thought. She was good at making herself believe he didn't exist, so to her, he didn't, except when she allowed her mind to wander off into obscure places.

Stephen was attending the preparatory programs at The Institute of Musical Art and was quickly elevated to more challenging classes and instruction. It seemed the only thing limiting him was the length of his fingers. That would come. He was just a young boy.

Carolina, Mary and Stephen were always talking about Montana. He wanted to live there. Like most women, full-time in the wilderness, no matter how regal your surroundings, was too isolating and during the winter, would require skills they didn't have. It was a dream of Stephen's and a crazy notion for the girls.

The next Summer, Mary moved into her own cabin and Carolina into hers. It was the first time for both. Intended as wedding gifts, Mrs. Kelley, who didn't see the immediate possibility of marriage for Mary, decided she should stay in her cabin for the season.

Carolina wasn't even thinking of getting married. She had her son to take care of and teach. That qualified her for early access to her wedding gift cabin.

The six cabins were all on Swan Lake, with the lodge as the centerpiece. They all faced the western sky that gave the bright afternoon sun a reflection off the still lake. The sun rays settled on the stone decks and the comfortably upholstered chairs facing west. Most of the log and stone cabins had a unique "eyebrow" covered roof over the doors. It was reminiscent of old English cottages or Swiss chalets of past centuries.

When they arrived in Montana, the two oldest girls and Stephen moved into their wedding gifts. This summer, they had some interesting guests on the calendar.

Queen Wilhemina of The Netherlands was scheduled to arrive at the end of June and stay for four days during her summer tour of North

America and Will Rogers for seven weeks in July and August. This was their first visit to Montana.

Mr. Rogers was one of the most famous persons in America. Known for his movies and syndicated columns in hundreds of newspapers across the US and beyond. He was also a humorist, and a political commentator feared by the Washington bureaucrats and elites, especially when he pointed his *plume* in their direction. His pen was more dangerous than a pistol.

Wilhemina was a Queen of the Netherlands.

"Uncle Will," as the girls would soon call him, stayed in Francis' cabin so he could focus on his writing responsibilities. Mr. Kelly, the secretary, would help him telephone and sometimes telegraph his columns to his editors.

He could entertain the household for hours as they huddled around the nightly fury from the great fireplace. It would heat up the room too quickly, though, and the seven sets of French doors were opened one by one as the night wore on.

Carolina's mysterious goosepimples when walking by Johnson Creek and the bridge were solved by Uncle Will. It turns out the site, where, Swan Lake, Johnson Creek and the Swan River join forces and flow together North instead of South, was an old sweat lodge site for the Kootenai Tribes. It was truly a magical pace. Uncle Will felt it immediately the first time he walked by. He knew something was special there. It was also the best fishing spot for a hundred miles.

Four decades later, when the property was sold, the caretaker who was left on the property year-round was asked about Will Rogers. A reporter from Missoula asked Mr. Stuyvesant to describe him. He told him he never stayed there. That infuriated Nicole when she heard about that news story.

Some of the girls' fondest memories from the lodge were interwoven with their Uncle Will. Nicole called the newspaper to tell that reporter that Mr. Stuyvesant wasn't even hired until the war ended, six years after Uncle Will was killed in a plane crash in Barrow, Alaska. She recalled sitting on his lap as he told the girls his stories. Funny stories, sad stories, love stories and western stories. He was half Indian and grew up on a reservation and his favorites were the western ones. She told the reporter that he was the kindest man she had ever met; ever. She told the reporter that the family was in New York when they heard on the radio that he had died, and how Johnson started a fire in the library fireplace, and they gathered around in a feeble attempt at recreating those special moments in Montana. They wept for hours as they recalled and retold some of his stories. Sometimes, they would have to stop crying in order to laugh at the fond memories. The Missoula newspaper corrected their story in the next edition.

Charles Lindbergh was a friend of Will's. He visited on two different occasions after his famous transatlantic flight to Paris. Francis had a photo of him riding a donkey in front of her cabin. He was wearing a tweed jacket and tie during the day while riding the animal. No saddle of course, his long legs dangling down and with his well-known grin stretched across his face. He was so famous that when he visited a nearby lake for lunch, the locals changed the name to Lindbergh Lake.

His wife didn't want to go to Montana. He married her the next year and moved to New Jersey. Mary wondered how things would have turned out if she had come to Swan Lake and loved it. Three years later, their baby, Charles Jr., was kidnapped from the second story of their New Jersey home. He was murdered by his kidnappers.

16

The girls, except for Mary and Carolina, were now all married. Mr. and Mrs. Kelley were getting older, but still made the yearly visit to their beloved Kootenai Lodge. So did the girls. The wedding gift cabins did their jobs and kept the family together each summer. Their husbands came too but because of business obligations, it was impossible for them to stay the entire summer without making multiple trips. The private train car was working overtime.

They all married well. Some arranged by Mrs. Kelley, some more organic. One spouse was the CEO of Brooks Brothers, an old-line, New York clothier to men. Another was the chairman of Phelps Dodge Corporation, the successor to the Anaconda Mining Corporation.

They all delighted listening to Stephen's violin and piano recitals. He now had a reputation in New York and New England as an up-and-coming instrumentalist and as a composer. His fingers kept growing along with his acumen.

Every night on Swan Lake, he would claim his cross-legged seat on the end of the dock and lay a bow on his old violin. The family, the guests and the universe, it seemed, would stop and listen to the heavenly sounds that travelled over the top of the still water.

One night, a large trout was chasing a fish just off the end of the dock. The little one launched into the air to avoid being eaten. It hit Stephen in the side of his head and almost cause him to drop his violin in the cold and dark water. The scream he let off startled humans and animals alike. Quickly composing himself he resumed playing from the beginning. After that episode, he always sat back a few feet from the edge. Nicole teased him later about the time he was in a piano recital. He was to play a very easy piano piece and quickly memorized it the morning of the performance. As he was playing, he started thinking about his new composition. He was creating colored notes in his head. They collided with the song he was playing on stage and everything went blank. He was frozen. He stopped and sat without moving for what Nicole thought was an hour. Stephen gained his composure, recalled he was somewhere mid performance and simply started from the beginning. Nicole decided at that moment that she would never perform on stage. She was a nervous wreck from that incident. Stephen decided to never again take a performance for granted. Each composition, no matter how simple, deserved to be respected by the pianist, violinist or any instrumentalist. He never forgot that performance or how important it was to stay focused during a recital.

As the summer wore on, Stephen regretted having to return to the city. When he first arrived each year to the Kootenai he was so excited and happy. Carolina noticed that his contentment declined daily until it crashed on the last week. It reminded her of the stock market crash the Autumn before. Carolina didn't want to return either. So many people were out of work and struggling. Soup kitchens and long employment lines were everywhere. The demand for copper declined too. Not enough for Mr. Kelley to be scared, but enough to be concerned. The value of their art declined too. Mr. Kelley thought it might be a good time to sell some. Mrs. Kelley thought it would be a good time to buy more. He agreed, not as much for the good deals that abounded, but more for the ability to continue to enjoy a scotch or two after dinner. He didn't want to upset that business arrangement made over twenty years ago.

Carolina told Mary about Stephen and her new desire to try out a year-round stay at the Kootenai. She was shocked when Mary told her she would stay with her and Stephen. It was her favorite place on earth, and besides, it wouldn't be fair if they stayed, and she didn't.

The scheme was launched. The three of them each had a part to play. It had to be rehearsed like a performance. Mr. Kelley would have to be onboard before they spoke with their mother about this crazy idea. He came along after a couple of hours and offered his help with the "boss."

It would start with Stephen. They all knew how much his spirit would decline as it became closer to leaving. He would start things rolling at dinner. Meanwhile, Mary talked one on one with her other sisters. She didn't want them siding with their mother if things went south at dinner. They didn't dare tell Johnson. He would snitch.

The sisters liked the idea. Everyone was on board except mother. She would find out that evening about the scheme.

"She doesn't stand a chance against all of us!" Carolina whispered.

"I thought you knew mother better. She was like a rock when she became stubborn." Mary reminded her.

"You're right." She knew that eight against one wasn't a fair fight when mom is the "one."

After a swim in the lake, the girls and two husbands came on the deck and dried off before getting ready for dinner. The husbands learned of the ploy and were all in. Ten against one now.

The girls suited up for battle in velvet and lace. Stephen put on his tweed jacket, tie and riding pants. He hated wearing them, but he felt it important that he dressed for battle, too.

They were already seated at the dining table when the object of this upcoming battle entered. Everyone rose from their seats as Mr. Kelley sat his wife at the opposite end of the long table. The girls sat down next followed by the "men."

Mrs. Kelley looked around the silent table that held the extremely well-dressed, for Montana summer visitors, gathered around it.

"Something is up!" she thought to herself. "Something's going on around here."

Johnson came in with the soup. Even he noticed something was going on. He tried, but he couldn't come up with any idea what the family had planned and who it was planned against. "They are sure are an interesting family." He mumbled to no one.

Mr. Kelley reached for his fork and stopped just before touching it. Stephen was duped. The girls were not. A few smiles were cracked when he had to return his fork to the table.

Mr. Kelley said he was sorry they had to go home. It seemed early to him. He reached for his fork again and stopped short. Nobody was fooled and the girls all started laughing. Daddy hadn't tried that joke for a while. It was a much-needed distraction. Soon Mrs. Kelley was laughing.

Stephen figured out his time was now, so he started.

"Nana?" That's what he called her when he was two. She loved it more than grandmother. It was not an accident. "Can I stay longer in Montana this year?" That stopped the laughter.

"And not return with us?" She was confused. "I don't think your mom would allow you to be alone in Montana."

"Of course not, mom. I would stay with him. We could take the regular passenger train back if we didn't like it."

Mary chimed in. "I want to stay too. Can I mom, Carolina will need some company. We'll be safe."

There it was, straightaway on the table for discussion. It would mean that she and Mr. Kelley would be home alone. The other girls were married and had their own homes and families. They lived nearby, but the house would be empty and quiet for the first time in decades.

"Did you know about this?" It wasn't a mean tone, but it was stern.

"Since last night when the girls put on the charm and told me about the plan. It took me awhile, but I gave in and said I would stand behind them." Mr. Kelley never lied to his wife. He sometimes was guilty by omission, but never lied.

"Does everyone at this table know about this?"

Everyone nodded as she looked at them individually.

"I'm outnumbered."

"No, you're not." Carolina countered. "I will abide by your decision and obey you. You are the most fair-minded person I know, and I'm sure you will make the correct decision for us and for you. I'm sure it will be fair, and I will happily live with it."

Stephen thought she was poorly negotiating. He would have tabled the decision and dragged out their case to whittle her down a little at a time. Carolina knew her much better than Stephen. She made the right choice. She looked at Mary and winked. Mr. Kelley saw it too.

"She's quite a negotiator." He thought.

"Why don't you just put a gun to my head? You're not very nice to your mom. I'm trapped!" She chuckled.

Now, Stephen was impressed by his mom's wisdom.

"Let me talk with your father alone this evening. I will give you an answer in the morning.

Now, can we get back to dinner?"

Johnson came into a chattering room. "Is it over? Did I miss it?" He thought quietly. He did."

There was no dock concert tonight. They all sat around the fireplace and Mrs. Kelley asked them about the best thing that happened to each of them in their childhood. One thing that they remember with the most fondness. They all moved in tight together. Mrs. Kelley wanted to remember this evening. She was worried they might not all be together at the same time ever again. She already had decided in Carolina's favor and would let them stay in Montana, she just needed to have her husband make her feel secure about her decision.

Nicole led things. "Remember when you took me and Erin to the pastry shop. I think we walked ten blocks to get there. You held our hands and swung our arms as we strolled. You bought us a bag of donuts. Mother never let us eat donuts. We took the bag into the park and sat on a bench and ate them all. We had powdered sugar and cream filling all over our faces. You told us we were the most beautiful girls in the world. Even with our faces covered with jelly."

"I do remember that." He hadn't thought about that day in a long time. "What about when we took you all to Europe for a month? What about the ponies we bought you?"

"I stand by my memories of that day in the park."

"That's my best memory too, dad!" Erin agreed.

Mrs. Kelley leaned over and kissed him.

Francis spoke up. "I remember when Paula Pierpont told me I was ugly when I was in the sixth grade. I came home crying, and you gathered me up in your arms and dried my tears. You had Stephanie come over to the house and style my hair. She did my nails with polish and then we went to Bergdorf & Goodman, and you bought me three new dresses. You got me new shoes and threw away my white, little girl socks. When school resumed on Monday, I walked in with ever so little makeup. Not enough to tell, but enough to notice. A new dress and shoes and a whole new attitude. You made me feel so much better. I must admit though I did feel a little jealous about those jelly donuts."

Mrs. Kelley now kissed Francis on her cheek. She remembered that like it had just happened.

"My turn." Said Constance. "My favorite memory was when you and mom took me to the Columbia football game against Yale. The Blue and White lost, but the way you tried to explain the game and rules, really made me feel special and smart. I just loved having you and mom all to myself on that cold Saturday. After the game we went to that steakhouse near the Flat Iron Building."

"Delmonico's. You had two deserts! Your mother's and yours."

"Mine's the best memory." It was Mary's turn. "Remember when I left my bedroom window open with my goldfish bowl on the ledge so they could watch the snow falling? I woke up freezing and found the water in the fishbowl was frozen along with my two fish, Goldie and Liam. They were my Christmas present. You took them to our doctor, and he revived them. When I came back from school, I couldn't believe they were swimming again."

"I couldn't believe you thought they were Goldie and Liam." Mr. Kelley blurted out before he realized what he just said.

"What!" Mary felt betrayed.

"Sorry honey, we thought it was the best way to deal with your grief." Mrs. Kelley tried to mitigate the mistaken disclosure.

The girls all started to laugh. When Carolina joined in, Mary did too.

"I guess I'll have to come up with another memory that isn't so gruesome."

"Your turn, Carolina." One of the girls said.

"I think you all know my best memories started the first day I came into your home. I was suffering, homeless and felt hopeless. Mom, you saved me. I mean it. I wasn't a child anymore, but I felt as safe as a girl could be. When I told you about what happened to me at the Bradbury home, and you all still loved me and my baby, it was like I had won the Irish Sweepstakes. Here I am with Stephen living in a world I couldn't even imagine. We both have a family now."

The next morning was beautiful. No clouds and sunny. It was 65 degrees at 8:00 am and no wind. It was a good omen for Carolina, Stephen and Mary.

They sat down for breakfast as Mr. and Mrs. Kelley came in and went to their chairs. Nobody said a word. No clues as to the decision.

The seating ritual ended, and Mr. Kelley reached for his fork and balked. All the girls laughed. It was a good sign.

"Mother has made her decision." He announced.

"I have, but with some requirements." She paused while Mr. Kelley picked up his fork and began to eat. Nobody else picked up theirs. They were focused on the forthcoming answer.

"I want Carson to stay next door. He can keep the generator running. They had power to the property now, but the generator, relegated to a backup status, was used at least once a week when the main power lines stopped carrying electricity. He can help with the fireplace and snow removal. He will have to bring his sleigh and horse in case of an emergency and to restock your food supplies. I want him to build a basket and rope pully across the river, so a vehicle won't have to attempt crossing the river in Winter. You'll need a cook, a laundry woman and a housekeeper. We will have to send out Stephen's school books and all his music and whatever you girls will need."

"Oh, thank you, Mom." Both girls said that in unison. Stephen jumped out of his chair.

The girls didn't need the staff. Carson, yes, but three more? One additional would be enough. They wouldn't fight their mom if she insisted. They would now be three of Montana's 500,000 residents. New York City had a population of 7,000,000. Their absence wouldn't be noticed except by the family and Johnson.

17

The three new Montana residents watched as the cars pulled through the iron gates of the Kootenai to Whitefish. The Pullman car was waiting to carry them back to New York. The goodbyes were difficult for Carolina, Stephen and Mary. Harder for Mr. and Mrs. They were on their own now with a staff of four. They didn't win that battle.

They had never been in Montana in the fall. Turns out, September is the best month of the year. Sunshine and cooler temperatures. October is about the same but with the leaves turning and the Larch trees beginning to turn, too. Larch trees are deciduous pine trees that drop their needles after turning yellow and orange in the fall. The surrounding mountains are covered with what looks like dying pine trees. They are perfect trees for the Kootenai. The velvety needles block the sun in the summer yet let the sun in during the winter months after they drop their "leaves."

The girls were getting driving lessons from Carson. The Model Ts had been upgraded to two Chryslers with the custom coachworks made by LaBaron. They were two beauties running down the road. So were the Chryslers.

Bigfork had a church, gas station, food store and a "bar" inside the Bigfork Hotel. Carson drove them into town one night. Stephen stayed with the staff.

They had fun. They even danced with a few locals who thought they were seeing a mirage. A few boys taught the girls how to cowgirl dance that night. Carson kept a watchful eye. He knew them both well. He knew they were pretty good kids, but he was the responsible adult and took his job seriously.

Prohibition was still the law of the land, but it didn't seem to make much difference. Evidently, the *Volstead Act* wasn't in force yet in Northwest Montana. Everyone brought their own booze in, and the hotel was happy to sell them mixers and glasses to use. The girls laughed on the way home when Mary remembered the underground vault that was crammed full of everything a bartender would need.

The girls returned with Carson the next Friday night. The trunk of the Chrysler was filled with dozens of different brands of real liquor. No bootleg for the Kelley girls. Carson was unaware. They soon became the Belles of Bigfork. The party moved out to the parking lot when they came into town in the evening. They always had receipts in the car for the booze. They didn't want to "break" the law or anything. Bigfork didn't have any policeman to interfere with the fun.

This went on for three weeks before the girls came to their senses. They had never been out on their own. Well, Carolina had been, but that was when she was a very young girl. This was more like the first month away at college or boarding school. The luster wore off rather quickly, encouraged by a few headaches and upset stomachs.

Two good things came from the second week while pouring booze for their "customers" in the parking lot. The girls met two brothers. They put their first weekend's dance lessons to good use with them.

They were two and three years younger, tall and handsome. They even smelled good. The owner of the hotel was known to stop people from joining in on the fun if they were dirty or smelled bad. Usually, a ranch hand comes in after finishing their chores on horseback all day. If the management didn't like what they saw or smelled, they handed the men a towel, a bar of soap and directions to the upstairs shower. Every now and then, he'd have to stop a woman that could use a little freshening. That was a problem because he'd have to guard the showers until she was finished and would take three times a long compared to a cowboy. At least women were good for business.

The girls made plans for the next Saturday afternoon to go for a sightseeing ride and dinner with the boys. They were a little embarrassed by their consumption of so much alcohol the night before. The boys noticed it. Next weekend would be without the booze and Carson to get them home safe. They felt they needed to repair their reputation. They joked about that all day Saturday.

They went to church as a sort of repentance the next morning. They wanted to be forgiven so they could forget their escapades. Just as they settled into the hard wood pews, sure enough, the two boys came in with their huge families. Carolina saw they had a bunch of kids, that they fought to sit next to them. That stole the wind from the girls' windmills. They had seven kids between them and two young and pretty wives. One on each end of the kids. Even mom and dad came along to help with the little ones.

Mary whispered to Carolina. "I guess we aren't the ones that should feel embarrassed." She said it as a joke, but it was a real let down. They sat through the service and took their punishment like adults. The sermon was about adultery, of course. Dancing and drinking with two married men meant all four were committing that sin together just two days ago. After the service ended, they tried to sneak out. Bobby saw them first and Tommy next. They both waved and said they wanted them to meet their families. "No shame with these two. I thought they were fairly honorable Friday night." Mary whispered to Carolina as they were marched over to meet their wives and kids. They were horrified.

"I'd like you to meet my parents. Mom, Dad, this is Mary, and this is Carolina." Bobby said. Bobby was Carolina's date for next weekend.

Tommy touched Mary's arm to turn her around to meet his wife. She tried to break that off. She was disgusted he would treat his wife so poorly. "Mary, these two girls are our younger sisters. Jennifer and Daisy." Mary moved back closer to her next week's, on again, date. She breathed out a little too loud and spoke. "You don't know how pleased I am to meet the both of you."

"I'll introduce the rest of the family to you at dinner next weekend." Bobby was really pleased to have his mom and dad meet their future wives in church. Both boys decided to keep that last night part a secret.

God sure is a joker sometimes.

The next week was spent picking apples and pears and outfits to wear the next weekend. The climate was as strange as the north-flowing river just outside the lodge. It didn't usually freeze until January. The moving waters and the mild climate caused by the easterly weather flowing off the Pacific Ocean created a little sanctuary against the much colder weather found around the Rocky Mountains, especially the Eastern parts of the state.

Carson was draining the water pipes in all the cabins except for his and the main lodge. The girls and Stephen moved their things into the lodge for the Winter. The staff moved into the vacant bedrooms near the kitchen. The cabins didn't have kitchens. Everyone ate together at the lodge. Besides, why heat another building with the fireplace? The Cabins weren't built for freezing weather.

They set up everything in the lodge. They made it cozier by moving some of the furniture closer to the main fireplace, which was guarded by the huge elk mount. Each bedroom and living area had large stone fireplaces that Carson would monitor three times a day and just before bed. After a few days of constant fire, the stones begin to emanate their own heat into the room. It was a big job and the only source of warmth. Carrying in the huge logs would have been impossible for them to do. January and February were the busiest for Carson. The other months were mostly mild. Stephen noticed that the back of seed packages had temperature zones listed for safe planting. The state of Montana was two zones colder than the little circle that was centered over the Kootenai. Carson was born there. He attested to the veracity of the seed company.

The girls talked and talked about their church experience, and they could never hold back a laugh. They had to avoid looking at each other when talking about it. Stephen was asking too many questions about all the giggling.

"We can't really be going to dinner at their home with their parents on our first date. Can we?" Mary lamented. "That was unusual in New York City," she said.

"That was normal in Germany," Carolina said. That started the giggling all over. "I feel like were being auditioned for wife potential." More giggles.

They both thought it was interesting. It's the first time either one of them ever thought about marriage. Sure, they thought about it before, but that was when no one was interested in them, or thought they had a chance with them. Now, it was a possibility. Why else meet the parents and the sisters? They would be sizing them up and making decisions just like mom and dad did with their four married sisters.

Carolina would bring Stephen along. If they were being ambushed, they felt the need to do a little ambushing of their own. Then, it dawned on Carolina. She would have to tell Bobby about Stephen's "father." She hated to connect in a straight line, her rapist to them. It disgusted her.

"What should I tell them when they ask about Stephen's 'you know who?'" Carolina worried.

"Tell them he went off to fight in the war and was never heard from again. You'll have to tell Bobby one day about that, if anything comes of this crazy thing."

"What are we doing, Mary? Talk about jumping the gun. Are we that desperate for a man?"

"Of course not," Mary said, less definitely than Carolina would have hoped.

"I'm still bringing my boy with us. If this is going to blow up over my son, I want to know the first three minutes into this strange dinner part of the "date.""

Saturday came with cooler weather and sunshine. The first week in October could go either way. Warm or Cool. The girls got ready and left in the Chrysler after lunch. They drove to the Bigfork Hotel and met up with the boys. They were glad to see each other. The boys really were handsome, and the girls really were beautiful.

They got in the car and Bobby drove. Mary and Tommy sat in the back. This was a real Montana double date, not the ones with two cowboys in the front seat and their hunting dogs in the back seat.

Bobby drove around Flathead Lake down to Elmo and had to turn around if they wanted to get back before dinner. They stopped along the way at little coves and hiding places that dotted the lakeshore. Carolina was correct about the boots that they wore. Mary was glad for that. Hiking wasn't on her mind at all that morning.

They drove through Kalispell to show off the big city. They thought it was nice the way they loved where they lived. How could you not? It was so clean and beautiful. The only smells came from the fireplaces that were started last night and fading away with light streams of smoke as the last of the night logs burnt off.

They showed the girls the Conrad Mansion and the Carnegie Library, just off Main Street. As they drove by the mansion, Bobby asked if they could even imagine living in a house that big. He stopped and laughed. They already did at the Kootenai Lodge. He didn't know that the house they grew up in was four times the size of the Conrad home and its library was about the size of the Carnegie Library.

"We better get home for dinner," Tommy interjected.

"Take the Chrysler," Mary said. "We'll drop you off to get your car later." Bobby and Tommy spent the whole morning cleaning and washing the old car. They wanted to show it off.

They agreed and headed home. Carson and Stephen were waiting about a mile from the farm they were headed to. Carson knew the family and was happy the other boys at the Bigfork Hotel were rejected. Carolina asked Bobby to pull over behind the matching Chrysler just ahead on the side of the road.

"What?"

"Pull up behind that Chrysler. I want you to meet someone."

He saw Carson and Stephen. He already knew Carson.

"This is my son, Stephen; I thought he should meet you and your family." Bobby jumped out and shook his hand.

"Nice to meet you, Stephen. I'm Bobby Harper. Get in; we were just heading home for dinner." He looked at Carolina to make sure that was okay. She smiled.

"Good sign." She thought.

Tommy looked at Mary to see if she had any surprises of her own. She didn't appear to be getting ready for any announcements. He got out to meet Stephen and say hello to Carson.

Carolina got back in the front set and moved closer to Bobby to make room for Stephen. They liked the new seating arrangement. Their hips were touching. She didn't move away. She was happy with his response, to Stephen's surprise. So was Mary.

They waved goodbye to Carson and headed home.

She thought back to when Mrs. Kelley recalled a playful conversation about her and Mr. getting older.

"Honey, you never sit close to me anymore when we go driving; I miss those days." She complained.

"Darling, I'm the driver; I haven't ever moved from this spot." He lamented until she moved back over to sit next to him and give him a kiss.

The Chrysler pulled up to the front of the farmhouse. The family came out to greet them. All of them. The young boys checked out the car as well as their dad. Those not looking the car over, looked Stephen over.

"I invited Stephen to dinner. He's Carolina's boy." Bobby told his mom and sisters.

"Oh, hi. Welcome Stephen. I'm Mrs. Harper. Hey boys, come here and meet Stephen." She complained. "You too, dad, where's your manners?"

After the introductions, they all went into the house for the compulsory tour of the boys' bedroom and the rest of the Harper home. The young sisters showed Carolina and Mary their bedroom. While inside, Daisy whispered. "Mary, are you on a date with Tommy?"

"Maybe, why?"

"They've never been on a date before."

"We were kind of on one last Friday in Bigfork. We were dancing with your brothers." Mary didn't mention the drinking in the parking lot. Way too early for that disclosure.

"They were dancing?" Both girls laughed at that thought.

"They sure were. Pretty good, too."

They laughed at that again.

"We hope you like them; we can tell that they like you two."

Carolina wrapped that talk up and suggested they go back downstairs and find Stephen. Mary wanted to hear more, but she acquiesced.

Stephen was playing Mrs. Harper's grandmother's piano in the living room. Every note that his fingers could reach was stretched to play the Rachmaninov preludes he found under the bench. Sergie Rachmaninov had extremely long fingers and Stephen used his more difficult pieces to gauge his growth. He was getting closer to being able to reach all the tortuous notes Russian composers were known to throw around like chicken feed.

Mrs. Harper had never heard that sheet music sound so perfect. It sat in the bench ever since her mom died.

She walked back into the kitchen, remembering her mother. She missed her.

"Come to dinner, everyone." Mrs. Harper called.

The evening was more fun than the girls expected. The Harper family was delightful. Bobby and Tommy were caught staring at Carolina and Mary more than once, and they were caught staring at the boys more than twice.

Stephen sat next to Mrs. Harper, and she soon realized that he was smarter, more well-mannered, better socialized, more educated and talented than any child she had met before. She knew that was a reflection of his mother.

"Tell us about your father, Stephen." Mr. Harper asked. There it was, along with a new bruise to his shin, delivered by his wife's shoe heel.

"He went off to the war in Europe and he never returned. I never met him."

Mary and Carolina looked at each other and marveled at the perfect answer to that question, handled by Stephen's brief response to that direct line of questioning.

"I'm so sorry, Stephen." Were the last few words on that subject.

Dinner was over and it was getting late. "Church in the Morning." Ended the evening.

The Kelley girls drove the Harper boys back to their spotless and freshly washed twelve-year-old Willys-Overland automobile. Stephen stayed in the car as the boys said their goodbyes and the girls thanked them for a wonderful day and evening.

Bobby held Carolina's hand and hugged her goodnight. Tommy decided he would try for his first kiss. A total failure. Mary turned her head after Stephen called out for them to hurry up. Tommy missed his target and kissed her ear lobe. Mary swung back and gave him a proper kiss on the lips.

"May we go dancing next Friday?"

"Let me ask my driver," Mary looked at Carolina for an answer she already knew. Carolina winked.

"We would love to. Thank your parents and family for treating us to such a wonderful evening."

Mary meant it. She missed her mom, dad and sisters very much. She would have missed Carolina more than she could imagine had she returned to New York without her.

The boys waited a few minutes and followed the girls home. They wanted to make sure they would get there safely. They watched the Chrysler pull through the gate and then turned back to their farm.

They drove through the gates and headed to the lodge. The first mission was to get Stephen out of ear shot so they could talk about what just happened in this cool and sunny and now starry Montana episode.

Sitting alone around the fire that Carson stoked back to life for them, they held their hands and giggled.

"Looks like we'll be going to church again in the morning!"

18

The phone that Mr. Kelley had installed in Mary's bedroom rang at 8:00 am as usual. Time to check in with the family.

The Kelleys were both on in New York. Mary called out to Carolina to come in. They always talked together before bringing Stephen on the call.

They rehashed most of the week and talked about the four girls in New York. No mention of Bobby and Tommy Harper.

"Carson slipped up last night when we called. He told us you were driving the Chrysler. He confessed to the lessons and the skill he thought you had when driving. Why wouldn't you tell us? We don't keep secrets."

Mary and Carolina felt bad about the omission, that qualified as deceit to the Kelley clan.

"I'm sorry, dad."

"Okay, anything else you want to tell us." He joked.

The girls looked at each other and nodded yes. What else could they do? They couldn't stack another lie on top of the first one.

"Yes, they both mentioned in a low voice."

"I can't hear you."

"Yes, they both said again but with more volume." The girls pointed back and forth at each other. They each wanted the other to tell them.

Carolina came up with the courage first.

"We have been dating." They both raised their shoulders and clenched their lips, waiting for the incoming artillery. The Harper boys were not pre-approved by mom and dad. All the husbands of their sisters were put through an intense grilling. As intense as any court proceedings and they were all quality "sign-ups."

After a very long time it seemed, Mr. Kelley responded.

"It's about time. Am I to understand you both have someone courting you?"

They answered in the affirmative.

They dropped their shoulders and unclenched their lips, removed their battle helmets and smiled at each other.

"Is it serious?" Mrs. Kelley asked.

"Who are they?" Mr. Kelley wondered.

"Two brothers who live in Bigfork." Mom's question was ignored.

They knew Bigfork very well. They Kelley family was credited with the construction of the small dam and electricity plant on the Swan River next to town. They had wires stretched all the way to the Kootenai. Everybody in between was allowed to hook up and electrify their farms and houses at no charge. Everybody on that wire route really liked the Kelley family and the endless free electricity. Until later, when President Roosevelt took over public utilities in the name of progress.

The houses and farms that were illuminated with way too many light bulbs suddenly went dark after their first-ever utility bill arrived.

To them, it was reverse progress. First world to the third world in one day.

"Okay, girls, don't do anything foolish. If you still like them next Summer, we would like to meet them."

"That went well," they both though to themselves. "Really well."

"Thanks, daddy. It's probably nothing," Mary said this to make him feel better. She always used "daddy" to make him happy when he needed a little extra care.

Stephen came on to talk next.

"Mom and Mary have boyfriends!"

Fall was winding down. It tried to snow the day before. Not much to show for it. Fog was billowing off the lake every morning now. Frost was finishing off the flowers and putting the landscaping to bed for the season. The grass was still green, but the trees had their foliage stripped away. You could tell the difference in seasons in Montana by listening to the wind. Summer always had a rustling sound as the warm breezes danced across the trees and ruffed their green "feathers."

Early fall sounds were sharper and higher pitched as the increased winds worked through the trees that were dropping leaves. Even the Larch trees had their own signature sound. The clouds travelled faster, and gray edges showed up to change the summer's pure white puffs of cotton into a different, natural, new fall cloud couture collection.

The squirrels were busy while the bats had abandoned Montana on their voyage to Texas for the Winter. Red fox, Whitetail deer and Bald Eagles didn't abandon their posts to search for warmer weather like the ducks and geese flying South in a precise, almost military-style formation.

The now continual fires in the huge stone fireplaces greeted them every late afternoon. Thanks to Carson. He was prepared for Winter. It wasn't his first one.

Mr. Kelley offered to send the train car if they wanted to come home for Christmas. They said they would think about it. He told them that their mother really needed to see them.

The girls didn't want to leave the "boys" behind. They wanted to spend Christmas with them. After all, they spent just about every afternoon and weekend together. This made Mary happy and Carolina sad.

Carolina knew she would have to eventually tell Bobby about Stephen's father. She hated calling him that. The time was clearly approaching to get it out and in the open. She hoped he would be as loving as the Kelley family. It hung over her time with Bobby like a dark veil. She was doing what she did before with the Kelleys. She was not giving him an opportunity to love her, hold her, and tell her it didn't matter. It's my German heritage, she thought, as if that would lift the blame from her.

Mary was all in on the trip to New York for the holidays. She wanted to go for a week. She couldn't leave Tommy for longer. But that meant two weeks with the train travel added to the calendar.

"Why don't we invite the boys?" Mary said as if she had just unraveled a difficult physics equation.

Carolina liked the idea, but that meant she would have to make her painful disclosure earlier than she had cared to do.

We can bring Carson as our chaperone. That would work for Daddy. He could find a replacement caretaker while we were away. The boys could get off work at the farm and their handyman jobs in December. Nobody worked anyway. Hunting was the only job most men in the valley performed in December. It was more than a sport to them. It was the time to secure food for the next four months of winter. It was a man's responsibility to his family. The Harper's had enough men left behind to fill in for their absence. The more Mary thought about it, the more her plan made good sense. The more Carolina thought about it, the more she dreaded the idea.

Mary looked over at her, perplexed. Then it dawned on her. She didn't want to tell Bobby her secret.

"Carolina, I just figured out why you're not happy with my idea. I'm sorry. I'm so callous sometimes. I understand why now. But don't you think this is like the first time you introduced Stephen to the Harpers? You said you wanted to know if he was a problem right away. You wanted it out to prevent everybody from wasting their time if Bobby or his family had a problem with Stephen, the boy that gave her so much joy."

"I know, I know!" she cried.

"Let's face it, we love our boys. All three. This is heading to marriage, as far as I can tell. Bobby loves Stephen and he loves Bobby. He's like his father. This is true love, just like the Hollywood movie star magazines show it to be. It's time to gather your courage once again. The same courage I've seen repeatedly in your heart and in your actions."

"You're right. We'll ask if we can bring them on next Sunday's telephone call. Deal."

"Deal. We can strategize a little before Sunday."

"You mean a lot of strategizing, don't you!" Mary said as she closed the deal.

Right on schedule, the call came into the lodge.

"Hi honey, did you girls give any thought to coming for Christmas."

"Yes, Momma." She coyly used the more affectionate version of her mother. "With two requirements, though."

"Ha," laughed Mr. Kelley. "You're just like your mother. How much is this going to cost me?"

"Not much," Mary said. "At least not now." She was thinking about the double wedding in the lodge next summer. She hadn't told Carolina about that fantasy.

"Okay, what is it?"

"We want to bring our boyfriends with us on the train to spend Christmas with our family. It's the perfect time for you to approve or deny our relationship. We will abide by your wishes. We don't want to be away from them for weeks, especially at Christmas."

"Girls, you can't travel without a chaperone."

"We thought Carson would make a fine guard. Besides, he knows the family well."

"A chaperon, not a guard."

"Oh, oh, right, momma, not a guard."

Mr. Kelley remained silent on the call. This one would have to be handled by the officer in charge and that person was not him.

"Okay, we will call you back tonight before your dinner. Now put Stephen on."

Mary thought that things went well. She overheard Stephen's call and could tell he was being questioned by the answers he gave.

"Yes, I really do like them. I know you will, too." Stephen smiled at his mom.

They said goodbye and waited for the answer. If they got the go-ahead, they would approach the Harper family and then Carson to tie up the loose ends. Mary wanted to be gone for the month. Two weeks to prepare for Christmas and another week for the New Year's parties. Three days of travel time each way.

Just before dinner, they got the call back.

"Yes, my dears, we would love to meet your beaus."

Mary doesn't remember the rest of the call; she wasn't even listening. She was busy planning things in her head. Stephen would have warned her to be careful if he had known. He learned that lesson during the fateful recital a few years ago.

They telephoned the boys. They just got a telephone at the house. Bobby pressed hard for their modern amenity.

"We would like you two to come for dinner Tuesday evening. We have things to talk about."

"Okay." He said with a tinge of nervousness in his voice. "What time?"

Tommy put the phone back on the wall hook and walked upstairs to tell Bobby.

"What did you do?"

"Nothing, I did nothing. We're always together, you know everything."

"Except for last weekend when you two went off to be alone. You were gone an hour."

"Oh please, I'm too chicken to get in any trouble. It was just a little kissing and maybe an accidental brush of the hand in places that they shouldn't venture."

"I guess we'll find out on Tuesday."

They arrived on time at the Kootenai and went into the main room to await their hearing. They didn't expect anything bad, but you never know. They talked about it more on that Sunday. Bobby wondered if they were going to make a play to get them to propose. Tommy wondered if Mary was planning to break things off. If that were the plan, they would have to do it to both of them. They always did things together, just like Bobby and Tommy.

The girls entered the room and looked so pretty, too.

"This is good. They wouldn't get gussied up to get rid of us." Their minds were synced in on that thought.

After they both received very intimate kisses, they knew they weren't in trouble. Their male minds ran immediately to the proposal scenario. Sure, they loved them, but they hadn't even met their parents. They would need time for family conferences first. Besides, they didn't normally carry engagement rings in their pockets.

Katherine brought in a tray with four glasses and set it down. She left to get the hors de oeuvres.

"These are called Manhattans. I hope you like them." Mary smiled.

"What is in them? I can see the dark cherry and orange peel."

"Whiskey, Luxardo liqueur and sweet vermouth. Finished with the aged Italian-style cherry, orange peel and a dash of Peychaud's bitters. The cherries are Flathead Cherries that were put up last year by the other Mr. Kelly when he bought them on his tour around the lake."

"Okay, they thought." Now, they were both really confused. What was going on here? What do they want? Are they seducing us? Are we moving too slowly for their New York time frame? Do they want to make love to us?

"I'm waiting for marriage before I'll go that far," Tommy declared to himself silently. He wasn't sure if his decision was based on morals or his virginity situation. He hoped Bobby was of the same mindset. They were good boys. He remembered when their dad took them hunting individually as they turned fourteen to talk about girls and babies. He remembers his answers to his dad's questions that were designed to teach them.

"Can I ask why you would want to date a girl?"

Tommy thought about that for a few minutes before answering. He had never thought about anything to do with dating before. His dad liked that he gave it serious thought before answering.

"To me, dating is for finding your mate, finding your wife. Not for fun as much as planning your future together." Good answer, he thought; it was genuine.

"When you do go on a date. How far would you go?"

"What do you mean dad."

"Would you touch them where you shouldn't?"

"What?" he replied.

"Would you kiss them? Would you touch their breasts, under their blouse?

This was getting really embarrassing and awkward for Tommy. But he gathered himself and thought again for a few minutes before answering.

"Dad, from what I can tell, most first dates don't end in marriage. So, no, I would touch them there."

"Why not?"

"Because they will probably be some other man's wife one day. I would hope someone who dates my future wife before I do would respect her like I would his future wife."

His dad was very impressed with his mature and carefully thought-out answers. He meant what he said. He didn't tell his dad that he got a head's up from Bobby after his hunting/learning about girls' trip. He had thought about his future wife a lot and he meant every word when he said them to his dad years ago. Nothing changed. He felt bad about brushing up against Mary's breast last week. He didn't go underneath her blouse, though. He was in the clear.

Katherine called them to dinner.

The answers to their questions would be put off for a short time.

Katherine brought in the main course. Trout in Flathead Cherry sauce.

"We are going to New York City for Christmas. Mom and dad miss us and want us home for three or four weeks. We feel obligated; none of their girls live at home. It will be Christmas. They need us. Will you forgive us? I will miss you, Bobby. I wanted to be with you this Christmas so badly."

Mary felt the same and told Tommy so.

"I, I mean we, want you to come with us. Will you, please." Mary pleaded.

"How can we? Where would we stay? Would your parents allow us to travel with you? How would we get there? How much will it cost?"

Dinner got quiet quickly. The girls had the answers; they just weren't ready to tell them. The girls knew that the boys would have to be involved in the solution. It would be important that they worked out some of the details. It would also confirm that they really wanted to be with them during the holiday. It would confirm their, dare Mary say it. "Love."

They finished dinner and the girls went off to freshen up. They actually wanted to leave the boys alone to work out a Christmas plan. They hid for ten minutes and met them at the fireplace.

"We have a plan. You ask your parents if they approve of our visit. If they agree, we'll talk with our parents. We'll need a chaperone. For my parents, for your parents' peace of mind and for your honor. If we get this done, we'll figure out the rest."

"We already spoke to our parents about this. They approved."

The boys smiled when they figured out that they were so expertly played.

"Okay, we'll speak with our parents tomorrow. If they say yes, will you both come for dinner?"

"Are you sure?"

"Yes."

They enjoyed the rest of the evening by the fireplace. Carson seemed to interrupt things at the perfect time to check on the fire. And perfect timing to break up the lovebirds from overindulging in things that can be difficult to stop when the passions of youth are challenged.

Carolina and Mary retired to their bedrooms just before midnight. They spent time in conversation before sleeping. There are times when you want to get to bed to regale in the situation that just unfurled and savor them quietly in solace. Other times, it can be productive to continue enjoying and honoring the important feelings and emotions in order to extend their memories by recalling them and repeating them, all the while looking for minor details to add to the event and improve those memories. That's what they did and they talked until 2:00 am.

The Harper boys did the same thing during the car ride back home. They joked about surviving a close call. That close call was a marriage proposal. The had fun with that. The joking, though, was just a cover story that guys conjure to avoid dwelling on things of the heart and acknowledging they're in love. The realty was that they both did love the girls, and both wanted to marry them. Hormones tend to work harder and overtime for good boys more than they do for bad boys. The girls slept well; the boys woke up tired.

The boys asked and received permission from their parents at breakfast. They were surprised. Bobby thought the message was: "You've overstayed your time in the house; it's time to find a wife."

Before going out, Bobby called the two of them to say, "we are going to New York City." He ended with a faint "I love you."

Mom heard him and smiled. "Dinner at 6:00, invite the girls."

19

Mary called home to tell her mother the good news. "We're all coming for Christmas. I'll talk with Carson this morning. I'm so happy to be able to see you, mom."

"So are we. I'll have two bedrooms made up on the third floor. They're staying with us, right?

"Perfect, thanks."

The two settled on a date to meet the train in Whitefish. After a relaxing train car ride, the activities for them and the boys would be a *contra punctus,* as Stephen would say, to Montana. He loved Bach's "counter point" musical style. It was popular in the 1700s and many composers tried to outshine each other. Bach jumped in and set the standard. Most were three parts. Bach had some four-part compositions. The astounding thing was that each counter point melody could stand alone as the basis of a composition. Four together was perfection. So perfect that other very good composers just stopped trying to create their own and threw in the towel. They acknowledged defeat. Stephen loved that.

The girls arrived just before six and the Harper's were waiting on the porch. The sun set an hour ago, so it was chilly. They hurried inside and sat by the fire. The boys were still getting dressed. Mrs. Harper said they had a rough day helping dad with the farm work. "A lot to do before the first hard freeze rolls in from Canada."

They saw the girls by the fire. The warm light gave them an angelic glow. They sat down next to each other's dinner date and gave a pathetic kiss. They didn't want to be teased anymore about having their first girlfriends.

Tommy went back for more and gave Mary a full-stop smooch. Now, Bobby thought he should do the same, but instead opted for holding Carolina's hand tight. Both signs of affection were appropriate for the time and circumstances, especially when you're surrounded by sibling spies watching from their stairway perch.

Why do sisters and girls delight in watching other lovers? Are they happy for them, jealous because of them or simply living substitutionally through them? Most likely, all three are just individually calibrated to suit each's needs.

They all went to dinner together and sat at the usual places. They talked about the upcoming adventure for the boys and the homecoming for the girls via the train.

"How much are train tickets?" Mr. Harper wondered. "You boys better start working extra hours."

Mary said the "tickets" were taken care of.

"Bobby, Tommy, you can't let them pay for your trip."

"We won't, dad. We both have plenty of money in the bank and we decided to pay for their tickets and Stephen's, too."

"How much do we owe you girls? Tommy asked.

"Nothing, it's free. Dad has a private Pullman Car that he is sending out to take us home."

"What?" Two or three people said out loud.

"I won't allow that to happen, boys. You can't be in a private train car with two young ladies alone. I won't have it."

"Mrs. Harper, my mother said the same thing to us; that's why Carson is accompanying us. And Stephen is a more watchful eye than your daughters hiding on the stairs." The sibling spies looked down and started eating.

"Good, I know Carson and his family. They are good people. I know Stephen will be a good backup." That was truer than she thought. Stephen loved his mother and was always looking out for her. He had strong morals and wouldn't let them bend theirs.

"Now we need to find lodging. Could you girls help us with a reasonably priced rooming house?"

"We already have two rooms awaiting."

"Where?"

"On the third floor of our home."

"Your house has three floors?"

"Five, actually."

Carolina thought back to her first day on the job. Making the beds that now her future husband would sleep in. She chuckled as soon as the two words "future husband" was thought. This was happening a lot in her mind. She was glad that Mary and she wouldn't have an arranged marriage. Her four sisters did and although she was happy for them, she was sad for them at the same time. Something is missing from the game if the hunting and chasing part is eliminated. She had learned from Bobby that the game you hunt and eat tastes better than the stuff passed over the counter and put in your market basket. Even if it's not better, it always seems to taste better.

"Carson can drive us all and leave the Chrysler in Whitefish. The train trip is three days. We get into the city around noon. Geoffrey will pick us up in the big car and another will carry our luggage."

"What about clothes? Do I need to buy anything?"

"No." Carolina lied. "Maybe a jacket for dinner. We can borrow a coat or two. You'll be fine." Mr. Kelley would take care of that. They needed a compete rehab before meeting friends and family and he would see to it that Johnson would smooth over that bump and prep them in manners along with the wardrobe make-over.

"How exciting." Mrs. Harper exclaimed. "We'll really miss you all for Christmas. But you boys sure will see new sights. Private Pullman train car to New York City, chauffeured cars to a five-story mansion in Manhattan. Oh my!"

20

The morning of the trip came early. They hadn't seen the boys all week. Mr. Harper kept them busy keeping their responsibilities and promises that he negotiated before running off to New York. Everything was completed and they were free as birds now. The Chrysler pulled up to the farmhouse and loaded up the boys, their toiletries and change of clothes for the journey. Their suitcases were already on the train and in the storage area.

Stephen was a little sorry that his first Christmas in Montana was subverted. That was made easier knowing he would be with his grandfather and grandmother. He had a few new violin concertos to perform, and they were expecting a heavy concert schedule from him.

The train pulled from the station on the first part of the journey through Glacier National Peace Park. The boys had never seen it up close. They could see the mountains from forty miles away. The always had snow on the very tops. You could judge the height by comparing them to the smaller mountains around Swan Lake. They only had snow in the winter.

Just before it was time for lunch, Tommy brought out sandwiches that his momma made for the trip. Just as he was unwrapping things, the trays with silver covers hiding the food were rolled in from the forward car. Tommy carefully put his sandwiches back in the bags. He would use them as late-night snacks.

When they finished, and the carts were rolled out, they settled onto the couches as the flat plains of eastern Montana approached.

"I have some ground rules you need to know," Carson said to everyone except Stephen. "You can sit close to each other, you can hold hands and even put your arms around your girlfriends' shoulders. Anything else and I'll blow the whistle and throw the penalty flag. Second warning will be followed by a benching. A third warning will get you suspended and thrown off the train."

Carson was the high school football coach in Bigfork before he started his caretaking career. He loved his football analogies.

"What about me?" Mary asked. "It's my dad's train."

"I don't think I have to worry about you girls. So, I don't plan on throwing you off the train."

"I thought you knew Mary and me better." Carolina was playing with Carson now. "We can be trouble."

Stephen rolled his eyes and went to the other end of the train and started to play his violin. "I wish we could have stayed at the lodge." He whispered to himself.

After three days of mostly behaving themselves, the train pulled into the station. The Bentley was waiting to take them home. Carson instructed them to leave their belongings behind. He would make sure everything got to the right bedroom. Geoffrey brought a driver and car for all the luggage. Carson was relieved he didn't need to drive. To him, the traffic was crazy and more frightening than the bucking bulls he used to ride back home.

As the car pulled up to the front of the mansion. The staff came out after notifying the family. Mrs. Kelley and Mr. Kelley came out to meet the car and to meet the "boys."

After a lot of hugging and kissing, the girls and Stephen, it was their turn to try and impress the parents.

They each gave a firm handshake and looked him squarely in the eyes. The staring into the eyes contest was won by Mr. Kelley, but he was impressed by how long they were able to stay in the "ring."

Mrs. Kelley was next. A gentler approach was taken using age-old complements on how she couldn't possibly be their mother, followed by a light handshake and bow. She couldn't help noticing how extremely handsome they were. That pleased her. It didn't please Mr. Kelley as much, but he liked them, even though they were "lookers."

They were led inside and shown their rooms on the third floor. Each was larger than three of the bedrooms back in Bigfork. Exquisitely furnished with a private bathroom. They never had one of those before.

Mary brought them back downstairs. The huge stairway that split into smaller side stairways was seen by Tommy before in a silent movie. He thought it was a Hollywood fantasy.

They all gathered in the library and sat in the deep couches and chairs. Carolina and Mary had their men next to them. Mrs. Kelley could see the love their daughters were feeling when she looked over toward them. The boys could feel the eyes of Mr. Kelley looking them over and watching them encroaching on his daughters' couch territory.

Mr. Kelley brought Johnson in to make arrangements for the boys to be properly dressed and "shod." Cowboy boots were fun in Montana, but not so fun in Manhattan during Christmas parties. The boys brought their church hats and their Sunday boots. They still looked new. Their western-style "funeral and wedding coats" they packed would not do. Johnson would handle things and leave their dignity intact. He learned how to be delicate from Carolina.

Dinner was interesting. All the staff somehow got involved with the dinner service. They all wanted to see the six-foot, four-inch-tall handsome cowboys from Montana with the two "spinsters." Johnson let them take turns with dinner. When two of the upstairs maids brought in the cheese service just before dessert, Mrs. and Mrs. Kelley figured out what was going on.

"You sure have a lot of helpers here with serving the dinner," Bobby mentioned to Mrs. Kelley. The girls laughed along with their dad.

It was all giggles and laughter in the kitchen, too. The staff didn't need to take a vote to approve the two boyfriends. They all asked Mr. Johnson if they could work in Montana next summer.

"I'll work for free, Mr. Johnson."

"Me too!"

"I'll pay for the privilege to work at the Kootenai, sir."

They wanted one of those brands of men. Not the dandies that lurked around Manhattan debutante parties, thé dansants, and balls.

They finished dinner and withdrew to the library for the after-dinner aperitifs and cigars.

Mr. Kelley had the two boys alone and started the "interview" process. After a dozen or so questions each, he would have them figured out and classified. Mrs. Kelley recognized what was going on and left them alone. He did the same thing with the other daughters' prospective husbands. It was their turn to face the firing squad.

Before he had a chance, the boys started to interview *him*. Here, he was being questioned about his daughters and family and he answered to the best of his ability. He finally figured out that this was backwards and started to ask questions about the boys and their families. The boys really didn't know much about the girls outside of what they saw in Montana. They were asking genuine questions and Mr. Kelley could tell they were sincere. He already knew a lot about the Harper family. He instructed Johnson to do some detective work. A little bit of the Pinkerton approach on them. They came up clean. He never had someone turn an interview around like that before. He really liked that about them and would tell that story over and over again. It was almost like they weren't too sure about the girls and their families and wanted to verify and inspect these New Yorkers. It was as if their wealth was secondary to information about their values and mores. After all, they met them in the parking lot of a bar and hotel with a trunk full of liquor during prohibition. When Mr. Kelley realized they weren't drawn to them by their wealth, he was satisfied with the girls' selections.

He liked them for a lot of different reasons. He liked the way they told him their jokes. They talked to him like he was an old friend. These two were not nervous at all; they were comfortable joking around with Mr. Kelley. They weren't there to fool him into giving them a high-paying job in his company after tricking his daughters into marriage. They were honest and straightforward, truly fine young men.

They joined the girls playing roulette. Mr. Kelley didn't like that secret that was revealed so early. He didn't want to jeopardize his daughters' marriage opportunity. They might not like gambling.

He stopped and caught himself worrying if the boys would accept his family. He laughed about that for the rest of his life.

They all retired around 11 and went up to their rooms. Mr. and Mrs. Kelley finally had a chance to talk about Mr. Kelley's talk.

"Well, what's the verdict?"

"I'm not sure; I still hope they like us after the gambling." He joked. "I really like them, and the funny thing is, I was the nervous one during their interview of me."

"What do you mean, their interview of you."

"Just what I said, they interviewed me before I had a chance to interview them. Never had I had that happen before. I even started answering their questions very carefully. I didn't want to make a mistake I couldn't recover from. By the time I figured out what they were doing, they were wrapping things up. It looks like we passed inspection!"

"That is hilarious. You met your match."

"Yes, but it was an unfair fight. There were two of them."

"Seriously, tell me about them."

"They are genuinely fine young men. They didn't know anything about us. The girls didn't have to lure them in by flaunting wealth. They didn't know much until the Pullman car delivered them to a chauffeured Bentley taking them to a New Yok City mansion. The girls didn't tell them anything about us. I think they must be ashamed of their gambling-addicted, soon-to-be, mother-in-law."

She slapped him playfully.

"I'm going to like these sons-in-law."

"Oh, they did not mention marriage." He teased.

"Plenty of time for that to come. Plenty of time."

They turned off the lights and they both quietly wondered if Bobby knew about the attack on Carolina.

21

The girls went first to Mary's room. They needed to talk about how things went this evening.

"I miss my room and our parents, but I miss Montana more. A lot more." Mary said. Carolina loved it when any of the "real" children included her in the "our parents" lineage. She never got tired of hearing that.

"I think our beaus left a good impression. I'll ask mom in the morning. She's probably getting the full story right now."

They would have to wait.

"Mary, now I must tell Bobby about Stephen's "father". I hate that word! It's time he knows. I think I have to tell him sooner than later. He has to know before he gets in any deeper with me. I have to know if he will still love me before I get in any deeper with him."

"You two need to go out to dinner together and talk about this. You can't do it here in the house. Dad can help if things turn bad. He went through the same disclosure when you told him."

"I just hope it doesn't destroy your relationship with Tommy if Bobby wants to end things."

"It doesn't matter. Remember when I promised to never leave you?"

"Yes."

"Why do you think I told dad I wanted to remain in Montana with you? Why would you think I would go off with Tommy if you weren't nearby? We are sisters, and we have a bond that is indestructible. No man can defeat that."

"Oh no, here comes the tears." She teased Carolina about how easily she cries, especially happy cries.

"Here comes my tears, it's contagious." Mary joined in.

They slept in Mary's room that night. Carolina needed her next to her once again. Mary needed to help her get through this.

The boys, on the other hand, went straight to their rooms to sleep. Bobby was intrigued by the huge bathtub and decided to try it out. He turned on the hot water and was shocked by how hot it was. He added cold water and then slid in. He was glad he was tall. The tub was six feet long. He put his feet on the end to keep from siding under.

As he lay there, he saw a long velvet, three-inch streamer with a fancy curtain ball on the end. What a useless decoration, he thought. It's going to get wet. He tried to pull it out of the way, but to no avail. He would have to be careful.

A minute later, a sixteen-year-old girl came into the bathroom and set towels down on the bench in front of the tub. He covered his important parts and wondered what was going on. He recognized her from dinner. Martha was her name. She filled the water glasses.

"May I bring you anything else, sir?" She said, diverting her eyes as she reset the bell wire attached to the velvet pull next to the tub. It was connected to the hall bells near the servants' quarters. It lets them know if any guests or families need anything. Every room, bathroom and bedroom had their own bell.

"No, thank you, Ma'am." He said as his wimpy voice trailed off from embarrassment.

"You look surprised, sir. You did pull the cord, didn't you?"

"I sure did."

That was the first time he was ever naked talking to a female stranger while taking a bath. He would laugh with Tommy about this tomorrow. Suddenly, he had a great idea. He would tell him that he had to try the bathtub in his room. He also told him about the velvet streamer cord that "opened the drain." He would tell him to pull it to let the water out when he finished his bath.

The house was quiet now. It had been a big day for every one of them.

They all gathered in the breakfast room at 8:00 am. Mr. Kelley had meetings at his office to attend and Mrs. Kelley would be taking the girls Christmas shopping. The three boys would be under the guidance of Johnson as they sought suitable clothing for the parties on the calendar.

"Stephen." Mrs. Kelley asked. "I have a surprise guest for you Friday evening."

"Who, Nana?"

"His name is Fritz Kreisler."

"The violinist?" She nodded yes. "He would like you to play for him this Friday night after dinner."

"I would rather listen to him play. He's really coming to dinner. The Austrian, Fritz Kreisler?"

"Yes. His star pupil recently accepted a position at Yale College in New Haven as an associate professor of music. They learned of your talent from teachers at The Institute of Musical Art. You left a big impression on them."

"What shall I play? I have to practice and memorize a piece. Help me, mom. What shall I play?"

"Play what you composed this fall. Play your "Montana Concerto.""

"Mother! Seriously, help me pick a composition."

"I just did. Play your own music; that's your best choice."

Grandfather concurred. He hadn't heard it before, but he knew that if Carolina liked it, it was exceptional. He told Stephen he should play his own work.

"Bumpa! I can't play my own work in front of the world's greatest violinist."

Mr. Kelley loved being called Bumpa. He hadn't heard it in years. "I certainly would prefer to play something he had never heard before. He couldn't compare it against the hundreds of violinists he's listened to over the years. He could only concentrate on your playing and your style. He wouldn't be burdened by comparisons."

Carolina looked over at "Bumpa" and added. "Daddy, you are a genius. You are exactly right." Now, looking at Stephen, she continued. "He is right, you know, your Bumpa is right."

It's hard to go up against those two when they combine forces. Stephen would play his *Montana Concerto for Violin in F Minor* in front of the greatest virtuoso in all the world on this Friday night.

The boys were useless in these matters. Nobody in Montana had ever had a conversation like they just listened to. Experience was the best instructor for these guys. They had zero experience in music at this level. They both heard Stephen play. They thought it was pretty good. No sour notes like the band at the Bigfork Hotel. They never thought about describing it. They just listened and enjoyed. I guess you could say they were unstifled by knowledge of music. That's what Carolina said.

They finished breakfast and before Mrs. Kelley left, Carolina and Mary asked to speak with her in private.

"Certainly; what is it, my dears?"

"Mary spoke first. "Carolina hasn't told Bobby about Stephen's father."

"He's not his father!" Carolina snapped back.

"Sorry, I know, I know. She wants to tell him today, and I suggested they should go out to dinner alone and then take a carriage ride home. What do you think?"

"Oh, honey. I know this is hard for you. Are you worried he won't want to be with you anymore if you tell him?"

"Of course, Momma. Of Course."

"Well, then, let's get this over with. I'll make reservations at the New York Yacht Club. You can sit in the main dining room. It will be better than a quiet room where people can eavesdrop. How about eight o'clock?"

"Thank you. You are too good to me; I don't deserve any of this."

"Just stop right now, stop what you're doing. It is not helpful!"

"Okay, okay."

The day played out as planned. New clothes for everybody, shoes, jackets, dresses, neckties and handkerchiefs. Everything the five

Montanans would need for Manhattan. They would be ready next week if the fittings went well.

Carolina and Bobby got dressed to go out to dinner. Mary, Tommy and Stephen were staying home with the family.

"What do you want to talk about tonight?"

"It will have to wait until dinner."

"I hope it's not bad."

"Me too." She worried silently to herself.

They gathered in the library for a cocktail. Mrs. Kelley wanted to spend time with Carolina before she sent her out to dinner. She wanted to come alongside her to shore up her courage and add to the small amount she was mustering on her own.

Bobby had his Sunday clothes on, his cowboy boots peeking out beneath the cuffs. A clean white shirt and bolo around his neck. His best belt buckle and, of course, his spotless cowboy hat in hand.

Even Mrs. Kelley thought he looked really good in his best Montana attire. She approved it to wear to their private club. Not many New Yorkers could pull that look off.

Tommy came down pretty mad. He took a bath and pulled the "drain cord." It didn't work. Shortly after that, he met Martha with the towels as he was standing up to get out of the tub. Martha had seen more of those boys than their girlfriends ever had.

Mary was still laughing since she heard the story.

Bobby decided it was time to go!

They walked to the New York Yacht Club. The weather was unusually warm for December. Bobby asked why they were walking away from the waterfront.

"There is no dock in the city. The club docks are called Stations. There are a few of them between here and Newport, Rhode Island."

"There it is. Notice anything interesting about the façade architecture?"

"It looks like an old wooden ship from the rear."

"Exactly, everyone loves it."

They entered through the main doors and lobby and walked to the dining area.

"Miss Kelley. Welcome back to the club."

Carolina's reservation was made in the family name. She likes that. The maître d assumed she was a grown-up Kelley.

He looked Bobby over, actually up and down, and asked for his hat. He didn't know what to think of his "outfit, but he let him pass."

"Here we are, the center table. Enjoy your dinner."

He tried to help Carolina with her chair, but Bobby wasn't going to let that happen; that was his job. As he sat down, he noticed this enormous silver trophy on a beautiful wooden stand right behind him.

"What is this?"

"The America's Cup is a sailing trophy held here for the winners. If another yacht club wins the race, they hold the trophy until the next challenge. It's been on that stand since 1851. The New York Yacht Club never loses."

He was impressed by that record. As he looked around the room, he was astounded at all of the models of sailing vessels covering every inch of the wall space.

Carolina didn't know anything else about the club. She told Bobby everything that Mrs. Kelley had taught her about it that morning. Now, they would have to talk to each other.

They waited until the dinner was served to talk. Mrs. Kelley had made arrangements for their dinner. They didn't even look at a menu. There was a flurry of table service and finally, the main course was set in front of them.

Lobster!

Carolina thought that was very funny. Of course, Bobby had never had lobster. Mrs. Kelley planned it so that Carolina could help her helpless boyfriend navigate a lobster main course. The waiter looked at Bobby and waited. Carolina took over and told him it looked very good and that he could take it back, remove the shell, and place the "meat" on a dinner plate.

"And you, sir?"

"Oh yes, please do the same."

"Right away, sir."

He brought back the lobster and butter and placed fish forks above the plate. Carolina noticed the correct placement of the fork between the salad and dinner forks. She thought of Johnson.

Mrs. Kelley even selected wine. Carolina explained where the glasses were placed and why. She explained the silverware settings and the proper place for salads and bread plates.

"I'm sure glad I'm not doing the dishes tonight." She was really good at reading lips now. Bobby always looked straight at her to make it easier.

"As I."

Carolina knew it was time to get serious. "Bobby, you know I love you, don't you?"

"Yes, and I love you,"

"Don't say that until I'm finished telling you what's been weighing so heavily on me. You may have a different opinion after I finish."

Bobby froze. He had to remember to start breathing again. He wondered what was so terrible that she didn't tell him already. They were best friends, too. She was ending things; he just knew it.

She reached for his left hand with her right and squeezed him tight.

"I need to tell you about Stephen's father." She hated to say that word, but she had no other replacement word she could use.

"There's no need. I know it must have been so hard on you when you had no word about what happened to him in the war."

"It's not that noble, Bobby." She lowered her voice and continued. "I hate him. He attacked me in the basement of the first home I worked in. He raped me, Bobby. He raped me and that's how Stephen came into being. I was never married and never even dated until you. I hope I haven't ruined what we have. I hope you can understand. I hope you won't desert me, Bobby. I need you and I pray you can get past my past."

Bobby was stunned. He thought for sure she was ending their relationship. Maybe her parents insisted; who knows? Maybe she was tired of him when she got back to New York and saw what she was missing. He had all sorts of scenarios, but none like this one.

He slid his other hand to touch her left hand on the table. "I am so sorry this happened to you, Carolina." She loved to see her name coming from his mouth and lips. "I love you more than ever. I really do." He stood up, and his commanding height, handsomeness, and attire caused the whole room to look at him and pause. He walked around to where she was sitting and lifted her up so he could kiss her and hold her. Carolina's feet were 18 inches off the ground.

"Will you marry me?"

"Yes, yes she answered." Now, finally, her "*liebestraum*" became real and not just a love dream.

The entire dining room erupted in applause. Now, the other members knew why these young people were given the best table in the room. One or both of them were pretty important to have been able to get that location.

Mrs. Kelley asked for that table, knowing it would be already reserved. She inquired as to whom had reserved it. The maître d knew her well and she was able to get the name.

"Mr. and Mrs. Philip Mallory, madam."

She called PR, as he was known by his friends and at his company. Mallory Battery Corporation was the largest supplier of batteries in the world.

"PR, I need to ask an enormous favor from you." She paused and then asked. "I need the center table for my daughter and her fiancé this evening. I know you have it reserved."

"Of course, my dear. We can sit off to the side. I'll introduce myself after dinner."

"Don't mention the fiancé part. It's not certain yet. Well, I should say that they don't know it yet, but I do."

"Okay darling, I got you covered. I'll call the club. It's for 8 o'clock."

"I can't thank you enough, PR. Goodbye."

Unlike Mr. Kelley, PR actually had a big yacht. A big one. He kept it in Newport and Fishers Island. His captains would deliver it to Miami each winter and would stay in front of their home on La Gorce Island until after the holidays and then take it on to Eleuthera Island, Bahamas. He had a 150-foot Trumpy. It was well traveled between Fishers Island, Newport and every yacht club on the way to Eleuthera. His great-grandfather was a Mystic Island boat builder. Whaling vessels, then eventually passenger ships. PR went on his own after graduating from Yale and then Columbia Law School.

PR and Corrine walked over to congratulate the "kids." They were happy they let them have the main table for such an important event.

Seven bottles of Champagne were sent to the table by some of the other members. The maître d opened them all and served the entire room. They were the center of attention and the unlikely party hosts in an exclusive Manhattan private club that they had never been.

"This is just like the Bigfork Hotel." Bobby laughed. It felt good to laugh and smile after the earlier uncertainty that evening.

They had so much fun, and Bobby noted how everyone seemed as friendly as the folks back in Montana. Carolina smiled at his naiveté.

The party went on for over an hour. They didn't touch their food. They were both too excited. They left to the applause of the members. He tried to pay for dinner. Carolina informed him that they do not accept payment. It was billed to the member account. The maître d was won over after that. He handed Bobby his hat and he perfectly place it on his head. He looked even taller now.

They hailed a carriage for their ride home. They snuggled tight and kissed in the cold night air. Carolina knew they needed to finish the conversation, but the hard part was over.

They rode around the park for over an hour before returning home.

Bobby asked her if she was cold.

"I've never been more comfortable and warm pressed against you tonight, Bobby."

They arrived at the house. Bobby paid the driver and they walked up the same stairway that she couldn't use at one time. The irony didn't pass her by.

Mr. and Mrs. Kelley and the entire family were waiting in the library. Mrs. Mallory telephoned to let them know how pleased she was to be a part of Mr. Harper's proposal. She also mentioned how everyone loved Mr. Harper's attire.

"Is there anything you want to tell us?" Bobby wondered how they knew already. He said, "Yes." But I need to talk with Stephen. He already knew, but he would let Bobby tell him, man to man. They went into the dining room and sat down.

"Stephen. I proposed to your mom tonight at dinner. It was unplanned. It just happened. I wanted to talk with you first and get your approval. I wanted to do that on the train ride home to Montana."

"Did she say yes?" Now Stephen was playing with Bobby.

"Why do you think I'm asking you now?"

"I'm joking with you. We already know about the whole evening. And of course I approve, Dad."

Bobby liked being called dad. He didn't have to worry about hurting Stephen's feelings or trampling over his father's legacy, now that he knew what really happened. He wondered how much Stephen knew. A lot of questions were lingering that needed to be talked about.

They hugged each other and Bobby said one more thing. "I will always protect your mother and you. Always."

Stephen felt safe with Bobby.

They left and went into the library to be with the rest of the family.

"He said yes!" Bobby yelled. "Stephen said yes. Now I need to ask you Mr. Kelley. I'm sorry I didn't before tonight, I just didn't know I would be proposing to your daughter. It just happened."

"I approve, young man. I approve.

Do we need Champagne?"

"Not for us daddy, for you all. We've had enough tonight. The whole club bought us Champagne." A picture would be in the New York Times society pages in the morning. Mrs. Kelley had already spoken to the paper and gave the correct names and spelling. When someone brought in a camera and had them pose during the "party," It didn't occur to either that it was for a newspaper. This wasn't her first daughter's wedding, she wanted to control what went into the society pages of the "Gray Lady".

Johnson was already on it, carrying a tray with chilled bottles of bubbly.

Mary and Tommy were sitting on the sidelines. If you thought Tommy was mad at Bobby after the tub incident, you probably wouldn't have noticed his knew found anger. All eyes would soon be on the other lovebirds and Tommy knew it. Yes, he loved Mary, yes, he wanted to marry Mary. He just wanted his proposal to be special. It would be pretty difficult to beat what happened tonight at the yacht club. He could already sense the pressure and so could Mary. He thought Bobby should have told him.

"Don't do it now, Tommy. Don't propose to me now. I don't want it right now. Let my sister enjoy her time. Let them enjoy it without distraction."

Mary didn't tell Tommy about Carolina's attack. Bobby would be the one to tell him, if he even wanted to. She was just happy that Bobby loved her and Stephen enough to push through this potential catastrophe. She loved Bobby even more now. He would be a wonderful brother-in-law.

Tommy felt better about everything. Mary's words gave him permission to congratulate his brother and offer his best wishes to Carolina, without worrying how she felt. She knew he loved her; it just wasn't their time yet. That made him appreciate Mary even more. He found a gem of a woman and understood her value and liked the way she defused his errant emotions.

The family went off to bed. Carolina and Bobby weren't ready yet. They needed to wind down and just sit next to each other and look into each other's eyes.

Now that they were engaged, certain liberties would be allowed. Chaperones were not as important. Not obsolete, just not so important after a marriage commitment was made.

They fell asleep in each other's arms on the couch. Yesterday it would have been inappropriate. Mary woke them up around 3 am and ushered them up to their own bedrooms.

It was a good ending to a long day.

22

Stephen was getting ready for his concert in the evening. He worked with Johnson to set up the room for his performance. "Keep this a secret, Mr. Johnson."

He was prepared for his audition. He assumed they wanted him to be a student at the Yale School of Music. Why would they want to hear him play? He would find out in a few hours.

Carolina spent the day reliving the dinner last night at the yacht club. She wanted to recall every moment and replay it again in her mind. She was overindulging in it. If it was eating or drinking, she would be committing one of the seven deadly sins.

Carolina was as happy as she had ever been. The boys were enjoying their Manhattan stay. Today they went to the museum to see dinosaurs and mummies. They loved seeing the Egyptian artifacts. Everything they saw was twenty times older than the oldest Montana artifacts, Indian art excluded. They were like two young boys.

Johnson and the staff were preparing for their important visitors coming to dinner. Mrs. Kelley looked in quite a few times to check on things. It was not necessary, Johnson had everything sorted out.

The guests arrived at six. Johnson showed them into the main salon where the Kelley's were waiting. Stephen introduced himself right away. He realized he violated protocol and stepped back. Mr. Kelley handled the introductions as he welcomed his guests.

Stephen noticed he brought his violin. He asked to see it. He opened the case to reveal a Stradivarius. "I brought it for you. You can play it later if you like."

"Yes, sir, I would love that!"

Mr. Kreisler had his student with him. His name was Ian Beamish. Mr. Kelley didn't like him. He didn't look him squarely in the eyes when they were introduced. Ian had recently taken a position at the Yale College School of Music. He was here to listen to Stephen play.

Dinner was taking way too long for Stephen. He wanted to hear Mr. Kreisler and his "Strad." The dinner seemed to never end.

"Stephen, Professor Donaldson told me about your musical acumen at such a young age. When did you first take lessons?"

"Not until I went to the institute. My mother helped me with the correct fingering and bow pressure when I was very young."

Carolina added. "He first picked up my violin when he was two. I played for him in the womb and before sleeping as a baby. Some people thought I was crazy. He instinctively knew how to place it correctly between his chin and shoulder and hold the neck. It was the same with any instrument he picked up. He just knew how to hold it and play it."

"No matter how badly they sounded!" Stephen added.

"I taught him how to read music. I found ancient handwritten music under the lining of the old violin's coffin case. It appears to be from the 18th century, maybe before. Most are concertos and some look like works in progress."

"How did you come by the music?" Mr. Kreisler asked.

"I'm an orphan and it was my only possession. The man I worked for kept it for me. I started to "play" and I do mean "play" with the violin when I was three. I must have had training; I just don't remember. There was a man at the church we attended in Germany than I can recall." Carolina hated to sound stupid about her past.

"You're German?"

"Yes, from Leipzig."

"Ah, the home of Bach. I would love to see the music and your violin. Is it as old as the music?"

"I am not sure."

"Your English is perfect. I am from Austria, you know."

He spoke to her in German almost as if to verify her story. Mary, Stephen and Carolina all laughed at his quip about her being the only other intelligent person at the table. The rest of the table was silently wondering what was so funny.

Now in English, he said. "I see you two are also intelligent," he chuckled as he looked to Mary and Stephen.

They finished their dessert and now it was time to listen to Stephen. They were all ushered into the ballroom by him.

"What's going on Stephen?" Mrs. Kelley was intrigued.

"The music will be in the ballroom tonight. It has the best acoustics." The ballroom was on the top floor and spanned the entire space. It was rarely used.

They all entered an empty hall except for the chairs lined up at the back of the room and the long red carpet rolled out to the opposite end of the huge room. The carpet was purchased a few years ago when

Queen Wilhemina visited their home. It was rolled out from the front door all the way down to the street when she visited in her carriage. It was never used again, until tonight. Since the ballroom was on the top floor, the ceiling was twenty-five feet at the peak. It was Johnson's idea to set up in this grand room after Stephen told him that he wanted to play his Montana piece.

Stephen went to pick up his violin from the red carpet in the center of the "concert hall."

"Play mine," Mr. Kreisler offered as he opened the case and carefully lifted the old instrument from it. It was a Strad from the "Golden Years." The Golden Years were the twenty-year span of violin building at the Cremona, Italy Stradivarius shop. Some say it's the tightly grained wooden tops that were used, and all sorts of other speculations as to why these were the best examples of their work. The Golden Years created the best violins the world had ever seen or heard.

It was a standard size, just like Stephen's. The bow was not curved like the old-fashioned style bows, it was almost flat. Stephen wanted the newer style when he was at the institute. It made him feel less sophisticated to have a hand me down bow. This newer style was from the 1800s.

"Thank you." Stephen carefully took the violin and ran through a few scales. He adjusted the tuning and played a short Paganini piece.

"Thank you so much." He said as he handed it back to the master.

"Keep playing, son."

"I will on my own instrument. My own feels a little different and more comfortable to me."

Mr. Kreisler nodded in agreement. "I know what you mean, I know what you mean. Mine is like my wife."

He paused for a minute to size up the room. "When we were first married, I didn't know how to 'handle' her. Now I am much more confident as the years gather steam." He said, smiling.

Stephen got the joke.

"Are you ready, Mr. Johnson?"

"Yes, sir, Stephen."

Stephen slowly walked to the end of the red carpet. It was the same width of the Kootenai's long dock and about the same length. He faced away from his audience to look out over his "lake." He opened his case that was resting on the end of his red-carpet dock. He picked up his violin and looked back at the audience sitting on deck chairs on the covered porch of the lodge. He raised his bow and Johnson, right on cue, extinguished the lights and turned the room into a quiet, dark night in Montana. The only thing missing were the stars and coyotes.

Stephen played his *Montana Concerto*. It was so quiet and delicate at first, barely audible. It subtly increased volume, as the two middle strings were being caressed by his well-rosined friendly old bow.

He looked up at the stars with his eyes closed and played as if he was alone on the dock at night and back home in Montana.

The colors in his mind were beautiful. Distinct and exact. It helped him to feel the music. His concerto was not a technical piece. It was not flashy. Any decent musician can play with technical skills.

It could not be played in a lighted room. It needed the attention that darkness provides. It required that all other senses were stifled and ignored to be able to feel and hear it properly.

The composer and musician ended his concerto with the same barely audible volume that he began with, as his bow dropped off the last note. He laid down and didn't move. No one else did. Johnson left the lights off as Stephen had directed him earlier. He didn't want any applause; it would only diminish the emotions.

The audience didn't move or make a sound. Stephen knew he could use the audience protocol of not clapping until the last movement was played. Since they didn't know the piece, they didn't know when to applaud.

On schedule, Johnson brought up the lights. Stephen was lying flat on the "dock." He stood up and turned around to see Mr. Kreisler and his assistant standing while applauding. He couldn't hear them; his ears hadn't shifted back to listening to mortal sounds yet.

He saw his mother applauding. He was sad she couldn't hear him. He bowed and walked back toward his audience. He didn't have to worry about falling off this "dock" in the darkness.

"Bravo, Stephen!" Mr. Kreisler shouted in delight. "Bravo!"

Ian was jealous of Stephen. He knew he was a better composer and musician than he.

"May I look at your violin?"

"Of course."

"Where did you get this?"

"From my mother."

Looking at Carolina, he said "This is not a German violin, It's Italian and it's very old. Could I look at your bow?"

Stephen handed it to him. "This is German. I know of the maker. Mid 1700s. Most certainly a replacement bow."

"The violin is original, it looks untouched. Don't repair this top wood crack. It's very small and could change the sound if repaired. I see a tailpiece repair; that's fine. The strings are new as is the horsehair on the bow."

"Yes, Carolina told him."

"Do you have the old strings and bow hair?"

"They are in the case," Stephen said.

"Good, keep them; they may help identify its provenance. You have a special instrument; you never know; it may be a Strad."

Mr. Kelley thought back when he offered to repair and refurbish the violin. He remembered Carolinas strict instructions to only lay back down the fingerboard and fix the crack on the back of the neck. Light cleaning only.

"Did she know the value of it? How did she know not to refurbish it to look like new?" Mr. Kelley was glad he didn't undertake the drastic steps he assumed were the right way to preserve the instrument.

He handed it to Ian to look over. Ian wanted this violin. He wanted Stephen's talent, and he wanted the fame and respect that Stephen's performances and composing would command in a very short time.

"Very nice Stephen, very nice. It definitely does the job."

Mr. Kreisler look at him with a perplexed face. "Definitely does the job." He thought it a strange remark.

He would understand what Ian meant in a few months.

They all stayed and talked for a while until Mrs. Kelley directed them back to the library. Stephen and Carolina stayed behind to thank Johnson for his help.

As they made their way back to the library, Carolina stopped Stephen in the hallway before the stairway.

"I could see your music. I could 'hear' what you were playing. It was so beautiful, my little boy; it was the most beautiful thing I've ever seen and 'heard.'"

She was crying.

"You did not!"

"Yes, baby, I did. Things are coming back to me now. I have been noticing slight changes and weird sounds. My hearing is finally returning. The doctors were right when they said to give it time."

They walked into the library and Mr. Kreisler was getting ready to play. It was stunning to Stephen. The brilliance from his bow across the upper register was striking, especially being so close to the violin. He wondered if he had a special rosin. It reminded him of his own.

He finished and set down his instrument in the case and looked at Stephen. "May I see the old handwritten compositions you have?"

Stephen opened his case and carefully lifted the instrument and handed it to Ian to hold. He took out the music and handed the pages to Mr. Kreisler.

He spent an enormous amount of time dwelling on the compositions. He played each one in his mind.

"You need to research these; perhaps Mr. Beamish could help you with that at Yale."

Ian asked to review them. He was handed the stack and sat at the large library table with lamps and chairs.

He noticed each one had the initials "SDG" on the last page. Mr. Kreisler didn't recognize the significance. He mostly played music written by Italians.

"Johann Sebastian Bach composed these pieces!" He thought to himself. "These are original handwritten compositions by the world's greatest composer."

Ian didn't say anything about them. He just said he would be glad to research their origin.

"They are German." Mr. Kreisler said.

"Yes, of course." Ian acknowledged that correct assertion. He was glad he didn't know who the composer was. Ian wanted the music and the violin now. They would make him famous he thought. He was right.

The gathering was coming to a close. The clock in the corner chimed midnight and soon after they all said goodbye. Ian asked Stephen to come to Yale before he returned to Montana. Stephen looked at his mom and now the new guy, Bobby for permission. Carolina agreed and Bobby did after waiting for his fiancé's response. He waited so he wouldn't make a false step on the first full day of his dad job. He also would need some training from Carolina regarding child rearing. He appreciated that Stephen acknowledged him. Bobby wasn't anywhere near as intelligent or mature as Stephen was. He was much taller and more handsome though and that meant they were equals in the eyes of the world. Life's not fair.

The house cleared out and the family went up to retire. Carolina told Mary about her hearing changes. Mary was so happy. So was Carolina. Mary spoke directly into her ear. Carolina could hear it, but the clarity needed was lacking. It was improving though.

23

Clara was back in the city and called on Carolina first thing. She brought Clara up to date on everything. The first autumn in Montana. Her new boyfriend turned fiancé. Stephen's music. Mary's new boyfriend. Everything.

"Did you tell your fiancé…"

"His name is Bobby."

"Did you tell Bobby about the attack?" Mary couldn't hold that question back. She needed to know. Men can be stupid and think all sorts of crazy ideas about rape. It could be warped ideas involving their ego, a perceived attack on their masculinity or ancient mores about virginity. There could be many insurmountable reasons to discard a woman who became a victim of a violent man. There was no reason for any of these excuses to come from a man that truly loved a woman. None.

"Yes, and he proposed to me literally right after I told him. We were at the New York Yacht Club for dinner. He stood up from the table and, walked around and pulled me out of my chair and lifted me up high and kissed me in front of the whole room. He said it didn't matter to him. He told me he loved me so much that nothing could break that emotion or bond."

"He said that?"

"Not in so many words, but that's what I heard coming from his lip movements. In the next sentence, he asked me to marry him! I don't really recall everything; it all seemed to trip over itself and just fall on top of me."

"I've got to meet this guy. Do you have a picture?"

"I have a newspaper article. Let me find it."

Carolina looked for the *New York Times* article. She found it on the desk and handed it to Clara.

"He is really, really handsome, Carolina. And really, really tall!"

"That always helps!" Carolina winked.

"What about Mary's boyfriend?"

"Tommy is Bobby's brother. He's in love with Mary. I'm sure he'll be proposing very soon. He's two years younger than Bobby. He's tall and handsome, too."

"He's your fiancé's brother? You always wanted a close-knit family!"

"Do they have another brother for me?"

"A bit young for you, but there's plenty more in Montana." They laughed. "Clara, you'll have to visit us in Montana. We are going to live there. Mary too."

Clara was sad that Carolina was moving to the Kootenai. She would have to settle for seeing her over holidays. Maybe she would travel west one day. The tall and handsome Montana men intrigued her.

"Where's Stephen?"

"He's at the institute. They call it Julliard School of Music now; he's catching up with his friends."

"Oh, okay, I'll have to see him later."

"He is growing every day. His hands are getting larger too. That's making him happy."

"What?"

"Longer fingers are good for his piano and violin playing."

"Of course. At first, I thought you were telling me that when you move to Montana, it makes you taller and more handsome!"

The girls laughed and talked about everything that was happening in both of their lives for most of the afternoon. Carolina learned that Clara had no boyfriend or even a hint of marriage in her future. That saddened her and she dialed back some of the wonderful things about her fiancé that she would have shared.

Carolina thought more about Clara visiting Montana. She could convince her to move out and expand her clique from two to three. Kalispell did have a hospital, and hospitals need nurses. "Maybe next summer we can convince her to visit." She thought.

Bobby and Tommy went to the Statue of Liberty in the morning. Carolina and Mary liked how they just got out and started doing things on their own. These boys weren't clingy. Everywhere they went, people turned to see the two handsome and extremely tall cowboys. Their large, brimmed hats were a perfect pairing, complementing their boots and silver belt buckles. Tommy even had a neckerchief wrapped around his neck. They almost looked fake. That's how authentic they were.

As they were walking away from the ferry boat that took them back to Manhattan, Tommy saw a police horse spooked by kids lighting firecrackers. The chestnut mare was running right to him. He took off his hat and started waving it and blocking its path. The horse slowed down and let Tommy hold her by the bridle. He slowly and calmly walked her back to the rider. Two young women who saw them before this happened and had giggled about the "make believe cowboys," quickly changed their opinion about the Harper boys' heritage. The only thing that would make his rescue better would have been if he had a rope to twirl and throw over the neck of the runaway horse. That's what the girls thought too.

"Those two are real." They said with a respectful countenance that was as genuine as the boys. The police officer was very thankful he didn't have to chase down his mare. He thanked his two helpers as he remounted his horse.

Stephen was surprised to see Professor Beamish at the school. He felt uncomfortable around him. He couldn't identify why, he just did. He walked around him to see his friends but couldn't avoid him. The Professor followed him into the practice hall and reintroduced himself.

"Have you considered coming to New Haven to look over the college?"

"We talked about it this morning. Maybe next week?"

"That would be great, Stephen. I'll have a lot of opportunities for you. Please come."

He gave Stephen his card and phone number in New Haven.

The boys were on their way back to the Kelley's house. Stephen had Geoffrey waiting outside Julliard in the Bentley to pick him up on his way to retrieve grandpa from the office. Mr. Kelley saw the boys on the sidewalk heading home and told Geoffrey to pull over and get them.

Three girls were following the boys when they got in the Bentley. One girl laughed and declared "I knew they were pretend!" as they watched the chauffer open the door for them.

The city was filled with Christmas decorations and window displays. The boys and the girls spent a lot of time walking around so they could show off their city.

They were going to a party tomorrow night at the Whitney family's home. Their wealth was unsurpassed. Mr. Kelley was involved in business with Mr. Whitney and Mrs. Kelley shared her love of art collecting and charity events with Mrs. Whitney. This would be the first test of their mettle in the minefield of New York City high society. Neither Carolina, or Mary, or Bobby, or Tommy could care. Their new clothes were not ready, but the Kelley's were not concerned after their yacht club premier. Everyone loved the honesty, sincerity and carefree attitude of the cowboys. Mrs. Kelley checked with Mrs. Whitney, of course, before the party to make sure. Mrs. Whitney heard from the Mallory's already and was hopeful they would not shed their western wear in exchange for New York society costumes. The boys were the talk of the town.

The next morning, the New York Times ran a photo and story of Tommy walking the horse back to the policeman. The boys were in town for five days and both had separate articles and photos in one of the greatest newspapers in the world. They could show up to the party in bathing costumes and probably pull it off, you couldn't underestimate the gravity of their charisma.

Saturday morning was sunny and cold. A dusting of snow "cleaned" up the area. The girls were already getting things arranged for the Whitney's party in the evening. The boys were ready the minute the staff unpacked their suitcases and hung up their clothes when they first arrived.

Mr. Kelley took his new soon to be son-in-law and Tommy to the Stork Club. It was his favorite. It was only for the elites and the "VIP Room" was only for the elite of the elites.

The boys had worn their second-best set of clothes and looked like millionaire ranchers from out west somewhere. When you walk in with Mr. Kelley, assumptions always go one way. Positive and straight up.

Jenson took their hats and overcoats, and Mr. Porter showed them the way. Mr. Kelley wanted to be with the boys alone. He wanted to have a time together without the females twirling around them.

"Bobby."

"Yes, sir,"

"I want you to call me Con. That's what my friends call me. Besides Cornelius is an old and out of fashion name. That goes for you too Tommy."

"Yes sir, Mr. Kelley," Tommy responded.

"Okay, let's try that again." Con loved the respect these two had for himself and his family.

"Oh, shucks Mr. Kelley. You're gonna have to give me a little time with that. It doesn't feel right quite yet. I'll get there."

"Ok, but Bobby, I insist you call me Con. I want you to practice, starting now."

"Yes Con." He would get better at it as time passed. It was obviously uncomfortable for him now though.

"Con?" Bobby asked. "Where is the bathroom? I need to wash my hands, sir."

"I'll just have to give it time," he thought to himself while walking to the rest room.

"Tommy, I want to talk to you about Mary."

"I appreciate that, sir; I mean Con."

"What are your intentions? As a father, I'd like to know your plan."

"I love Mary very much and I want to marry her someday. I want to spend the rest of my life with your daughter. I can't stand being away from her. I guess I don't know what to do. I am new at this. I never even dated before. I don't have the handbook. Even a new ranch hand gets a sheet of paper with the rules. I've got nothing here yet. I need to talk with my dad and mom, I need their guidance."

Con really appreciated his reliance on his family. He was truly a "family man." He thought.

"I don't even know if she would marry me, sir; I mean Con."

"You can't be that stupid, son. My daughter is so in love with you. You need to know that." Con couldn't believe he was coaching a prospective husband for his last daughter to marry. Except for Bobby, he hadn't been much of an encouragement to the future husbands, even the ones that did eventually marry his girls.

"Thank you for encouraging me. I do want to marry her right away; I just don't want to get in the way of Carolina and Bobby."

"I understand, you are the younger brother and probably yielded to Bobby your entire life. It's time to step out and do what you want to do."

"Sir."

"It's Con."

"Not right now Sir." Tommy asserted himself.

"Sir, will you give me permission to marry your daughter? I promise to protect and love Mary for as long as I live. I will remain faithful to her. I will keep her safe and happy until my last breath. The last word I will utter on my deathbed will be 'Mary.' I promise you that."

Con didn't say a word for over twenty seconds. He didn't want Tommy to think he already had an answer. Noticing how excruciating the delay was to Tommy. He finally spoke.

"Mr. Harper, I want you to know how happy I am to hear you tell me how you will take over my job and keep my daughter safe and happy. I want you to understand that you can call me any time, day or night, if there is something that you don't know. Something that bewilders you. Sometimes you need to talk with another man that isn't your father or brother. I will be there for you unless you hit her or cheat on her. Then I will have you killed!"

Tommy's head jerked up to look him straight in the eyes. There was a little smirk on his face and Tommy relaxed a little.

"Just kidding, son, I wouldn't have someone kill you. I would do it myself!"

Bobby came back to the table. Just in time, as far as Tommy was concerned.

"Welcome to the family Tommy. Welcome."

24

They all got into the Bentley for the short ride to the Whitney's home. It started to snow again and made everything brighter and prettier. They arrived at the home and the footmen brought umbrellas to protect the Women's outfits from the falling snow. As they entered the main floor, the Whitney's welcomed them, and Mrs. Whitney was glad to see the Montana boys wore their cultural garb, as she called it.

"My oh my." She thought. "They are an impressively handsome pair." As they removed their "Sunday" cowboy hats to not run into the foyer chandelier, she expected their height to be reduced. It didn't make much difference. She greeted the family and asked about Stephen. He popped his head around Mrs. Kelley and greeted her. She heard about his skills from Fritz Kreisler at dinner a few nights ago. "I hope you will play for us sometime. We want to hear you before you become rich and famous!"

"Come with me boys," she ordered as she grabbed an arm from each Harper boy and escorted them into the ballroom to meet her friends and guests. The boys looked back at the girls with a terrified expression. Mr. Kelley took the arm of his wife and Mary. Carolina was on the other side of Mrs. Kelley sacheting into the room following Mrs.

Whitney's lead. Mary's father noticed a little sway to his daughter's stride. He approved.

They watched from their prominent table as the young men and women danced in a fairly formal promenade style. Nothing like that at the Bigfork Hotel. The boys taught Mary and Carolina the Ten Step Polka and the Cowboy Travelling Cha Cha. The closest dance to this was the Cowboy Waltz.

The boys mustered some courage, grabbed the girls and danced along with the society folks, as they referred to them.

Their unusual western dancing seemed to stop the room. They didn't care, these weren't their friends anyway. These were daddy's business associates and their children. They knew the families. The Vanderbilts, the Du Ponts, the Carnegies and the Morgans. They weren't friends with any of them, unlike the younger sisters.

Suddenly people started to follow their lead, and they were trying to dance this "new" western style. They had never seen it, but they thought it must be the latest dance. It seemed like a new dance every week was becoming popular in the 1930s and this must be one of them.

They were leading the dancers in new steps and waltzes, cowboy waltzes.

Stephen stood up and watched the room turn into the Bigfork Hotel dance floor. Mrs. Whitney came along Stephen and smiled at the show.

"The music isn't correct, but fairly close during the waltzes." Stephen lamented.

"Why don't you show the band how to play?" She said grabbing his arm and walking up to the bandstand.

There was Stephen on the stage holding a volunteer violin and bow. He talked with the band. Told them the note progressions, time signatures, keys and chords he would be playing. They were surprised by his knowledge. Most of the impromptu musicians at these events were pretty basic, drunk and couldn't explain what to play. They just had to listen a little and join in fairly blind.

Stephen directed the them like a band leader. They started on his lead and sounded like they had rehearsed. Stephen played the violin like a fiddle. That's what this music called for and he had the notes and skill to pull it off.

After two songs, the entire room was dancing "western style." Even the older dancers joined in on the fun. The society photographers were working to get just the right photos. They would have to be approved by Mrs. Whitney before any were published.

The Harper boys escorted their fancy-dressed "cowgirls" off the floor and sat down exhausted.

"I didn't see that coming," Mrs. Kelley said.

"May I get you boys and girls some refreshments?" Mr. Kelley asked.

Tommy was the first to respond, and out it came. "Yes, Con, I think we all would like Champagne." The table froze at the utterance of the name Con coming from the mouth of one of the boys. Mr. Kelley signaled a waiter and ordered for the table.

Mary looked at Carolina and started to laugh. Soon Mrs. Kelley was joining the fun. Stephen had never heard the name Con uttered, except between him and the Mrs.

"That was good Tommy, that was good!" Con laughed.

Now that the boys were famous with New York society, couples came over to talk with them and tried to make plans with them. One young woman came over and started to talk with the boys and invited them to one of the many New Years Eve Balls. Her boyfriend was watching and was not amused. They deferred and deflected to Mrs. Kelley and to the girls. She returned to her boyfriend.

"She's a du Pont," Mary complained. They made their fortune from gunpowder. "They marry their cousins." Mrs. Kelley gave her a look to stop it. Her boyfriend was a Vanderbilt. He was a volatile young man. Wealth has a way of infecting a boy with unwanted side effects. He collected many unwanted things along his golden path.

Bobby and Tommy excused themselves and walked to the outside patio through the French doors. It was cold, but not too bad for a Montanan.

"You sure shook up the table with one word."

"Con."

"Yes, that was perfect. He liked it and so did the girls." It was a milestone in the relationship between the Harper boys and the Kelleys.

They were interrupted by the Vanderbilt boy. Evidently the whole table was talking about the two Harpers from Montana. Since nobody knew a thing about them and couldn't figure out their sudden and unexplained notoriety at parties and newspapers, they awarded them with much more respect than they were due. The unknown always works that way in the sphere of the wealthy.

"Hey, are you really cowboys?"

They turned around and looked at this slightly drunk and inconspicuous monkey in a fancy set of tails and a white tie.

They ignored him and that infuriated him. He was a Vanderbilt after all.

"I'm talking to you!"

"You're not talking to us you're yelling at us. We are having a private conversation. Please leave us."

"Do you know who you are talking with?"

"No and we don't care."

"I'm a Vanderbilt."

"Oh, the gunpowder guys. We just heard that from someone earlier. Thanks, we use gunpowder a lot in Montana."

"I think his girl boss is the gunpowder people. Is she your cousin?

That did it for the Vanderbilt, who never worked a day in his life.

"Do you two actually ride horses or is that a costume, too?"

"Yes." He didn't deserve more words.

"Have you ever played Polo?"

"Of course not, that's a stupid sport. You should either play croquet or ride horses. Not at the same time."

"I would like to challenge you to polo."

They both started to laugh, and the volatile Vanderbilt tried to land a punch on Tommy. Tommy blocked it and later said his return fist that connected wouldn't have hurt a girl in Montana.

"May I bring you another punch?" Tommy said while looking over at the large punch bowl inside. He was standing over him and smiling.

Mr. Whitney was told about the altercation and grabbed Tommy and leaned into him. "I must act like I'm mad right now. I'm going to take you around the corner and act like you're in trouble. Play along please. I like you young man. All of us have wanted to do what you just did. Thank you."

That cemented the fame of the Harper boys in New York City society. For the rest of their lives, they were welcomed into any home, club, yacht, horse race or event that the wealthy were apt to congregate.

The boys just shook their heads and laughed at these funny and strange people. They actually liked most of them. They were so entertaining on multiple levels. Some subtle, some obvious.

The family left the ball as the first few people started to leave. It was important to show up thirty minutes late and leave thirty minutes early. The boys understood the protocol. They remembered the revivals that came to town to help Jesus spread the truth. They always came thirty minutes late and left thirty minutes early from those events.

Geoffrey dropped them at the front door. Everyone was headed to bed. Mrs. Kelley was so happy with the reception her cowboys received. So was Mr. Kelley.

Tommy asked Mary to stay behind and sit with him in the library.

She liked that idea. She had been sitting respectfully next to him all night, as any society girl would do. She needed to touch him. She needed to kiss him hard. Tommy became famous that night for putting a Vanderbilt down and calling her dad Con. Only one took courage.

They sat down on the deep couch upholstery and looked at each other. Mary put both hands on his face and turned it toward her. She kissed him like she meant it. He kissed her back like he meant it.

They sat quietly looking into each other's eyes and savored the moment. The boys not only survived the society event of the year, they redefined what a party should be. Fun and filled with surprises and new things to try. Also, a little Montana whoopin' for the smart alecs when needed.

They just held each other and closed their eyes. Each dreamed about different things. Tommy thought about marrying Mary. Mary thought about marrying Tommy. Then it happened.

"Tommy?"

"Yes darling."

"I want you to know that I love you so much. I want you to know how much I care for you and cherish you."

"Do you really love me?" He sighed.

"How stupid are you cowboy?"

"Could you say it out loud?"

"Oh Tommy, I love you more than anything. I want you more than anything and I need you more than anything."

"Mary, will you marry me so we can get this part over with. I want to be your husband. I want you to be my wife. I want to be with you forever."

"Will you say yes and pull me out of my uncertainty and end my worries about you and me being together until the end? Will you?"

She grabbed him again with two hands, lifted up his face, and landed an even firmer kiss on those two cowboy lips.

"Yes, yes, yes!"

"Where's the ring?" She knew he was unprepared for this moment, but she loved to tease her new "husband." They just looked at each other and fell asleep on the same couch Carolina and Bobby did a few evenings ago.

They were awoken by Carolina around 4 am. She helped them up to bed. Mary winked and Carolina knew exactly what had just transpired on the "marriage couch." Her sister was engaged!

25

The morning brought the good news. During breakfast, Tommy stood up and proposed an "orange juice toast" to his future bride. Johnson quickly brought a battle of Champagne and glasses. They repeated the toast the correct way.

"My word," said Mrs. Kelley. "I don't know if we can invite you back here."

The entire table looked at her, confused.

"Because I don't think I can handle all the fun and excitement. Welcome to the family Tommy and Bobby. Welcome!"

Stephen made arrangements to meet Professor Beamish in New Haven. He took the train with the Harper boys for the day trip to visit the school. They left in the early morning hours and arrived around 10:00 am. They would leave New York for Montana the next morning.

The school looked impressive. Some of the buildings were from the 1700s. Most were less that twenty years old, they just looked like they had been there for a hundred years.

The Gutenberg Bible, housed in the library, was only one of the 48 surviving copies of the first printing. As they walked past Calhoun College, actually a dormitory, they walked two more blocks to the School of Music and entered the lobby.

Tommy saw the Vanderbilt Building next to Calhoun and laughed.

Professor Beamish saw them and came out to greet his guests.

"Hello Stephen. Hello Bobby and Tommy." He confused the faces with the each other's names.

"I'm Bobby, and he's Tommy."

"Oh, sorry." His apology was phony. "Which train are you taking back to the city?"

"The 2 o'clock."

"We have three hours, then."

Professor Beamish showed the boys around the music department. He was new here but seemed to know his way around. He took them to the classrooms and all the private practice rooms. They ended the tour on the performance stage. Stephen stood and faced his imaginary audience and was impressed.

"Play something for us, Stephen."

Stephen opened his case and brought out his violin and tuned it. He started with some progressions to warm up his fingers before playing. He played Bach's Violin Concerto in A Minor. Bach was his favorite; he felt a bond with the beauty of the precision and passion. His passion inspired parts of his Montana Concerto.

He liked the sound of the room. The acoustics in concert halls were somewhat of a mystery to architects of the time. Some of the more beautiful and ornate halls sounded the worst. This one was intimate and didn't have the return sound delay of the larger venues. He liked it. He like the school more than Julliard. That surprised him. He thought the professor would want to hear more of his playing. He didn't seem to need anything more from Stephen.

"Let's finish our tour and have lunch before you head back to your train."

The Harper boys were bored with the tour. They loved music in what could be best described as in a superficial way. They didn't care about the keys and chords; they just knew what they liked. Bach was beginning to move up the "charts" the more they heard it. It was okay that you couldn't dance a polka to it.

"Leave your things here. We'll return on your way to the train station."

The professor took them over to the faculty dining room. The school was on Christmas break. Only a few people were in the room eating.

The professor excused himself to lock up the building. He was the only one there and forgot to lock up.

He returned and they dined together. Stephen thought Professor Beamish would be recruiting him hard at lunch. He didn't. Stephen liked the college more than the professor. He thought maybe he wasn't wanted anymore. It was a strange turn around.

Bobby noticed the time and thought they should leave. He didn't want to miss the train back. The professor kept talking and delaying them until Tommy said, "we've got to run."

Professor Beamish walked back with them to gather their winter coats and Stephen's violin, that was left in the recital hall. He unlocked the door and led the way in. He stopped to show them photos on the wall of the famous students that Yale had taught and groomed.

"Is this guy trying to get us to miss our train?" Bobby was irritated at his nonchalance. "Come on, guys, it's going to be tight."

They quickly said goodbye and ran to catch the train. They made it just as the locomotive was pulling into the station.

26

The last night in New York was fun but sad for the Kelleys. They wouldn't see their daughters and Stephen until the summer. They would miss the Harper boys too. The girls promised to call as soon as they returned. The girls had a lot of planning and would need mom's help.

They left early for the station and the waiting Pullman car. The six of them said their goodbyes to the family and boarded the train. Tears and waves from the car windows and the station floor were exchanged. They kept waving until they couldn't see them anymore.

Tommy and Bobby claimed the couches that would be headquarters for the soon to be married couples. Carson was less concerned and yet more concerned about their behavior now that they were formally engaged. He kept his eye on things. Stephen knew his assignment too and loved to interfere with things that he had no business in knowing about.

They all settled in and relaxed until lunch was rolled in from the kitchen car. The porter served them all and left them alone.

They finished and sat back and looked out the opposing windows as the landscaped changed into farmland. In three days they would be back home. The new Kelley clan wanted to experience winter in their paradise. They were headed to Montana to find out.

Stephen left the four lovebirds as they were officially known now, to play his violin. He hadn't played since visiting Yale college.

He retrieved it from his bunk bed and closed the door to play. The girls yelled for him to leave the door open. They love to listen to him.

"Ok, ok!" He yelled.

He opened the case and screamed this time.

"It's gone, my violin is gone!"

Everyone rushed over to look at the substitute violin he was holding like it was a disease.

"This is not my instrument." He looked at his mom. She knew it immediately. Someone had switch violins on him. He took it out to look for the music. That was gone too.

"Who did this? The only time I left it alone was in the house. It didn't leave my side. How could it be gone?"

"You left it alone in the recital hall at Yale." "Everyone wondered who could have replaced it with an inferior practice instrument and steal the music."

Stephen knew. "Professor Beamish!" he screamed it out loud.

Bobby and Tommy knew he was right. He was the only one in the building. They recalled how he got up to "lock" the building. He was gone a little too long. "You're right Stephen that professor was a thief. He replaced it with one of the student violins and stole your music. He kept us running late so you wouldn't check it before leaving. We were running late because he delayed us. He planned this before we even arrived in New Haven."

"Carolina." She turned away from Stephen to Bobby as he spoke. "We need to get a telegram to your father. The sooner the better. Stephen's violin must be extremely valuable for this scum to steal it."

"It was more than valuable to Carolina; it was the only direct link to her 'old' family. It was all she had."

Stephen came over and hugged his mom and apologized for losing her violin.

"That's nonsense, Stephen, it was stolen. You did not lose it. We'll get it back, Bumpa will get it back for you."

The porter returned to remove the lunch cart.

"Sir, could you get a message sent by telegram from our next stop?"

"Of course, write it out and I will take it to the conductor. Our next stop is in 15 minutes."

They took stationery from father's desk and wrote him the details of the violin saga. Bobby wrapped it up with a five-dollar bill for the cost of the telegram and a tip for the porter. It was way more than enough.

"Thank you, sir." The porter smiled; he knew he just received a very generous tip.

At the next stop, they watched the conductor walk it over to the station office. A return telegram would be sent upstream to the railroad and eventually reach the Pullman car.

Stephen was destroyed by the thefts. He was angry, too. He lost his mother's most precious possession, and he couldn't do anything to get it back.

The violin was actually her sixth most precious possession. Stephen and now Bobby in second place. Mary and mom and dad had been elevated in that order over the "precious" violin. She could survive this, but she wasn't sure about Stephen. She had her Bobby now; Stephen had his mom and his violin until yesterday.

They checked for telegrams at each stop. Nothing yet. The next morning, they received word from Mr. Kelley. He promised to get it back. He hired the Pinkerton National Detective Agency, same ones that his company used. He paid them a lot of money over the years. He made this their number one propriety. He asked that Stephen stop worrying, he promised he would get it back.

The porter asked if they wanted to send a reply.

"Yes," Carolina said. The porter thought that was a good idea. It would give him another nice tip.

They wrote back saying they received his telegram and that it comforted Stephen. That was a half-truth. All they could do now was to wait.

Two detectives were on their way to Yale to speak with this professor. They showed up unannounced at his office. He was shaken to see someone confronting him two days after the violin went "missing."

He wasn't a very good thief and certainly not a good liar. They checked around the post office in town to see if any package that would match the size and weight of a violin and case was recently sent from their office. Nothing.

They went to the college post office and inquired there. Nothing.

They followed him home and pushed their way into his apartment as he unlocked his door. The searched everywhere. Nothing. The professor threatened them and they just laughed back.

"Do you know Mr. Cornelius Kelley?"

"Of course, I had dinner with Fritz Kreisler and ten others, including Stephen."

"What do you know about his missing violin?"

"He played it for us. It seemed very nice. It sounded beautiful."

Did he play it for you when he visited you two days ago?

"Yes, he played a concerto. He came with the two cowboys from Montana."

"Who had access to the violin besides the four of you?"

"I don't know. It was locked in the recital hall when we went to lunch. The last time I saw it was when they left for their train." He was getting mad at the cross-examination. "You can't just break in here and search my home without a warrant. You're not even cops."

"File a complaint with whomever you like. We will personally follow up during our next surprise visit."

He backed down and became quiet.

"Are you from England? You have an accent."

"Yes, from London."

"Are you here on a visa?"

"None of your business!"

They knew they had their man. Now it was just a matter of time before they would have him arrested, convicted and deported. He would never be able to play the violin in public. He would not get to enjoy his stolen instrument without looking over his shoulder.

Their next visit was with Mr. Kreisler. He would be leaving the city soon and they setup a meeting with him the next day. They went to Julliard and spoke with the people Stephen knew. They knew nothing. The stolen manuscripts were hand copied by two students while Stephen was a student. At least he could get copies of the original handwritten manuscripts. 'That wasn't much of a consolation, though.' He wanted the violin back and the original music too.

He felt good about Bumpa running the retrieval operation. He knew he had a chance to find his stolen property with him involved.

The meeting with Kreisler went well. He suspected Beamish too. He told them that he felt the violin was very old and very valuable. He suspected it was a Stradivarius. He felt that Beamish knew the provenance of the instrument, the first time he saw it. He also thought he knew the composer of the unidentified music. He thought it was J.S. Bach. If so, they would be priceless and unpublished.

They sent over a report right away to Mr. Kelley. He then sent a Telegram to the upcoming scheduled train stop. Stephen would have the info in an hour when the "Empire Builder's" flagship train rolled into Minneapolis/St. Paul.

The detectives had his last address in London, England and his parents' address in Liverpool. They had an agent already working on the trail and visiting high end auction houses asking about upcoming sales. They left cards with contact info to wire if a Stradivarius came up to auction. Sotheby's and Christies would be on the lookout.

Agents in Italy did the same with the auction houses. It wouldn't be easy to move this "hot" violin.

The train arrived in Whitefish, Montana without any new updates. They would call New York when they returned to the Lodge. It didn't look good. If Beamish stole it, he wasn't cracking yet. He was trapped and he knew it. It would have easier to sell the Mona Lisa. No collector or legitimate seller would touch it. Even Scotland Yard had it on their workboards. Mr. Kelley was a formidable opponent, and Beamish knew he made a mistake. A big mistake. Detectives were following him wherever he went. He felt it and realized he could never visit his prize.

The detectives interviewed the other instructors and the dean of the Music School. Now, his reputation was under scrutiny. They didn't want him fired; they wanted him to stay in the U.S. so they could arrest him when the violin turned up.

They spoke with the man who refurbished the violin to see if he could offer any clues to the violin's provenance. He had taken photographs to show clients. The photos revealed enough information to have the origins of the instrument identified. He gave the detectives the photos to make copies before they returned them. This was a big break. Packages would be mailed around the world with the photos and a detailed description from the repairman's notes was included. These were sent to experts in the field and especially Italian experts. They hoped someone could identify the maker. One package was shipped to the record keeper in Cremona, Italy that had Stradivarius records for most every instrument built and sold.

They were leaving nothing to guesswork. The detective agency was relentless and that's how Con wanted things.

They dropped the boys off at home and they invited the girls and Stephen for dinner. Bobby and Tommy's parents didn't know that their boys were engaged. They were happy the boys invited the girls.

They loved them both and knew they would hear better stories from the girls.

Two very important announcements were on the slate. Weddings and Carolina's slow healing of her hearing. They had Christmas gifts to give and get after dinner. The two Harper sisters were thrilled to see their brothers back and safe from the big city. They worried the city would be too much for some Montana country boys to navigate. They not only navigated it with ease, but they also earned some fame. When they showed the two newspaper articles to them, they looked at the photos and just shook their heads and laughed. Daisy grabbed them and was going to show them to their parents. That's when Tommy realized that one article talked about the marriage proposal. He grabbed it back and held it until after the engagement announcements were made. He didn't want to spoil things.

The girls arrived for dinner and were ushered into the living room to see the Christmas tree. It was puny compared to the one back at home in New York, but they loved it. They both talked about their first tree in Montana and how they would decorate it. They wouldn't turn that job over to staff.

"Dinner!"

They all went in and sat at the table. It was big enough for everyone. The youngest filled the water glasses to help the hostess. Mrs. Harper brought out the smoked ham and potatoes. The boys missed mom's cooking. The fancy food in New York was good, but not as good as their mother's fare.

"Stephen," Mrs. Harper asked. "We were hoping you brought your violin over to play for us."

Stephen took in a breath and slowly let it out before speaking. "It was stolen." He didn't want to think or talk about it.

"I'm so sorry, Stephen. What happened? In the city?"

"No. It happened at Yale College when I visited the School of Music. Grandpa hired detectives to find it. They think it was the Professor who invited me to the school. He was the last one to see it. They think he switched it while we ate lunch. Even Mr. Kreisler thinks he took it."

"Whose Mr. Kreisler."

"Fritz Kreisler, the violinist. His real name is Friedrich Kreisler. He's probably the best in the world. He seems to think it has great value if the Professor stole it. I didn't even know it was gone until we were on the train the next morning. I'm so very sorry mom." He lamented. "I know it was so important to you. I never thought someone could do such a thing. I was just stunned when I opened my case and found an inexpensive student violin. He took the old bow, too."

Carolina recoiled when she "heard" Stephen utter the name Friedrich. She didn't like that name leaving Stephen's lips. She clearly was not missing much of any conversations nowadays. Her hearing was returning, and her ability to read lips was almost perfect.

"We were with Stephen when it happened. He pulled a fast one." Bobby explained.

They told the whole story and when finished, moved on to the next topic of the evening.

Carolina and Mary planned the announcement to please the boys' momma. It was part joke and part serious. They loved their momma and the girls wanted to make sure the transition from mother to wives went smoothly. Mrs. Harper was familiar with the Bible term "cleaving" of the husbands to their new brides and the new brides to their husbands! It had a rich dual meaning of breaking apart and coming together.

"Mrs. Harper, Mary and I have something to ask of you."

"What is it, my darlings, what?"

They walked over to her and motioned to the young ones sitting on each side of her and took their chairs. They both looked at her with serious faces.

"Mary and I would. Like to ask you for your sons' hands in marriage."

Daisy shrieked and Jennifer shook with excitement. It took Mrs. Harper a little longer to try and process what she just heard.

"What? Are you going to propose to my boys?"

"They already proposed to us in New York!"

"You're both engaged to my boys?"

"Yes, Mrs. Harper, yes!"

They each put their arms around her and hugged her.

"Please say yes; they would be very sad if you say no."

The men, including Stephen, were shaking their heads and rolling their eyes.

Mrs. Harper started to cry and smile. "Yes! Yes!" Looking at Bobby and Tommy."

Mr. Harper came alongside his boys and, shook their hands and hugged each of them. He then walked over to the girls and hugged and kissed them both. The two young boys play acted like they were going to throw up, until momma put a stop to that with one glance.

"Sorry, Dad." Bobby started. "It just kind of happened spontaneously. I was going to ask for your advice and wisdom when we got back to Bigfork and then propose to Carolina here in Montana."

"Did you ask her father?"

"After the fact."

"How did that go over?"

Bobby recreated the entire night for his parents. He didn't leave out a thing. He did skip the part about Stephen's father.

"My Bobby sure is a romantic. What about you, Tommy?" She asked.

"I don't 'know what Mary is talking about. I didn't propose to her!"

Mary play slapped him. Not very hard, but hard enough to leave a red mark.

"Ok, my turn." Tommy started with the bathroom/towel girl incident that Bobby masterminded. Mom frowned and Dad laughed. He went through the lead-up and ended with his spontaneous proposal.

"Maybe not as dramatic as Bobby's, but definitely more private and romantic. After all, she said yes."

Mary kissed him on the cheek.

"See!"

Carolina kissed Bobby on the lips.

"Oh yeah!"

The young ones made their throw-up faces again. Mom laughed this time.

"Well, we have some planning to do." She said, looking side to side at the girls. "I couldn't be happier."

27

The detectives had a lead. It came from the village of Cremona, Italy. The records were held in the city archives. It was the missing Bach violin. The photos confirmed it when compared to the drawings. None other than Johann Sebastian Bach's violin given to him in 1712. It was from the Golden Age of Stradivarius and one of the rarest violins on Earth for two reasons. First, it was Bach's violin and second, it was a Strad from the Golden Years. Bach was the greatest composer on Earth and Stradivarius made the finest violins on Earth.

The report listed the last known owner in the year 1862. That owner's name was Bach's granddaughter, Carolina Augusta Wilhelmine Bach. The detectives didn't realize that Carolina Augusta was a direct descendent of J.S. Bach. She was Carolina's grandmother. She died in 1871. No record of her mother had been found yet. That was the missing link. That information meant that Stephen was the last branch on the Bach family tree. The Bach family line ended with Stephen.

The report also noted that the initials SDG were under the tailpiece, visible from one of the repair photos. It meant "Soli Deo Gloria." It is Latin and translates into English as *Glory to God Alone*. Bach was known to inscribe those initials on the last page of his finished compositions.

The photos confirmed that the Alpine Spruce top was genuine. 1709 was known as the coldest winter, going back to the 1200s in Europe. The Stradivarius wood top on Bach's violin was from that period and the tight growth rings from that era were the reason for the extraordinary sound of the finest Strads. That era was known now as the "Little Ice Age."

The detectives forwarded the information to Mr. Kelley. He would have it in a week.

Carolina and Mary were as happy as two people could be. They looked forward to married life as any women who held worries about their age and their pent-up sexual tension would. The boys had the same affliction and like most marriage proposals, these were pushed forward by those same symptoms and hormones. These emotions, unlike some men's, were fortified by a fountain of love and adoration.

Carolina worried about Stephen. He was affected by his violin theft. He felt so devastated about it and felt he had let his mother down for allowing it to happen. He knew he should have taken it with him. He didn't account for an inside thief's trickery. Carolina sensed it and tried to console him. It didn't work. Stephen was inconsolable. It exposed a terrible comparison between her happiness and his sadness.

Mr. Kelley purchased another violin and sent it to the lodge. It would arrive by train in three days. That was a blessing to Stephen and Carolina and helped to heal their misplaced emotions.

The detectives wanted the replacement violin sent back to them to analyze. It was left at the station to be put on the eastbound train.

The winter months surprised the girls. It was milder than they thought it would be. Stephen's seed package description was accurate. Swan Lake didn't freeze solid enough to allow for ice skating this year. The swiftly moving water of the Swan River interfered with that. When February arrived, they enjoyed the sunny "Big Sky" once again.

They decided to get married all together in the lodge in the third week of July. They all would have elected elopement to release all the pent-up—how do you say it politely?—emotions that youth run up against. They satisfied their passion with a lot of hugging, kissing and pushing boundaries that naturally expand during the engagement period. Mary wasn't as careful about these things as Carolina. Bobby wasn't as careful as Tommy was. That saved a rushed marriage or two. It was truly two engagements made in heaven. Both girls were even happier with the boys' choices. It kept the "playing" field level.

Mr. Kelley called the lodge with news about the missing violin.

"We have identified the provenance of your violin, Carolina. Sit down; I have many things to tell you."

Carolina was surprised by that statement. Was it destroyed, lost forever? What could it be?

"We know that your violin is a Stradivarius. Antonio Stradivari crafted your violin in 1712, during the height of his skill and the quality of materials used to make it. It was constructed in the middle of a twenty-year period that set the standard for the world they lived in and for the future. A finer violin has yet to be built. It is perhaps the most valuable violin on Earth."

"Did you find it?"

"Not yet, but now that we know about it, it could never be sold to someone who didn't intend to hoard it. The detectives agreed that this was good news. They also felt they had the correct "methods" to get it back to you."

"Let me call Stephen in!"

Stephen came running when he heard his mother screaming for him.

"Mom, are you okay?"

"Talk with Bumpa."

Bumpa retold everything to him. He was astounded to learn that his favorite composer once owned his violin. Its quality, value, and rarity were certainly nice, but the man who owned it before him was the most important part of its history and value to him. It was the single most important fact. Besides, he would never sell it anyway. The high value had made it a target. If he ever did get it back, he would always be worried about the next theft attempt.

"Thanks, Bumpa. I feel a little better now. I know you will find it for me. I just know it. Oh, thank you for sending the new violin. It is so much better than the one left behind in my case. I promise to be a better steward and custodian when you find it. I love you, Bumpa!"

"Oh, the violin that was put in your case is from the Yale School of Music."

He liked the way Stephen understood his role was to be a custodian of the famous violin. He didn't feel that he owned it; he felt he had to protect it for the future. "Put your mother back on."

Stephen handed the phone to Carolina and filled Mary in on the details they were revealed.

A second report would be forthcoming after the research was completed on the previous owner's names and residences. Mr. Kelley was hoping to find a path that linked the violin to Carolina. He was very interested in anything he could provide to his daughter that would unlock the mystery of her family history. He knew it was unlikely. Many records were destroyed during the war. Finding records pertaining to the lower class was even more unlikely.

The Montana Kelleys enjoyed the winter much more than they thought. It wasn't as cold as they expected, and the snow stayed white. New York City snow started out white, but soon turned dirty brown as it mixed and melted with the soot caused by coal fires used to heat the homes and rooms.

Especially unexpected were the hundreds of trails in the snow left by the winter animals that stayed behind and scoured the lawns and grounds of the Kootenai. The trails and paths changed from the fall when deer would sleep under the food and shade of the apple trees.

During their first Autumn in Montana, the girls noticed the apple trees near the natural spring-fed pond were so full of fruit that the branches were breaking off and falling to the ground, spreading the red apples across the croquet court.

They were telling the boys about the broken branches and speculating about the deer feasting on spoils of the trees that donated thousands of apples. Mary said she would listen for the crashing of the large limbs so she could run out and compete with the deer.

"Oh Mary, you be careful. Those branches are being pulled down by very large bears. The deer hear them break and rush over to get their share. They are smart enough to know how close they can get to the grizzlies." Bobby wasn't kidding.

"You're serious?"

"Go into the main hall of the lodge and look at the grizzlies hanging from the towering log walls. If that doesn't change your mind, then the deer are smarter than you!"

"Don't worry, I suddenly lost my appetite for fresh apples."

"The bears will be gone as soon as the food is gone. For now, keep alert and if you see a bear, slowly back away. Most important, if the sow has cubs, you are at a high risk. They will protect their young ones from threats that are real and not real. You girls are not real threats, but to a momma, you could be and that puts you in danger." Bobby didn't crack a smile or any facial expressions. He looked serious.

"Those bear mounts in the lodge are from this area. The story I heard was that the log builders that were hired traded them from the Salish Indian tribes. Ammunition, blankets and tarps were valuable currency back then. The workers presented them as a gift to the Kelleys. I have no idea where the polar bear came from; their habitat is at least a thousand miles from here. It must have been trapped because its front right paw is missing."

The times were different back then. If you wanted to fish, you went fishing and if you wanted to hunt, you went out hunting. No licenses, permits, or tags needed. No season was off-limit to any fish or animal. The only regulations were applied to alcohol and gambling.

"No more apple pies for you boys."

"Don't worry, we'll get the apples for you."

28

The morning call from Mr. and Mrs. Kelley came early this Sunday. It woke the girls. Mary picked up the phone and asked if everything was ok. They never called this early.

"Yes, sorry, honey. We have exciting information for Carolina and Stephen."

"You found the violin?" Mary exclaimed.

Mary heard the word violin and ran into the bedroom.

"No, not yet. I do have information about Carolina's family, though. Johnson brought a package from the detectives that was delivered late last night. He just brought it to me a few minutes ago."

Mary thought Daddy was talking too fast and breathing at the same speed.

"Put Carolina on the phone for me." He was very happy sounding.

Carolina was handed the receiver.

"Hello, Dad, what's going on?"

"Carolina, I know about your family and how you came into possession of the Stradivarius. We still have some missing pieces, big pieces."

Carolina had mixed emotions. She knew who her family was. She was on the phone with her dad. He might not have been a blood relative, but he was just as good to her, even better. The whole family was hers now and she didn't want to be anybody else's daughter.

"Okay, darling. Are you ready for this?"

"I guess, Dad. You know you're my only daddy, right?"

"Of course I know that, and you are my daughter. Nothing will change that." He felt the same way when he learned parts of her lineage from the detectives. He felt it interfered with her new bloodline as a Kelley. He wasn't going to abdicate his father's throne to some distant relatives that had never met her.

He took a deep breath before he unlocked her unknown past.

"We know who your grandmother is, and we also know about your family history for nine generations. The only missing part, for now mind you, is the identity of your mother and father."

He didn't like to have important information missing in any of his business reports. The hole in this report gave him some consolation. He was less worried about his role being replaced for right now. They still didn't know her father's identity and that eased his silly fear of being replaced.

"Your grandmother's name is Carolina Augustas Wilhemine Bach."

"I remember Wilhelmine was removed from my name at the immigration facility when I disembarked from the ship that took me to America. They shortened it to Carolina Augusta. I never used my real last name. You're saying my real last name is Bach? That is certainly a famous last name. Especially to a musician. Stephen will really like that his mother's last name is the same as his favorite composer."

"Carolina, we have every reason to believe that you are Johann Sebastian Bach's 6th generation granddaughter."

"What?"

The room became silent as they focused on the call.

"Put Stephen on the phone for me.

She called to Stephen, and he rushed in.

She handed the receiver to Stephen."

Carolina was whispering to Mary the amazing story she just heard.

"What, Bumpa?"

"Stephen, who is your favorite composer?"

"You know, J.S. Bach."

"What if I told you that you are the last known relative of Bach? Yes, the J. S. Bach." He paused to let that sink in.

"Johann Sebastian Bach. He is your grandfather, seven generations back. That's how your mother came into possession of his violin. It's a family heirloom, an inheritance. Your mother's mother, your grandmother, must have given it to her to keep. Maybe to keep it safe during the war that was coming to Germany. I don't know. I intend to find out, though."

"This is incredible. I always wondered about who my grandparents were, but I never thought they could be famous. Mom didn't know anything about her. Did you tell her yet?"

"I just did. Here's another possibility about your heritage. We think your mother is royalty. Not sure yet, but it seems likely."

"Put her on for me, *Prince Stephen David Gabriel.*"

"Just call me Prince SDG for short," Stephen said before handing the phone over to his mom.

"Stephen, Stephen!"

Carolina picked up the phone before Bumpa could finish. He told her the other findings of the detectives. She was shocked to think that she was a royal.

"My oh my, Carolina. You started your life as a little German orphan girl, Then a charwoman, a little girl charwoman at that. Then, an upstairs maid in New York City. A tutor next. And then our daughter. Next, a Granddaughter of Bach. Now, you may be a Princess. I always thought of you as one."

"Oh, Daddy, you know I always thought of you as my King! I love you so much. You forgot to mention my engagement milestone!"

"And I love you, darling. I pity poor Bobby, married to a princess and all!" He liked that combination. As an American, he thought that a cowboy was just what a princess needed to keep an even keel.

Does the life of an orphan child get any better than what has been given to and earned by Carolina? Who could have predicted such an outcome after the absolutely inauspicious early beginning. As time rolled through her life, she would appreciate her lucky fate even more.

"Tell Stephen that when he asked me to call him Prince SDG instead of Prince Stephen David Gabriel. I realized his initials are the same ones that Bach wrote on most of his manuscripts. How did you know that?"

"I didn't know Bach used them; I just liked the biblical names and the initials on the compositions in the violin case.."

"Strange, can you put on my other daughter, Mary, please? Don't rub in your royalty and heritage too much." He laughed.

A lot of laughs and a lot of jokes about the Kootenai Bachs were tossed around. It was a happy time for Carolina. The ribbing was okay and silly, but it couldn't harm the joy she felt in learning who she really was. She had a hole in her life that she thought would never be plugged. She played with different new expanded married names that she could choose. She decided that "Carolina Augustas Wilhelmine Bach Harper" would be her new legal name. It was a mouthful, and she knew it. She would go by the name Carolina Harper. It was a proper American name she thought. She wouldn't tell her dad, she worried he'd want to add Kelley into the mix. It was long enough she chuckled to herself. She thought about the immigration man taking a name away from her. Now she would put it back and add another two.

29

Clara had become friends with some of the police officers who had mistreated Carolina years ago. They were genuinely sorry for their behavior and the escape of her attacker. They were happy to hear she was engaged. They were also glad to learn about Stephen over the years and his musical success.

Life sure has a way of doing whatever it wants. Bad things can sometimes have happier endings than expected and the opposite can happen to things perceived as good.

Clara met Officer McMillan one afternoon when he came into the hospital to question an injured robbery victim. He was about her age and had bright red hair and freckles. She was amused by him and thought he was sort of cute. He noticed Clara immediately and came over to talk to her about his "case." That was not the reason, and she knew it.

Officer Michael "Mackie" McMillan was awestruck by her beauty and personality.

"I'm Officer McMillan, my friends call me Mackie."

"Nice to meet you, Officer McMillan." She cleverly responded.

"Please call me Mackie."

"You're not my friend. Officer McMillan. I know nothing about you."

He knew this was going to take some effort and he always enjoyed a challenge. Carla was curious how he would respond now. Would he give up or keep trying?

"I like you." Was all he said after that.

Clara liked him too and liked his determination. She decided it was time to slowly reward his efforts.

"I like you too, but probably not as much as you like me."

"Does it show?" He asked.

"What do you think?"

That was the start of their romance. He asked her to dinner on Friday night and she said she had to check her calendar and get back to him. He asked if he could stop by tomorrow. She liked his no-nonsense approach. She realized she was playing "calendar" games with him and decided she should stop.

"I would like that very much. See you tomorrow for my answer. I must get back to my patients now, Mackie."

"See you tomorrow," he said as he walked out with a slight kick to his step.

He ran back to Clara. "I forgot to ask, what's your name."

"Clara. Clara Barton."

He turned around and smiled. He loved the alias last name she gave him. He knew who Clara Barton was, everybody knew that name.

Clara walked back to her station with a smile on her face. She was asked out on a date by a cute cop. He was not as tall or as handsome as the Harper boys, but close enough. She couldn't wait to tell Carolina and Mary. She felt more of a part of their happiness now that she had her chances greatly increased to find what they had found.

Friday couldn't come fast enough for Clara. She confirmed her availability to Mackie that next day and asked about where they were going.

"I hear the New York Yacht Club has wonderful lobster!" She thought back to Carolina's night at the club. She loved that love story.

"I'm not a member yet."

She enjoyed joking with him. He was confident and she liked that even more. She suggested they go to one of his favorite places.

"I'm sure I'll love it."

"It's too early to walk into our precinct hangout with such a pretty girl. My cop friends can be rough at times."

"I can handle them." She wanted to see who his friends were. She wanted to observe him in the "wild." She handled the cops with Carolina just fine. Now she had even more experience with male bravado. It came with her nursing job. "Sometimes you have to take charge and set the tone," she thought.

"Okay then, Paddy's Tavern it is."

"I know where it is; meet you at seven."

"I can come and get you and we can walk together." He didn't want the travel time to be deducted from his evening with her.

"I'll meet you there." She wanted to spend some time with him before she gave out her address. It was a precaution that men never had to think about. To a smart, single and pretty young woman, it was essential.

"Okay, see you there." He conceded defeat and deferred to her wishes.

The Pinkerton Detectives were following Beamish now and he knew it. He was intimidated and was starting to wish he had never gone down this road. The violin and music were not worth it anymore. They knew too much. Yale was wary of him too. They had a detective from Scotland Yard go to his parents' home in Liverpool to inject a little fear into their lives. Maybe they knew about it, and if not, they would let their son know that the investigators had "long arms" and were not going away anytime soon.

Professor Beamish was getting desperate to be finished with this. He met a shady guy at Frank Pepe Pizzeria. He decided to set him up and pay him to turn the contraband over to the police. It was dark out and he lowered his hat and put up his collar. This guy was inebriated. They made plans to meet tomorrow night in the city park across from Calhoun College. He would improve his disguise and retrieve the hidden violin and music from the observation deck of Harkness Tower. It was safely hidden there. He would get it tonight and bring it to the park to give to Fritzy along with a note to give to the New Haven Police. His accomplice was a pensioned war veteran. He didn't need the $20, he was simply a bad person, Beamish needed his problems solved.

Clara left for Paddy's Tavern. She arrived at 6:30, a half hour early. She wanted to see what this bunch of "troublemakers" was all about.

She wanted to meet his friends on a level playing field before they saw the two of them together.

She opened the door and walked up to the bar. She looked around and noticed a few rascals, but overall, a lot more "nice guys" from the precincts, and still in uniform.

A couple of cops came over and offered to buy Carla a drink. Prohibition ended a few weeks ago, not that it had any effect on Paddy's Tavern.

"Thank you, I'm waiting for my date."

They respected that. He's probably a cop they thought.

Clara ordered an Old Fashioned. She had one at one of the charity parties and liked it.

"Here you go Ma'am." He welcomed her and asked. "Have you been here before?

"No, I'm waiting for Mackie."

That announcement changed everything.

"It's on the house if you're a friend of Mackie."

"I'm going on a date with him. What's he like."

"Stay away from him and go out with me instead. I'm a much safer bet!"

He liked Mackie a lot. He was a straight shooter and a good cop. He was happy he was going out with such a pretty girl with a personality.

"Okay, Mackie is a great guy, ask anyone in here or in the neighborhood. I'm glad he brought you to Paddy's. It's a real pleasure to meet you. My name's Paddy and this is my place. I've never seen him on a date before. I promise the boys will be respectful."

"Oh, sure they will. I've been around enough to know a little bit about cops. I'm a nurse in the hospital two blocks down from his precinct."

Clara was having fun playing a toughie. She always liked cops, not all, but most. She thought back to the jerks who mistreated Carolina. They were an aberration.

Two other cops came up to Clara to try their luck.

"Leave her alone, boys. She's with Mackie!" Paddy was watching over her. She liked that.

Mackie walked in ten minutes early so he could tell the boys to lay off him when

Mackie came in. He looked over at Paddy and was surprised to see Clara enjoying a cocktail at the bar. He laughed out loud and quickly walked over to her.

"You seem to be holding your own in this joint. How long have you been here?"

"Only a couple of hours!"

"I like this gal, Mackie." Paddy really did.

"I got here a few minutes ago. I like it here."

Paddy rang the tip bell and stood on the step ladder behind the bar that he used to reach the upper shelf bottles.

"This beautiful gal is Mackie's date, and I want all of you to behave yourself and not say a word about all of his other dates in front of her!"

The place roared with laughter, especially Clara. Mackie wasn't as amused as his friends.

He passed the date test. His friends were funny and cared enough to tease him. They all liked him, and she knew why. He was normal and fun. Clara was pleased.

"Can we find a table over in the corner?" Mackie winked at her and she followed him to a table away from the Friday night madness.

"It's nice I don't have to worry about being robbed in this place!"

They talked for hours. Clara had another Old Fashioned and Mackie nursed a Jameson that now was on melted ice. Mackie shared his history with her, but he always threw it back to Clara. He wanted to know more about her and why a pretty girl like her was not "taken."

She asked him the same question to him. He had no answer, except that he was starting to think it was time and he wanted a family.

His answer seemed too perfect. What woman could resist a man who was cute, wanted to settle down and raise a family. Oh, and he had a good job during an economic depression.

Her answer was identical, but she couldn't say it now. He wouldn't believe her.

What a predicament she was in. She wanted what he wanted. She wanted what Carolina and Mary wanted.

"May I come over and sit next to you?" she didn't wait for an answer.

"Mackie, I want what you want. It just seems like it's a little early for this conversation."

It was the correct and truthful response. Mackie was okay with that. They both told the other what they wanted, and it was a match. It felt normal and unforced.

"Are you hungry?" he changed the subject. There would be plenty of time to get serious. Now wasn't the time.

"Yeah, let's go."

Mackie went up to the bar to pay and Paddy wouldn't have any of that. "It's on the house," he said, "I'm just glad your wife and kids didn't come in and find you here alone with this beauty!"

"Thank you, Paddy," they both said at the same time while walking to the door.

They went to a small Italian restaurant nearby and dined on pasta, bread and shared a glass of Chianti. To Clara, it was the perfect date. Enough serious talk mixed with fun, food and playful rhetoric.

Anytime a woman can't get all her questions answered because time runs out, is good. Any time a man is captivated by a woman's questions and her answers, is even better.

Mackie looked across the table at Clara. He studied every part of her face and decided it was perfect. Any changes, he thought, would diminish her beauty. Clara looked at Mackie's face too. Not perfect, with a little hair dye to tone down the bright red hair, it would be. She chuckled inside.

They walked home together. He "accidently" touched her hand and held it for a few blocks. Clara loved that he did that. She had no problem sharing her address with this man. He took her key and opened her door and asked if he could see her again.

"Yes, I'd love it."

"How about tomorrow night? We could see a movie." He wanted more of her.

"Oh, ah, Okay."

"How about *King Kong*?"

"I was thinking more like *Little Women*."

"Our first fight."

"The last time I went to a movie with a guy he tried to kiss me."

"I hate that, don't you?"

They both laughed at the joke and the possibilities of a future that included the two of them happily ever after.

They said their goodbyes and Clara went in and up to her apartment. She dressed for bed and jumped in. Clara loved her bed.

"I wonder what our kids will look like?"

Does every woman say that sort of things to themselves? Do they all move ahead that deep into relationships. It must be exhausting to think like that. Is it only because she is in her early thirties and sees that time is running out on the "clock." A woman's window to have children is not like a baseball game. It can't go into extra innings. It's like football when the clock's running. Clara felt she was in the fourth quarter. Still time, but clock management would be essential.

"I like the freckles; the bright red hair might be a bit much, but I do like freckles." Was the last thought she had before they turned into dreams.

30

Mary and Carolina were getting tired of winter. Not because it was colder than New York. It was because of the diminished hours of sunlight. They would make up for it in the summer's long days, but they could use some right now.

The wedding plans involved both sets of parents now. Mr. and Mrs. Harper talked with the Kelleys many times to discuss the wedding and also to try and figure out what the kids planned for their future together. Everything is in duplicate when two sisters marry two brothers. It was obvious that they would be duplicating each other's lives too.

Living in Montana was a given. The Harpers loved that and the Kelleys did too. Just not as much. At least they would spend time with them in the summer. Mary explained that they would see their two Montana girls more than their New York girls. That helped a little.

It was decided that a Montana wedding in the main hall of the Kootenai Lodge would be perfect. Mrs. Kelley preferred the first week in September. The girls put their feet down on that idea. July was just about as long as they could stand up to their hormones and lean on their moral character. They were having a rough time as it was. September was way too far off for them to survive the unforgiving purity test they were taking. There were no multiple-choice answers on this one and the sooner they would lay down their pencils and hand in their papers the better.

It wasn't any easier for the boys. They relied on hard work and being "tuckered out." It was a guise. They were getting pretty forward with their girls. At first, they resisted most of the boys' advances. Not so much anymore. They knew to be more careful now that the girls were abdicating their throne of "rules and responsibilities."

September was not in the cards for these four gamblers. When it was explained to Mrs. Kelley about the dangers, she wholeheartedly agreed that July was just fine.

The detectives had no new information. The investigation would have to move toward a more physical approach to obtain the answers they wanted. Mr. Kelley gave the "go-ahead" for them to visit Professor Beamish at Yale. They made plans to stop by and "talk" to him in the next two days. It would be a surprise and cozy get-together.

They would place a notice in the New Haven and Yale newspapers that would put the thief on notice that the Pinkerton agency was on the case and that the valuable Stradivarius should be turned in to authorities immediately. The school was informed that the "replacement violin" was stolen from the college. That put even more pressure on Beamish.

Beamish dressed in a disguise and left his apartment to get his hostage violin and music. He didn't need a disguise. The detectives were not in New Haven and wouldn't be for two days.

He met Fritzy in the park across from Calhoun. They sat down together on the bench behind the old church, as they had planned. It was a full moon.

Fritzy was nervous that Beamish could easily see his face and describe it if he needed to. He could see Beamish's too. He supposed that mitigated things a little.

He took the violin, the music inside the case and the $20 along with a typewritten note explaining that the thief had no idea of the value. He would later read the New Haven newspaper advertisement describing the instrument.

He told Beamish he would drop it off on the steps of the police station at 3:00 am.

The professor returned to his apartment and Fritzy to the car he inherited along with the house from his uncle in Hamden.

He opened the note to read it. He would not be dropping off the violin as planned. He found a newspaper and knew what he had and decided he would be the next custodian of such a fine and valuable instrument. He put it in the trunk and drove home to Hamden. The only person that could turn him in was the man who obviously stole it and got cold feet. That was the only untidy thing. He would avoid New Haven for a while.

He took the instrument into the house and opened the case to see it. At first, he thought he was duped. It was an old violin, not a shiny new one like he expected. The next day he went to the Hamden Library and researched the name Stradivarius that was in the newspaper. He smiled and went back home to carefully hide his expensive and old violin. He didn't think much about the old music under the instrument. He left it and the bow in the case just as he found it.

The next day, Professor Beamish was visited by Pinkerton. They roughed him up pretty badly. He was surprised the New Haven Police hadn't informed the detective agency that they had the violin and music. Unless……

Clara had a wonderful day at work. All she could think about was her movie date with Mackie in the evening. When she thought about the real chance of this relationship surviving, it took away some of her happiness. She was able to conjure an enchanting ending in her mind and she clung to that in order to push the negatives aside.

Mackie came bounding into the hospital just as Clara was going to eat her lunch.

"Hi, Clara!"

She turned around to see a bright red head that had a very big smile. She smiled back at him. No coquetry, no games. She was glad he came by to see her.

"I'm just going to eat my lunch." She held up her brown bag to show him. "Care to join me?"

"Yes, Clara Barton. I'd love to."

"You know that's not my real name."

"Of course. It's Strickland."

"How did you know that?" she wondered.

"I'm a cop, you know. It was at the entrance to your apartment. It was the only one without a first name. The others had first names, and they were all male."

"Evidently, you're not a detective," she smiled.

"Isn't that your last name?"

"Yes, but it's a lucky guess. Two of the male first names are actually women who didn't want someone to think they lived alone. They thought the male name would deter problems."

He smiled back and acknowledged his rookie mistake. Clara offered half her lunch to Mackie. He didn't have an appetite. Sitting next to her and looking at her beautiful face interfered with his hunger. He declined and suggested they go to the seven o'clock showing of *Little Women*.

"What about *King Kong*?" she asked.

"I can always go see that with a different girl. Besides, I think I'll have a better chance at a kiss if I take you to the one you want to see."

She tried to conceal her smile, but she couldn't. It was as big a smile that her face could hold.

"Not on the second date!" they both knew it was a lie.

Mrs. Kelley felt lonely in the big house especially during the day when she was all alone. The four married sisters were providing grandchildren on a regular basis and that helped ease the uninvited solitude. When her five girls were young, that was all she wanted. A little solitude. She would gladly trade that for the hectic schedule of a young family again. She rethought that and decided that the hectic schedule of grandchildren was a perfect balance of chaos when they visited and solitude when they departed. She appreciated how God had that all planned. He never doled out more than one could bear in the Bible. Noah, Job and Jonah came to mind.

Mr. Kelley was still in his prime and increasing his wealth and companies through acquisitions and expansions. The times were tough for the working man, but they also provided great opportunities for him along with great price reductions form the companies that were having a difficult time navigating in this "new" economy.

31

The Pinkerton boys stopped by to visit the Professor every day for the last four evenings.

"I'm telling you I don't have the violin, and I don't know where it is!" That was recited every visit, just before they started punching him. The boys were beginning to think he was telling the truth. That's because he was telling the truth, and it sounded convincing. If he was lying, he was one of the tougher suspects they had run up against.

They stopped by the next night.

"You might as well just start hitting me, boys; I still don't know anything."

That was the last visit for them. He convinced them he was innocent, or at least didn't know where it was hidden.

They really didn't have any leads yet. The next report to Mr. Kelley wouldn't be a good one.

Beamish thought about Fritzy and his blood boiled. "I'm gonna find that crook."

It's interesting how the hierarchy of the underworld can operate with such irony, how things can change in a heartbeat and get turned upside down. At first it seems like such a strange and different world that evil people live in. It's not, though; even good people can be hypocritical and lack any self-awareness. Now, Beamish saw himself as the victim. That was as absurd as a wayward wife blaming her husband for her adultery.

He went to the pizza joint every evening, hoping to find him there. And then it happened. Fritzy couldn't resist the best pizza in America. That's what the critics were saying anyway. Pepe claimed to have concocted the first pizza in America.

Beamish walked in behind him, stuck a short-barreled .38 revolver into his back and said two words.

"Follow me," he led him out.

"You better still have it," he added.

They were outside and got into Fritzy's inherited car for the drive to his inherited house to get his stolen violin and the music.

Twenty minutes later, they were there. He opened the garage door and drove his cousin's car inside. The two of them went into the house through the kitchen door.

"I'll go and get it."

"Not so fast; I'm coming with you," he kept the gun on him as they went down to the basement and retrieved the "loot" from behind the coal box next to the furnace.

"You better not have overheated it here next to the furnace."

He took it from Fritzy and felt it was cool. That relieved him.

"Let's go upstairs." He ordered as he followed his man.

He intended to kill him and leave the violin with the body. He wanted this whole thing to end. He didn't want to get another visit from the detectives.

Fritzy never thought this somewhat mild-mannered man would hurt him.

"So, what's the deal with this violin, anyway? Who are you?"

"I'm a Professor at Yale." He didn't mind talking about it to a dead man. He never had the chance to brag about his violin to anybody. He couldn't ever do that. This was his only chance.

"I stole it from a young protégé who lives in New York City and."

"What's that?"

"That's a young man with a great musical talent and bright future."

"They must have a lot of "dough" to have such a valuable thing sittin' around."

"It's from the Kelley family in Manhattan. I stole it from his grandkid in New Haven."

"I know the house. I used to deliver ice in that neighborhood. Before the war." He thought about Carolina and wondered if she still worked for the Bradburys. I knew a girl back then, Carolina Augustas, I think."

"It's her son's violin; he's a talented eleven-year-old."

"He's the pro-ta-shay?" he tried his best to pronounce the foreign word.

"Yes, why? Do you know them?" he was confused.

"She is Mr. Kelley's daughter, now. Word is that she worked as a housekeeper and also tutor to his daughters, and they "took" her in."

"Is she married?"

"I don't think so," Stephen told me his father never returned from the war. I think she is engaged to a cowboy from Montana. "Why so many questions about the Kelley family?"

"Rich people always interested me."

Beamish was annoyed by all the questions. It interrupted his crime story that he wanted to brag about.

Fritzy saw how uncomfortable he was holding a revolver. He kept it pointed at him the entire time. When he turned on his inherited lamp next to his inherited chair, he could see into the chamber. It was unloaded. He knew it was possible to have one cartridge in the chamber hidden by the barrel, and it seemed likely. He knew his hours or even minutes were numbered.

"Get me a piece of paper and a pen. You're going to leave a note behind."

He got him a pen and paper from the desk. He thought he was being very careless. He could have had a weapon in the desk. He wished that he had.

"Start writing," he began to dictate the note. It was a suicide note that simply stated that he didn't want to keep the violin or go to jail.

"It's my only way out," was the last sentence before he signed it. He purposely misspelled his name in case his theory about the cartridges was incorrect and the police found his body. It wouldn't take long to find the spelling error on the note and discount the suicide theory. Now he had to find an opportunity to jump him. He decided he would strangle him instead of shooting him. Too messy and too loud for the neighborhood.

He wanted to be careful and not get himself killed. He wanted to personally give it back to Carolina and meet his son the protégé. She would be so grateful that she would take him into her life along with his son, Stephen. Sure, he felt a little bad about what he did, but she would have forgotten about Bradbury house "incident" a long time ago. He was certain he could win her over with the violin. He hoped she was still as beautiful as he remembered her.

Some people might call this "dumb love." technically, it's "stupid love." Stupid and very frightening. Carolina's rapist was a deranged maniac, and he was planning to pay her a social visit.

Beamish realized he hadn't looked into the violin case. How stupid am I he thought. He opened it and the old bow horsehair fell to the floor. He bent down to retrieve it.

Fritzy saw his opportunity to take down Beamish, and he took it. "That was easy," he thought. It was, compared to the strangling part of his plan. He was holding the gun. He checked the chamber. It was loaded with five cartridges. "Almost blew that one," he thought.

He was trying to figure out how to strangle him with his right hand holding the gun. He needed a new plan.

"Get up and follow me to the garage. Gimme the keys."

Fritzy opened the trunk and grabbed a towel hanging on the wall.

"Get in."

"Where are you taking me?"

He wrapped his revolver with the towel and answered the professor's question.

"To Hell."

No one ever wanted those two words to be the last ones they hear. Maybe Fritzy would. He was evil and crazy enough.

He decided to drive to the front of the Yale School of Music and drop the body on the steps. It was midnight and cloudy. He wasn't thinking about that when he decided to get rid of the body. He wasn't a thorough or thoughtful person. He did like the dramatic effect that the music school and professor provided.

He drove home and fell asleep in his inherited bed. The sheets were filthy.

The detectives were notified within hours of finding the body. Two music students were going in early when they saw the body. It was still dark out. They ran to their dorm and called the police. That was the last time they went in early.

They took the first train back to New Haven and rushed to the music school. No violin. Not enough blood either. They concluded the murder took place somewhere else. They grabbed a taxi to his apartment and pried the door open. They spent an hour tearing the place apart. No violin. No blood. To no one's surprise the cause of death was a bullet to the head. Dr. Dan DeMaio certified the results in his coroner's report.

The cops were anxious when they finally arrived at the apartment. It was broken into. They assumed the violin was stolen.

The detectives left the New Haven jurisdiction and later in the day, let the cops know about their visit to the apartment. The Pinkerton Agency could get away with their conduct. They were the best in the business.

"You mean it wasn't stolen again?"

Doesn't appear to be the case. We're back to the beginning. We have no leads."

It was a big story in New Haven and soon would be one in New York City. No one could figure out who had possession of the instrument and music. Now, the detectives worried they would never see it again.

32

Mackie pushed the buzzer at 6:30 and Carla didn't hesitate to let him in. He was early. She wrote it off as excitement. She was correct. He liked her apartment. It was neat and tidy. Everything was clean and straightened.

"Can I get you anything?"

"No thanks."

"I'll be ready in a minute; I just need to put on a little makeup for my date."

"No, you don't. You're perfect, absolutely perfect just the way you are.

"Slow down, copper," she laughed.

She came back out and grabbed her coat. Mackie wouldn't let her put it on by herself. He opened the door and held it for her.

"You sure are a gentleman."

"I have to be. My grandfather would crawl out from his grave, find me and slap me if I wasn't. And his grave is in Ireland."

They walked out the front and down the stairs. He held her hand the whole way to the theatre. They came up to the *King Kong* theatre and Mackie feigned going to buy tickets.

"Just kidding. I want a kiss from you."

They went inside the next movie house to see *Little Women*. He knew the story as much as his memory allowed. It was required reading in his high school.

She picked out her favorite candy. A Tootsie Pop.

"I guess I won't be getting a kiss until intermission."

"You never know. Might not get one at all."

As they went to finds seats, Mackie led her to the back half of the theatre.

"Pretty dark up here," she wasn't complaining. Mackie smiled.

The movie started slower than the Tootsie Pop. After a half hour or so she dropped it on the floor. Mackie jumped up to get her another. She pulled him back down to his seat and gave him a kiss.

"I dropped it on purpose," she whispered. "I couldn't take it any longer watching you looking at that Tootsie Pop in my mouth. I just wanted to put you out of your misery."

It was his first real kiss. It was hers too. They would laugh about it later when they entered the confessional part of their relationship. Clara was fairly certain it was his first because of the rapid improvement she experienced early on in the kissing department. She even noticed improvements during the last half of *Little Women*. They missed most of the movie after intermission.

They walked back with a different stride and attitude. They were in love already. Two dates and they were in love. He held her hand with a confident but gentle grip.

They arrived at her place, and he took the key and opened the door to say goodbye and give her the last kiss of the night. She yanked him inside the entrance and gathering together all the skills that she had learned in the theatre, kissed him almost unconscious.

He stepped back to gather himself and said, "Woah! Can I see you tomorrow?"

"How about right now?" She grabbed his hand and pulled him upstairs to her clean and tidy little apartment. Tomorrow was her day off.

Mr. Kelley was not happy with the Pinkerton report. The only suspect they had was dead and the violin was still missing. He was smart enough to know they only had a sliver of a chance to get it back. He felt bad for Stephen and Carolina. Not for the thief murdered last week in New Haven. The thief that was a guest in their home.

"Stephen said it out loud," he remembered him saying it. "He didn't like the guy the moment he first saw him. I pushed him to visit Yale; this is on me," he solemnly thought.

Friedrich "Fritzy" Schmidt was on his way to the city in his, yes, inherited car. The first stop was to be the Bradbury house. He would ask about Carolina to see if they knew where she lived. He looked a lot different now. Worn out a little you might say. He wouldn't be recognized.

His delusion was incomprehensible. He thought of himself as a father returning home to his family. He actually believed Carolina and Stephen would welcome him back to the fold. He would fill the void left from not having a man around. She would break off her engagement. He thought the violin would make it all possible. He could have sold it, but he is such an "upstanding man" that he didn't.

His good conscience wouldn't allow it. Yes. They would see what a good man he really was. The murder thing, that was just an outlier, a fluke, a "flyer." It shouldn't affect things going forward.

The first warm day of winter arrived at the Kootenai. Sixty degrees. The snow was rapidly melting. Little rivers of thawed snow flowing off the wood shingled roofs of the cabins. The lodge had a copper shingled roof, eves troughs and downspouts of course. Grass was exposed on the croquet field. It was green underneath the melting snow. Johnson creek was almost at flood stage, and the Swan River had a tumultuous and angry look to it. Runoff was flowing into Swan Lake and the water rose to the tops of the stone breakwater that was in front of the main lodge before it choked it into a wild and rushing river. The ducks and geese would soon be reuniting with the small courageous birds and wildlife that stayed behind to manage things while they were off to warmer weather. The bats waited until their food supply showed up in late May along with the explosion of green. It was like the wildlife hides in the winter. The snow-covered lawns were full of thousands of animal tracks. Some small and some big and some really big. The mountain lions had a four foot stride that ended in huge paw prints. Fox, rabbits, and deer were everywhere. The deer tracks were everywhere, and they were around all seasons.

The girls and Stephen survived their first winter in Montana. "Not too bad," thanks to Carson and his fireplace skills.

The girls sat by the fireplace each and every night. So did the boys. Stephen went to bed early many a night. He couldn't take all of the hugs and kisses being passed back and forth. The fireplace had the same fire in it since January. Carson never let it go out. He just kept adding logs. The stone on the fireplace was very warm from the continuous fires. It heated the room as much as the fire. The fireplace was large enough for Stephen to walk in without hitting his head. It passed the test this winter.

Stephen was happy to see the warmer temperatures. Bobby promised to resume teaching him to shoot this spring. Shooting skills were more favorably look upon than violin playing to the junior high school kids. He would take him hunting when he was ready. Carolina and Mary were learning to shoot. Not to hunt, but to make her feel safer as she walked around the lake on the animal trails. She was always thinking about bears and felt a little irresponsible walking alone with Stephen without an equalizer. That's what she called a gun. The boys called them by the old western gunslinger moniker---widow makers. Carolina was quite the sharpshooter already. She could group 6 shots in a four inch circle on her target. She had a .38 Smith & Wesson Triple Lock revolver. She could handle it better than most.

The wedding plans were under the control of Mama Kelley now. It was getting to be too much work to run things by the "group." It was too big to manage. Mary, Carolina, Bobby, Tommy, Mrs. Harper, Mr. Harper and Stephen. They would only be consulted on the more important items going forward.

Friedrich showed up at the Bradbury home. He walked in the servant's door and was stopped by the housekeeper. He asked about Carolina. "She hasn't lived here in ten years. Who are you?"

"I'm her cousin visiting from Germany. We lost track of her."

"She worked at the Kelley's home, and they adopted her, I guess. You best ask them. Do you have their address? She spends a lot of time in Montana now."

"I know the house."

She thought that was strange. "He's visiting from Germany and knows the Kelley's house." As soon as he left, she called Johnson to tip him off.

Johnson was ready for him. He watched him pass the front entrance and walk around the side of the house.

"He's going in the servant's entrance." He ran downstairs and locked the door just before Friedrich got there. He turned the doorknob to enter and found it locked.

Johnson yelled through the door. "Why are you trying to enter without knocking? Who are you?"

Johnson asked Martha to alert Mrs. Kelley and check all the door locks.

"I'm looking for my cousin, Carolina. I heard that she used to work here. The family lost track of her when she left Germany."

"I have no idea who you are talking about. Now go away before I call the police." Johnson knew he was lying now. The iceman came immediately into his thoughts. It was Carolina's attacker.

He picked up the phone and called the precinct on the next block. Mackie heard the name and rushed over. Friedrich was gone.

"What happened Johnson?"

"I'm glad it's you Mackie. Can you wait until I call Mr. Kelley. He may want to talk to you."

"Yes, of course."

Johnson telephoned Mr. Kelley at his office. He was in a meeting.

"Get him out please, this is his butler, Johnson."

"Certainly, Johnson. Is everything okay?"

"I don't know, just get him right away."

"Johnson, what is it?" He ran out of the conference room to take the call and was a bit winded. "What happened."

Johnson told him everything about the visitor. He frightened him.

"Call the police!"

"I did; Mackie is here now."

"Good job, Johnson. Do you really think it could be him?"

"It seems so. What do you want me to tell Mackie?"

"Tell him I'll be right over."

Johnson asked Mackie to stay for Mr. Kelley and then called over to the Bradbury home. He talked with his counterpart about the strange visitor. As soon as he described his questions, especially the lie about her family losing touch with her, he knew it was the iceman who raped Carolina in the basement. He saw him leaving and now could see the resemblance as he thought back to that terrible day. He was certain it was Friedrich Schmidt. He never forgot the name.

"Mr. Kelley's home now. Thank your housekeeper for the warning."

Mr. Kelley walked in his home, but not without looking around first. A Pinkerton detective was on his way over. The house would have a full time, armed guard in ten minutes.

"Hello Mackie, I'm glad it's you. We have a delicate situation here."

"What happened? What is going on, Mr. Kelley?"

"Please sit down."

Johnson left them alone. If he was needed, he would be called in.

"How long have you been on the force?"

"Five years, sir."

"Then you don't know about a man named Friedrich. I don't know his last name. It's German. He raped a girl in the Bradbury basement years ago. He ran off back to Germany to escape the law."

"I know about this case, Clara told me about it."

"Then you know that he raped Carolina."

"No sir. Clara just told me how the policeman didn't help her until she almost bled to death. Clara said she nursed the poor woman back to health. That's all I know. Are you saying that it was Carolina he raped, and he just showed up at your door?"

"Yes."

Mr. Kelley was impressed that Clara said nothing about Carolina.

"Would you find the old files and bring them over to me. I want Pinkerton's to look over the case and track this guy down. For Carolina's sake please tell no one. Please help us."

He thought about police procedures and how removing a file was grounds for immediate dismissal. He didn't want to jeopardize his career, but he wanted to help the Kelleys. His new girlfriend was a close friend to her. He thought about it for a minute longer.

"I'll do it, Mr. Kelley. Please don't mention my name to your Pinkerton man. I need my job; I want to get married soon. I can't if I don't have a job."

"I will protect your identity and if for some reason you are pinned with giving me the files, I will hire you at ten times your salary! I promise you."

He walked over to shake Mackie's hand and told him how indebted he was to him.

"Is Clara the lucky girl?"

"Yes, sir. Word sure travels fast in this part of town."

"Mrs. Kelley was visiting the hospital this morning. When is the wedding?"

"No date set, she doesn't know it quite yet." Mackie smiled a nervous looking expression.

"I'll wait here until the Pinkerton guard shows up. Is Mrs. Kelley home?"

"Johnson has her sequestered upstairs."

This was Mackie's first time in the house. He was astonished.

"He's here now." Mr. Kelley let him in and introduced him to Mackie. He didn't mention the files. He would give them to him later to protect Mackie. He thanked Mackie for coming over so quickly and showed him to the door.

"Thank you, again, young man. Please excuse us, we need to talk in private." He opened the door and winked at Mackie. "He's a good kid," he thought. He was happy for Clara.

The armed guard was stationed just off the servant's entrance. They set up a desk and ran telephone wire over to him. The servant's entrance was the weakest link in the home. He knew what he was doing.

Mr. Kelley stayed home to be with his wife. They had a lot to talk about. "Carolina doesn't know about this. I dread reopening those wounds. I won't let him attack her all over again. Just the mention of his name would feel like he attacked again. I don't want you to know about my plans. I intend to have Pinkerton's find him and do what's right."

"I don't want to know, but you be careful."

"We have to call her. What about her safety? What if he knows about Montana and goes looking for her? What if she…?"

"Calm down, honey; he can't get there any faster than the train. She's safe for now. Johnson told this guy he didn't know who he was talking about before he sent him away."

"I'm not involving the police. I don't want this case reopened. Mackie is helping me from the inside. That's between you and me only."

"He seems like a good man. He knows Carolina and Clara and they like him. I told you Clara has a boyfriend."

"He's more than a boyfriend. Mackie is going to marry her."

"When did that happen? When is the wedding?"

"That's the thing, she doesn't know it yet."

33

Clara and Mackie made plans to see each other again tonight. This would be their fifth date in five days. Their second one was with a little scandal. Mackie stayed overnight after Clara yanked him up the stairs to her "neat and tidy" apartment. They left their clothes on but slept together until Mackie had to run home to get ready for work. He left in the darkness. They held each other and kissed each other most of the night. They fell asleep in Clara's bed, arms and legs interlaced. I guess you could say they were "going steady."

Tonight, they would be going back to Paddy's. She liked it there. They had a lot to talk about. He had already found the file and had it hidden in his apartment. He didn't want Clara to know. He knew she would approve, but it was better if she didn't know.

He picked her up and they held hands until they reached Paddy's. They went in and immediately, the room erupted with hoots and howls. It was like you had twenty brothers and came home with your date. You couldn't sneak in. After five minutes of men teasing men, things calmed down. Clara ordered a shot of Jameson, kicked her head back and slammed the empty shot glass back down on the bar. That started it all over again.

Mackie looked at her and asked, "Who are you?" He was starting to figure out who would be wearing the pants in their soon to be marital household. She laughed. She loved to laugh, and Mackie was good at helping her.

Things settled down again, and the two of them found "their" table in the corner. Mackie had a lot to talk about.

"I learned about Carolina's rape today."

"How?" She didn't expect that or the follow-up sentence.

"Friedrich Schmidt is back in town and he's looking for her."

Clara froze and was shaking. He went over to sit next to her and hold her. The boys saw the romantical (as they would call it) stuff and started up again. Mackie gave them a look to kill. They stopped.

"Mr. Kelley told me. Johnson called the precinct, and I heard the Kelley name. I told the sergeant that I would handle it. I ran over and waited for Mr. Kelley to come home from the office. Johnson said someone may have tried to get in the house."

"When he got home, he took me into his office and asked me if I knew about the rapist from years ago. I said yes. I told him you told me about the cops that didn't believe the poor girl."

Mackie told Clara how Mr. Kelley assumed that he knew about Carolina. He thought you told me about it. I told him I didn't know who it was until he told me. "Clara kept it a secret." He said.

"Did they catch the guy?"

"Not yet." She started to tremble again.

"Mr. Kelley has Pinkertons on the case. The precinct doesn't even know about it. They think it was an attempted break in. He wants to keep this quiet for Carolina's sake. He wants to take care of this guy himself."

"I want to call Carolina. I won't do anything until they tell her. This is going to upset her so much. I'm glad Mary and the boys are there with her. Poor Stephen, he doesn't need this creep trying to find his mom."

"I'm frightened, Mackie; I'm scared."

He held her tighter and tried to comfort her.

"Will you stay with me tonight? Please."

This was the easiest question anybody had ever asked him. "Yes. We can stop by my place and pickup work clothes for the morning. I'll stay with you baby. I'll let Mr. Kelley know I'm going to drop off some information about this guy on the way."

She kissed him for a long time. The boys behaved themselves.

Mrs. Kelley remembered Mr. O'Sullivan from his other job to protect them during one of the worker strikes. She liked him.

"Hello Craig, nice to see you again."

"Yes Ma'am. Sorry it had to be under these circumstances."

Johnson monitored the main entrance door and Craig remained on the lower-level staff entrance. He noticed a shadow outside the door. He was sure something was out there. He stayed in the house to protect the Kelleys and the staff. He wanted another agent assigned. He asked Martha to get Mr. Kelley for him. He came downstairs right away.

"I need to get another agent. I think I saw something moving in the shadows. I can't go out and investigate without an agent staying behind to protect you. It's too risky."

"Call for a backup, whatever you feel you need."

He thanked him and called his office. He knew it was unlikely to find anyone until the agents working the railroad strike got in tomorrow. He got his answer. "No go."

He gave Martha a note to give him.

The doorbell rang and Johnson looked out the view hole. It was Mackie and Clara. He let them in.

"May I speak with Mr. Kelley?"

He went to get him as they waited in the small parlor near the entrance hall.

"Thank you, Mackie, for stopping by so late."

"No problem, we were on our way back to Clara's apartment."

He took the file as Martha walked in with the note. He read it and thought about it.

"Mackie, would you stay here tonight and watch things for us. We have one agent here and I think we need two. I would be happy to pay you.

"Mr. Kelley could Clara stay here too. She's frightened that this guy's on the loose.

"We'll run back and get her clothes and whatever she'll need. Is that okay Clara?"

"What's in the suitcase you have?"

"My things," Mackie responded, a little embarrassed.

"Oh, I see." Mr. Kelley understood.

Now Clara was embarrassed.

They quickly returned and Mrs. Kelley was waiting for Clara.

"Thanks for staying with us. It means a lot. I think we need to call her right away. I know she's safe, but she needs to know."

She couldn't get a line through. She would keep trying.

She took Clara up to her room to get her settled in. Mrs. Kelley went to her own room to freshen up as they say. Clara went back down to be with her boyfriend. Not what they had planned, but this was for a good cause.

Mrs. Kelley tried to call again. Mary answered the phone in her bedroom.

"Mom, what. Is dad ok."

"Yes, were fine.

"Are you alone?" she said yes.

"Good, I want to talk to you first before Carolina gets on." She paused for a moment. "The man who raped Carolina is back in New York City and he came by the house looking for her. Johnson called the police, but he got away. He tried to get in the house. We have a Pinkerton agent here and a policeman, it's Mackie, you know him."

"Oh, momma, no!" She was panicked for Carolina.

"Clara is staying with us. She's very scared."

"Remember she took care of Carolina after the attack. This guy is a still attacking her family and friends."

"Daddy is heading up the search. He'll get him. I'm glad Mackie brought Clara over tonight."

"Did you know they're engaged?"

"What?"

"That's what your dad said."

"Ok, Ok, let's figure out telling Carolina about this first."

"How is she? Is everything okay with her and Bobby?"

"Yes, she can take it. I'm glad Bobby is her fiancé. He'll keep her safe and comfort her. Do you want me to talk to her first?"

"I think it should be in person and not over the phone. Yes, I think it would be better if you talked to her first. Have her call us right back. We need to try and comfort her."

"Ok mom. I'll tell her now. We'll call you back. I love you."

Mrs. Kelley came back down. She used the Otis Elevator they installed two years ago. She had a long day, that was no way near to being over.

"I spoke with Mary. She's talking with Carolina now. She'll call back when she's finished." Clara was nervous for her dear friend. She never wanted this day to ever happen.

The phone rang. They were all in the library. Mr. Kelley answered.

"Hi daddy. Are you Ok?"

"Don't be silly; how are you, darling?"

"I'm a little shaken, but Bobby and Mary and Tommy and Stephen are here next to me."

"Honey, I have Pinkerton working to find this guy. We'll get him. I'm glad you're in Montana. He's in New York; you don't have to worry about him."

"Mom told me Mackie is staying at the house with Clara to help keep you safe. I didn't know they were together. When I heard that I was so happy for them. Can I talk with mom?"

"Carolina, I'm so sorry this bastard is back."

That caught the room by surprise. She never used course language before.

"I apologize, but this is war! Your father is outraged. I pity this bastard!"

34

Up until this moment, the girls led an easy and comfortable winter life in Montana. Now the upcoming days would be clouded by worry and even fear at the detection of any weird sound or strange shadow. Not exactly the "premium experience" they had enjoyed before the phone call.

Carolina had to tell Stephen, and the girls had to tell their fiancés. They had three days of safety before things became more serious. They wondered if they should move in with the Harpers. What about the staff? They couldn't leave them alone at the lodge. Should they all go back to New York City and close down the Kootenai until summer. They had made plans to talk with their father the next day to figure out their options. Hopefully this miscreant would be quickly captured and finally jailed for the rest of his life. Nobody cared about the violin anymore. The same violin sitting in the blood-stained trunk of his inherited car, five or six days east of Bigfork.

Schmidt knew his cover was blown. He also knew that Carolina was in Montana. He needed to see her in person and give her the violin. His delusion was frightening. He was looking forward to becoming a father and husband. He didn't know where they were in Montana. He had to figure out a way to get the address. And then find a way to get there.

The Pinkerton man had the file, and the information wasn't very helpful. It did mention a possible relative in Hamden, Connecticut. They would check him out in the morning to see what he knows. O'Sullivan called a friend in Hamden who worked for the city. He gave him the info and asked for his help. He called him back within an hour with the news that he had died a few months ago. O'Sullivan slammed his fist on the desk and thanked him.

Schmidt needed the Montana address. He would try calling the Kelley's office to get it. He would simply ask them because he needed to "send a package."

He called Mr. Kelley's office and spoke with his secretary.

"I'm looking for an address in Montana to send a package. Can you help me?"

"Who are you, and to whom are you sending a package?"

"Let's see here…Carolina August." He mispronounced her last name intentionally.

"Augusta. Is this for the wedding?"

"I don't know about a wedding, Ma'am. We're just trying to get a package to her."

"What company is this?" She wasn't ready to give it up yet.

"Saks Fifth Avenue." He drove by it the day before and saw expensive cars parked in front and expensive dresses in the windows. That worked. The secretary gave him the address in Montana: The Kootenai Lodge, 1000 Sunburst, Bigfork, Mont.

Fritzy was going to Montana and claim his wife and son. He had money that he inherited. He needed road maps for the trip and found them with the help of an automobile club. He cleaned the blood from the trunk and packed a suitcase he found in the closet. The violin was placed in another suitcase to keep it from bouncing around during the hundreds of miles of asphalt and dirt road driving and also to conceal it. More ammunition was purchased and put in the glove box with the revolver. He fueled up his Dodge Bros. automobile to begin his journey at first light. In six or seven days, he would be in Bigfork.

O'Sullivan's friend called him the next morning.

"Craig, I have more information. All of his possessions were willed to a man named Friedrich Schmidt."

"Do you have an address?"

He gave it to him and that started the Pinkerton machine into high gear. He immediately left with another agent and headed to Hamden. He would surprise Schmidt and take him in, hopefully with the violin. Mackie and Clara stayed at the house with the Kelleys. O'Sullivan's replacement took over his position near the rear entrance.

Mr. Kelley waited for the news from O'Sullivan. It would be hours. He thought of calling the girls but decided it would be too early and scare them. Everyone's nerves were rubbed raw. He said another prayer as he sat at his desk waiting.

The agents arrived at the Hamden house. They parked a couple of houses away and O'Sullivan went to the front door and the other to the back of the house. Their guns were drawn.

He was going to break the door down and rush in. As an afterthought, he twisted the doorknob. It was unlocked. He carefully checked out the first-floor rooms and then let his backup in through the kitchen door.

They moved up the stairway to the three bedrooms and hall bathroom. No one was home.

Where was he? They saw food in the electric refrigerator that replaced the need for ice delivery. Ironic. The master bed was slept in and filthy. Did he know they were coming? Did he leave the area? These men were looking for answers, and all they had now was more questions.

He saw the rolled-up horsehair on the floor next to the chair.

"He was here, and so was the violin." The two of them began an intensive search now. They had a fresh lead.

They found nothing in the house and headed for a pay phone to call Mr. Kelley. He needed to know right away.

"You need to put men at the train station. We need to know if he is on his way west. We need to get him before he leaves the area."

"I'm on it."

The Kelleys' called Mary and Carolina. They needed to make some contingency plans if they lose track of Schmidt. He was reluctant to leave anyone behind at the lodge. Too dangerous.

The girls would call back later in the day after talking with the Harper family and Carson. Carolina didn't want to tell everyone the whole story. Here she was again, suffering at the hands of this monster.

Mary just wanted her to say he was a crazy man who had attacked her a long time ago and that somehow he is involved with the violin theft and a murder. She felt that said enough and raised the level of fear that was needed to properly alert the family and outsmart this dangerous enemy.

The boys wanted to stay at the lodge alone and wait for him to show up.

The girls and the Harpers' wanted everyone to stay at their house and be together. It was easier to defend, and they felt the safest option. They still had time to decide; it was a long way from Connecticut to Bigfork.

They called their father before dinner to tell him about their plan and see if any new information was available. He liked the idea of everyone clearing out of the lodge. He said he would gladly pay for the staff to stay at the Bigfork Hotel or even buy the train tickets to return to the city.

"Shut it down and make it look uninhabited. No heat, no electric. The animals will have to be fed. I want two, armed men to handle that. There were plenty of cowboys and ranch hands in the area that would love that high paying job. The barn would be a logical outbuilding to try and get a jump on Carson or whomever was taking care of the animals.

Carolina told her dad to not worry about them. They were in good hands with the Harper family.

"I know, I know. There's more, darling. The detectives believe he's on his way to Montana now. They interviewed the Bradbury's housekeeper, who saw him. Before she realized he was a threat, she told him you spent a lot of time in Montana at our summer retreat. She didn't tell him what area of the state because she didn't know.

"Oh. Oh no."

"They believe he murdered Professor Beamish and stole the violin. They found the original horsehair from your bow on the floor of the house he was living at. They think he's armed and of course very dangerous. He inherited some money, too. I would have you home right now if we didn't think he was on the train to Whitefish right now. We just don't want you anywhere near this homicidal maniac, even on a passing train."

He wished he hadn't said that last part. He didn't want to panic her into making bad decisions.

"I know it's unlikely, but dads think like this when their family is in any type of danger."

"I know, Dad, I know."

"We will have men at virtually every depot from Chicago to Whitefish. We've already sent telegrams to each station with a description of him. If he's on the train, we'll get him. The conductors know about this too. They've even been ordered to not slow down between Havre and Malta, Montana to get their usual growlers of beer delivered train side from a local bar. That would seem a lot funnier if this wasn't so serious. If James Hill was still alive, he'd probably have every passenger searched."

He said all he could. They had no other information.

"Let's talk at least twice a day. If I hear anything, anything at all, I'll call you immediately."

"We'll do the same from our end. I love you, Dad. Here's Mary she wants to talk to you."

Mr. Kelley was heartbroken that his daughters and grandson were going through this. He dreaded the thought of any harm coming to them. He stopped short of taking his mind into places he couldn't imagine.

Schmidt was out of Connecticut and traveling through New York State. In fifty miles he would cross into Pennsylvania headed toward Ohio. He would find a motor hotel outside of Pittsburgh to avoid the larger cities.

35

Monday morning, Mr. Kelley went into his office to collect what he needed to work from home for the near future. He explained everything to his secretary as she helped him. She stopped and froze.

"Mr. Kelley, I think I gave him your address at the lodge."

"Gave who?"

"A man called Friday trying to get an address to send a package to Carolina. He was from Saks Department Store. I thought it was for the wedding. I'm so sorry if I told the killer their address. I'm so, so sorry sir".

"Can you get me O'Sullivan at Pinkertons for me?"

She located him and connected the call to his desk phone.

"Craig, he has the address of the lodge. He knows where to find her. Any word from the train stations?"

"Nothing yet. We have no idea where he is. He hasn't boarded a train yet. I'll send a guy back to Hamden to speak with the neighbors."

He hung up and finished packing up his papers. Geoffrey came up to take them to the car. He said goodbye to his secretary and tried to make her feel a little better. She was devastated.

"I'm so sorry." Followed him to the elevator.

He arrived home and called the girls. Carolina answered.

"He has the address of the lodge and we don't know where he is. I want you, Mary and Stephen to get out of there now. Get all your stuff and go to the Harpers. What do the staff want to do?"

"The girls are a little frightened; I think they want to come back to the city. They'd just be in the way here. Carson can take them to the train in the morning. I guess that will put them in the city on Friday. I'll let them know. They can stay with Carson and his sister in Bigfork. We'll all clear out by this evening."

"Do the Harper's have any handguns or rifles?"

"Yes, daddy. I own a 38 revolver, and I shoot better than most!"

"Good, keep it with you at all times. You shoot guns, huh? You really fit into your new surroundings quickly."

"Mary and Stephen shoot too."

"A week ago, I would have been worried about having guns around. I'm glad you have them. Get a holster. Okay, call me tonight when you get to the Harper's house, no matter how late. Give my love to Mary and Stephen. Ask Carson to call me."

Carolina told Stephen and Mary to get packing. She called Bobby's house to tell him. The boys were working in the barn with their dad. She went out to get them.

She explained everything that was going on. The boys would come right over and bring some guns. Neither wanted their girls to be alone until this guy was captured. Mary joked that this would put their marriages at risk, being with the boys around the clock and all. Carolina smiled at Bobby and said it was a risk she was willing to take.

They started packing while waiting for the boys. The girls felt a sort of relief now that they were going to be in the Harper house. Much safer over there.

The farm truck rolled up in front of the lodge to take the suitcases for the girls. Carson would take the maid, chef and laundress in his car. They would stay with him and leave very early in the morning to catch the train. He would return to close up the lodge and his cabin.

Soon, the plan would be in play as the waiting game began.

The truck and one of the Chryslers pulled up to the farmhouse. The girls would stay in the boy's room and the boys would stay on the couches in the living room. Everyone breathed a little easier now.

Carolina asked to use the phone and called her dad to tell him they were all safe and sound. No news from the detectives yet. She wondered how long it would take to get him.

Dinner with the Harpers was peaceful. Both girls loved their soon to be in-laws. They were kind, generous, fair and had a toughness developed over their lifetimes in Montana. Things were a lot easier now compared to their wedding day in 1901. They now had electricity, a well pump, a farm truck, a car and a "monitor top" refrigerator. They were "in the chips" as Mrs. Kelley would often say to the winners at her poker table.

A week passed with no sightings or new leads on Schmidt. It was as if he was holding the family hostage. Carolina was holding her temper. She wanted him to show his face so they could give him the "recompense" he had coming. The Smith & Wesson kind was not ruled out.

Schmidt was leaving South Dakota after passing the rough-cut construction of Mt. Rushmore. He crossed from Rapid City into the Treasure State. Montana wasn't what he expected. Endless grasslands for the last 500 miles. He was looking for the American Bison he read about when he was a child in Germany. He saw an Indian and a couple of cowboys. He was still waiting for the mountains. They were nowhere in sight.

Mackie and Clara got to know the Kelley's pretty well. He got the file back into the precinct right away. No one noticed they were missing. They stayed for a week and now things were loosening up. Pinkerton was still in the house, but Mackie wasn't needed for the night shift anymore. One agent would suffice at night and during the day. Mackie was noticeably tired at work. The sergeant knew he was volunteering at the Kelley house and he let it pass.

Clara wanted him to stay with her because she was "scared." Mackie felt "obliged." He went back to his place to get his pajamas, fresh clothes, and toiletries. "I better be careful," he thought. Not for Schmidt, but for his attraction for Clara.

He came back with his things, and Clara let him in. "We need to get you a key."

"How long am I staying here?"

"Until I'm not scared anymore."

"Let's go to Paddy's."

The gang was there and gave them the usual greeting. Paddy rang the bell to quite them down. "One Old Fashioned for the lady and."

"A Jameson for the gentleman." Clara chimed in. The tavern honeymoon was over. Paddy charged for the drinks.

They sat down next to each other at their table and Bobby gave her a kiss. He waited for the harassment, but nothing really materialized. Clara looked at him and started to cry. She had held it in all week. She was so sad for Mary and Carolina. This animal was ruining her wedding plans. She wished she could be there and come alongside her for support. It was a good thing she had Stephen and Mary and of course their boys.

The detectives got a hit from one of the neighbors. He was driving a black Dodge. They had a plate number from the motor bureau.

"CF 244" white lettering on black background.

The first calls went out to the Flathead County Sheriff and the Lake County Sheriff. It was given immediate attention because the request came from Pinkerton. A statewide highway patrol didn't exist yet in Montana.

"It shouldn't be hard to spot a Connecticut plate on a Dodge in Montana." They all knew where the Kootenai Lodge was, and patrols were implemented. Some of the neighbors were surprised to see sheriff's cars on their roads. They had never seen one before. They had a large territory and only a few cars to spread around.

Mr. Kelley called the Harper house to let them know the latest news. It was kind of a weird relief to be able to identify his vehicle. At least the enemy had a face, so to speak.

The boys let everyone in town know what to look for. He gave his new phone number to a lot of people. Bigfork had no police department; they were on their own. They left handwritten posters describing the car and license and a phone number to call. It would be hard for him to get through the dragnet. The Harpers' and now girls' church was on high alert. Any Black Dodge with a Connecticut plate would earn a call to the Harpers' and the sheriffs. It seemed everyone was on the lookout and happy to help.

Carolina kept a gun in a holster hidden under her sweater, just like her dad told her. The boys were armed as well as Mr. Harper. Stephen had his rifle at the ready as he "patrolled" the farm. He was a good shot. Even Mary had her revolver. It wasn't loaded; she kept the bullets in her pocket.

Mr. Kelley wished the girls were on the train coming home now. They never thought he would be driving from Hamden to Bigfork. Pinkerton was sending two agents from the Denver office. They were scheduled to arrive the following evening and check into the Bigfork Hotel. They drove two cars to give them better coverage on the manhunt. They were well armed with two Thompson Sub Machine Guns. The same ones the Chicago underworld favored. They didn't have violin cases like the mob. Even though they were on a "violin case".

The town would be locked down by the next day. Schmidt was walking into a trap.

Clara and Mackie walked back to her apartment and rolled into each other's arms on the couch. Their kisses and touching were different now. A few notches down on the lust scale and a lot of notches up on the love scale. They both knew where this was heading. The only question was when would he pop the question?

They talked about their future together. Children rose to the top. They settled on three. She wanted more. No problem, she thought; as soon as a little boy or girl puts their arms around his neck and gives him a kiss, he would be a dead duck.

Mackie looked her square in the eyes and said he wanted to marry her before the summer.

"I hope you don't call that a proposal! If you do, then the answer's no, Casanova."

"Oh, I was expecting you to propose to me. You're the one who tricks me into your bed."

"Like this?" She gently took his hand and walked him into her bedroom. Tonight, they would wear pajamas.

Tomorrow, Mackie would look for an engagement ring.

<h1 style="text-align:center">36</h1>

Schmidt had just entered Flathead Country. He pulled into a gas station and after filling up, he noticed a sign about a black Dodge with Connecticut plates. He looked around before taking the poster with him back out to the car.

He parked on the side to conceal his plates and went back in to use the bathroom. One employee was all he could see. He went back to his car and got out a screwdriver to remove the license plate from the old car next to his. It had not expired yet. He quickly removed it and replaced the one on his car that would surely give him away. He did the same with the front plate and drove off to find a motel.

He pulled into Whitefish and checked into the Cadillac Hotel located "downtown." The new attraction in town was the golf course that was built with government funds intended for airport construction. The first hole was a straight line and level par five. It was technically a runway and even had a windsock off the tee box. Players knew to move out of the way if a plane circled overhead. The airport "terminal" was the restaurant and bar and, of course, an airport operations office. It passed the government's inspection, and no one was ever chastised for such an obvious hoax on the feds.

He left the Cadillac Hotel and walked down to the Great Northern Bar. It was a railroader's hangout. It became a legend when Carrie

Nation was traveling around the country on railroads to various prohibition rallies. She got off the "Empire Builder" and was walking down Central Avenue to the Presbyterian church six blocks away to meet with her supporters. She was stopped and surrounded by the railroaders that poured out from the Great Northern Bar, and they forced her back onto the train and out of town. She said later that she feared for her life.

He walked in and noticed more signs about his car tacked on the wall. This one had his name on it. His ego was already bloated; now, it was ready to explode. He thought he was Jesse James or some other famous criminal. He had a few beers and got along great with the railroaders. "His kind of people," he thought.

He left early in the morning to scope out Bigfork and the lodge. He was careful not to tip off any locals. He saw the signs everywhere in this little town. He never got out of his car.

Next stop was the Kootenai Lodge. He drove down Sunburst Drive and saw the stone and iron gates. "This must be it," he thought. He slowed down and noticed everything was closed down. No tracks in the snow or footprints anywhere. "They aren't staying here."

Schmidt needed to find her hideout. He drove back to Bigfork and parked in front of the Garden Bar. It had just opened after prohibition ended. He could hang out here and maybe find out about the people putting up the signs.

He saw a pay phone and thought he'd call the number on the poster. It rang twice and was answered. "Harper residence," the young lady politely answered.

"I must have the wrong number," was all he said before he hung up.

Mackie woke up and leaned over to Clara, pushed her hair back and kissed her forehead. He lingered, staring at her. He noticed everything about her face. She had some tiny moles that could be mistaken for freckles. He liked that since he had a lot of freckles. He looked at her closed eyes and wished he could see them open. Her nose was adorable to him. So different from a man's. Her lips were so beautiful and soft. He wanted to kiss them without waking her. He loved her chin and her ears and her neck. He couldn't believe she loved him.

He left for work and left Clara sleeping. He wanted to shop for engagement rings. He was ready to propose.

Schmidt walked away from the telephone and went back to the bar and ordered a beer. The rotund bartender lived in the area his entire life and bragged about it. When Schmidt learned that, he had one question. "Do you know the Harper family?"

"Sure do. I went to school with Bobby and Tommy Harper. They sure struck gold!"

"What?"

They met some rich girls from New York City, and now they're getting married. Those boys are set for life. I wish I seen the girls before them, I would've been the lucky rich boy."

Schmidt didn't like him talking about his "wife" like that. He ordered another beer, and this time, he gave him a big tip while noticing his front teeth were missing.

"Keep it."

"Thanks."

"Do they live around here?"

"Yeah, I heard the girls moved in with the family because some crazy guy was looking for 'em. Have you seen all the posters in town?"

"They're everywhere. I hope they live out in the woods. I wouldn't want some nutjob trying to find me."

"They don't; the farm is right off the Highway 83. You can't miss it; it's next to the Milhous Horse Farm."

He left the bar and headed out to the highway. He was getting closer to finding his family.

He drove past the horse farm and saw the mailbox. "The Harper Family."

"These people sure make things easy for me."

He drove back to his hotel room in Whitefish. The Cadillac Hotel had two unmarked identical police cars in front. It wasn't the police; it was the Pinkerton detectives. He drove past and headed east toward Columbia Falls and then turned south on 206. It was now or never. The lawmen were closing in on him. He was taking a back road to the Harper home and reunite with his wife and kid.

He stopped for gas about three miles from the house. After filling up, he grabbed the poster from the car and put a nickel in the payphone outside and called the number.

"Hello," Bobby answered.

"I just saw a black Dodge with Connecticut plates driving down Sunburst Drive. A man was driving very slowly and looking things over. I called the police already. They won't get there for twenty minutes."

"Thank you. Who is this?"

"You don't know me, I'm Steve Smith." He hung up and drove to the Milhous farm and parked near enough to see any cars leave from the Harper's place.

"Dad---He's at the lodge. Police are on their way. Come with me and Tommy. Let's go get him."

Stephen, call the Bigfork Hotel and tell the detectives to meet us at the lodge. "You stay here and protect the girls," he yelled upstairs to Carolina. "He's at the Kootenai, stay in the house, Mom and the kids are in town at the market."

Stephen learned the detectives were not in the hotel. He left an urgent message to call him.

Schmidt watched the Overland pull onto the highway. This was his chance. He slowly pulled out and drove to the driveway and pulled in and around to the back of the barn.

He opened the glovebox and took out his revolver and headed to the back of the house. He looked around to satisfy he was alone. No one noticed him. He wondered if Carolina was even in the house. Then he saw Stephen walk out the back door to patrol the area. He got down low and retreated to the back of the barn and waited.

Stephen came around and was startled by the black car. Schmidt grabbed him and put his gun to his back. "Don't make another sound."

Stephen froze and thought "what a strange way to meet my father." He was a musical genius, and his mind didn't work like most people. He deducted he wouldn't be killed by his "dad." He approached this like a recital. Don't rush anything and play him with the skill of a trained violinist. Start slow and lull him with your voice.

"Put the rifle down," he complied

"Turn around and look at me," he complied again.

"Do you know who I am?"

"My father, I assume."

"Mein sohn!" Schmidt said as he reflexively returned to his native German.

"Ich bin nicht dein Sohn," Stephen replied to mock him in his home language.

Carolina yelled from the window, "Stephen, where are you!"

He looked at his captor for direction. Schmidt turned him around and shoved the gun into his back again.

"He's out here Carolina."

He walked him out into the open area next to the barn holding the gun on him.

"Come out and talk to us. I have something to tell you."

Mary told her not to do it. It was too dangerous.

"I have to, he's got Stephen."

She opened the door and stood on the small back covered porch shaking. She knew this was no time to panic.

"Come closer, I want to see you. That's it, I won't hurt anybody, I just want to talk. I have something for you."

Carolina walked a little closer to him and a rush of anger filled her. She had to keep it together for Stephen. She knew he was crazy and didn't want to push that out in the open.

"You sure are pretty! How long has it been?"

"What do you want?"

"I brought your violin back for you. I have it in the trunk of my car behind the barn. I was hoping you'd give me a chance to be a father and a husband."

When Stephen heard that insanity, he became very frightened. He would gladly die for his mother. He would never let this animal touch her again. This was a showdown and he was willing to stand up and take a bullet for his momma.

"I want you to know how sorry I am for what I did to you. I was an idiot, I know now. I just want you to give me a chance to make things up to you."

Nobody spoke.

"Take the keys and open the trunk and look at the violin. There's music in the case too. I was hoping you would be so happy that you would give me a chance. That's all. That's all I want. The keys are in the car on the front seat. Go ahead and open your gift from me to you. I want to see you smile."

"Go ahead, I won't bite."

She walked around them and went to the car. He turned around with Stephen to watch her. Carolina found the key and walked to the back of the car and opened the trunk. He couldn't see her pull her Smith & Wesson from her holster, cock the hammer and slide it under the violin case.

"Come on bring it out, I want to see you when you open it."

She walked over to him, holding the case flat. She had her finger on the trigger, and it was pointed at his stomach while concealed under the case.

"Will you please let Stephen go? It would make me even happier right now," she gave him a coy glance.

He moved the gun away from Stephen's back and turned to look at Carolina. "This is going well," he thought.

Stephen moved away. He knew his mom had her revolver under her sweater. He knew what she was going to do. He located his rifle and slowly moved toward it.

"Stay over there son."

"I just want to see the violin and mom's excitement when she sees it again."

"Just stay over there and sit down."

He moved closer to Carolina while pointing his gun loosely in her direction. This was her chance.

The first shot hit him square in his stomach and cause him to roll over on his back. Stephen jumped up and grabbed his rifle, pushed the safety forward and pointed his 12 Gauge at his forehead.

Schmidt started to curse Carolina in German and then tried to point his revolver at her to take a shot.

The shot from Stephen removed most of his face. He ran over and kicked the revolver to the side and picked it up.

"It's over momma, it's over forever."

Mary came out screaming and hugged Carolina and Stephen with everything she had. She was certainly relieved, but worried for them getting over this. For now, she just hugged them.

"Call the police, Stephen."

'Right away," he said.

As he was going in the Harper men came barreling down the driveway and saw Carolina and Mary standing over a body.

Bobby screamed to them, "Where's Stephen? Where's my boy?"

Stephen ran back out and yelled. "Over here, we're all fine, but he's not."

Two black cars came down the driveway and the two Pinkerton detectives jumped out and ran over to the girls.

"We'll take it from here. Go inside the house."

"We'll take it from here, huh?" she said quietly. "We'll take it from here."

Mr. Harper was a mess. He knew they made a mistake when they rushed from the house because of a call. Bobby figured it out the moment he got to the Kootenai. "We've be setup, we need to get back home!" He was right.

Now a police car was driving up very fast with the siren blaring. "Lake County Sheriff" was painted on the doors.

"Is it him?"

"Yes, everybody said."

Carolina called New York as soon as she walked in the house. She asked permission first. Mr. Harper gave her an "of course" nod.

"Daddy, we got him, he's dead!"

"What do you mean we got him?"

"We got him. Stephen and I shot him, he's dead on the lawn!"

Mary was listening and her earlier thoughts of Carolina having to deal with killing a man vanished into the air. Stephen didn't seem phased either. "Why should I then," she thought.

"Hold on, Daddy, here, talk to Mary."

She went outside and told the Sheriff he may want to listen to her conversation with her father in New York. She didn't want to repeat it to the cops.

She stood by Mary jumping up and down a little waiting to get the phone back. Mary saw her and said goodbye and gave it back.

"Mary told me what you did she told…" Mrs. Kelley grabbed the phone.

"Carolina, I'm so glad you're okay. I can't believe he tried to hurt you again."

"Don't worry, mom, he's in a place you don't want to go to!"

"Where's Stephen?"

"Good question, I'll get him."

She went outside and found him leaning on the trunk of his "dad's" car playing the Stradivarius once again. He checked for the music. It was still in the case. It played as well as he ever heard it. His lost lamb was home, and he loved her now even more.

"Come in and talk to Bumpa."

They ran back with the violin and got on the phone. Nana was on the library phone listening in.

"Bumpa. We have the violin back. We got it back. It's as good as ever!"

"Nana here's Stephen, I am so happy for you. I'm happier that you and your momma and Mary are okay. My prayers have been answered. I love you, Stephen."

"I love you too, Nana and Bumpa!"

Carolina grabbed the phone back as the Sheriff walked in.

"Daddy and momma, I have the Sheriff here with the Pinkerton detectives so they can hear the story as I tell it to you."

Carolina described the whole episode and left no details out. Mr. Harper and the boys had their mouths open listening to her and Stephen's bravery. The Pinkerton boys were pretty impressed and maybe embarrassed a little. One of them should have been at the house and they knew it.

The ambulance drove in and picked up the body and took the unrecognizable Schmidt to the morgue in the Kalispell Hospital. He would never be seen again by the Harpers' or the Kelleys'.

They wrapped up the police report with Carolina and asked Mary for her statement.

"Mom, will you call Clara and let them know, Carson too?"

"I will dear, I'm so glad and relieved this whole thing is over for you and Stephen."

"For everyone momma."

Mrs. Harper came in the drive as the ambulance was leaving. She ran screaming into the house. She even outran the younger ones that were with her. She saw everyone in the living room and became faint.

Tommy caught her and sat her down.

"I was scared. I was so scared."

The three sisters and brother came in and were confused.

"We got him," Stephen said, "He's dead!"

Now that it was over, Mary and the two Bachs all had the same idea.

"When can we go home to the Kootenai Lodge?" They were all polite enough to not say it out loud. Tommy and Bobby had the same thoughts. They liked the idea of getting their own beds back, the real reason was so they could hug and kiss their girls without their sister's and parents prying eyes.

<h1 style="text-align:center">37</h1>

Mackie found a ring he liked from the uncle of one of his precinct cops. He owned a very nice jewelry store on Madison Avenue. He told his friend he couldn't afford that address. His buddy told him he could. His uncle was expecting him and would take good care.

He was right, his uncle gave him a good deal. He had a budget of $150 and walked out the door with much more valuable diamond ring and $40 in change. He hoped Clara would like it.

He stopped by the Italian restaurant they loved and made arrangements for the dinner and proposal. He told a few friends from the precinct and bar about proposing there tonight. He even told the Kelleys when he stopped by to show Mrs. Kelley his ring. He wanted to run it by a woman before he proposed. She liked the idea of proposing in a small Italian restaurant. And she liked the ring.

She told Mr. Kelley how cute that Mackie was. "He's so nervous about proposing. I can't believe how stupid men can be at love and marriage. Clara loves that boy to death." He is proposing at that Italian restaurant a few blocks away, this evening.

"Let's go and surprise them," Mr. Kelley said, completely out of character.

"What?"

"Come on, the worrying about our two girls and Stephen is over. We need to do something fun."

"I take back what I said about men being stupid about love."

Mr. Kelley went into his office and called the restaurant owner. He told him that he wanted to pay the bill for Clara and Mackie and any of their friends that might come in.

"Are you sure?"

"I am, why?"

"The whole restaurant is full tonight with his friends. He must have told a lot of them about his plans. I couldn't even seat you as it is, but since you're paying for the whole night, I'll make room sir, I'll make room. May I have your name, sir."

"Kelley," he spelled it for him.

"Cornelius Kelley?"

"Do I know you?"

"No, but I know you. My name is Frank Giancarlo my wife Jeanie helps with the serving."

"Nice to meet you. Could you make arrangements for flowers to be placed everywhere, I want them everywhere and on every table. How many tables do you have?"

"Fourteen tonight, including you and Mrs. Kelley, I presume."

"Yes, she will accompany me. Can you also round up 15 bottles of Dom Pérignon Champagne for the tables?"

"Yes sir, I'll have to send out for those. I don't have enough champagne glasses. I'll have to borrow at least 40, from other restaurants."

"No worry, I'll have my man bring over 70 glasses within the hour. Do you need me to prepay? I'd be more than happy to."

"No sir."

"Are you sure? Oh, and tell everyone as you seat them that their meal and drinks and tip are paid for. They can order anything they want. Just don't tell them who's paying."

"Yes, sir!"

"Three other things: what time will Mackie and Clara arrive?"

"Eight o'clock, but his friends are arriving at seven thirty so they can surprise them."

"And I'll need a photographer for the night."

"I will make all the arrangement sir."

"Do you have a table that a phone can reach?"

"We have a long cord that we can use. Will you be needing to make calls this evening?"

"I want my daughters to call Clara after Mackie proposes. They're in Montana, they'll be sad they couldn't be here. When she calls, if it's too early. Just tell her to wait and call back or come get me and I can call her at the right time."

"I'll handle it."

"Fabulous, see you at seven thirty, thank you Mr. Giancarlo."

"Yes, sir!"

The Harpers were so relieved too. Tonight's dinner would be a feast just like Clara and Mackie's. Mr. Kelley called, and Carolina and Mary were now in on the planned telephone congratulations.

Stephen couldn't take his hands from his rescued violin. Carolina thought it reminded him of Bobby after a while on the couch together. "He did kiss it when he opened the case," she laughed.

Everybody was laughing again. That's what everyone noticed first. They missed laughing and now they could. Schmidt must be turning over in his grave on his way to the lower Hell floor of the long elevator ride down on his final journey.

Stephen was so happy to be playing his own instrument. This was the first time since learning its heritage. The relief he felt tonight allowed him to enjoy his Bach music, his Bach violin and his Bach name. He hadn't thought about it much until today. He imagined his ancient grandfather playing this instrument in the early 1700s. It gave him chills. He still didn't believe he would ever see it again or the music that great grandfather wrote two hundred years ago.

Mr. Kelley had everything set for tonight. Mrs. Kelley was impressed with his hosting skills. This was his first solo soirée planning.

The Green Bentley pulled up in front of the restaurant and Geoffrey ran around to help Mrs. Kelley. Mr. Giancarlo greeted them before they reach the door.

"Mr. and Mrs. Kelley, I am honored."

"That's so kind of you," Mrs. Kelley said. "I hope you and Mr. Kelley have everything arranged. He's never made arrangements for a party before," she laughed when she saw his nervousness. "I'm certain it will be wonderful."

"This way please."

He sat them next to the future Mr. and Mrs. McMillan's table and noticed a telephone placed just behind it. The flowers were beautiful. Mrs. Kelley was impressed so far.

Another table was seated just before they arrived. Mr. Kelley went over and introduced himself and said that Mackie and Clara were good friends. Mrs. Kelley waved and smiled. He was a policeman from Mackie's precinct.

Two more couples entered, and Mr. Giancarlo seated them. When he whispered that the bill was taken care of, his customers exhibited huge smiles. They thought Mackie was the generous patron of the night's festivities.

Soon the place was filled. Mr. and Mrs. Kelley enjoyed speaking with all of Mackie's and Clara's friends. They had been to hundreds of fancy parties over the years where the guests weren't as polite and gracious as this group. They were having fun here.

"Everyone, sit down and cover your faces with your menus," Jeanie yelled out. "They're coming in."

Frank welcomed the young couple. "Your busy tonight, Frank." He nodded and had them follow him to the center table. Clara was the first to notice the tables were filled with their friends. Mackie was in a different world of nervousness and lightheadedness. When Clara saw Mrs. Kelley, she ran over and kissed her. Everyone else dropped their menus and gave up their terrible disguises. The room erupted in applause. Finally, Mackie realized what was happening. Now he was really nervous. Lord knows, Clara wasn't. She knew what was going to happen this evening the second she saw the Kelleys seated next to their table.

"Did you invite everyone to join us tonight?"

"No, but I did tell the boys at the precinct what I was planning."

"What are you planning?" she knew she was being a little playful and a little mean. She stopped and held his hand and said, "I love you, copper." He felt a lot better that she knew and was still sitting at his table.

"You better get this over with, so we can have champagne. Did you see all the bottles of French Champagne?"

"How could you miss it."

Mackie stood up to make an announcement. It was time to propose. It would be silly and weird to wait as if something more spontaneous was planned. It was actually planned to be a surprise, but they had gone way past that possibility.

"I want to thank you all for coming tonight and ruining my proposal." Paddy laughed the loudest. I'm going to excuse myself and go into the back with Clara. I have something to ask her in private. I hope you will all understand."

"Do it here, Loverboy!"

"We want to watch you stumble and mumble."

"I want to see her say no, so I can ask her out!"

They walked through their roomful of friends and laughter and went into Frank's office to be alone.

He had Clara sit on the chair in front of him as he stood.

"Clara, I wanted to do this quietly at our table, but that's not possible now. He reached for both of her hands and spoke into her eyes.

"I want to be with you forever. I want my last breath to be with you next to me. I want to die in your arms a happy man with his children and grandkids surrounding me.

"I promise to always be faithful to you, no matter what. No excuses. I want you to know that I will protect you and gladly die for you if that is what it takes to keep you safe.

"I promise: To never mistreat you. To never strike you in anger or at any time. To defend you and cherish you. To provide you with a family and a safe home for us to live. I will respect you and love you for as long as I live."

Clara started to cry. She couldn't stop. He got down on his knee and spoke the four words she wanted to hear.

"Will you marry me?"

"She jumped up and screamed Yes!" the kitchen staff listening by the door were relieved and went back to work.

He pulled the ring box from his pants pocket and opened it facing her. He took it out and put it on her finger. It was a little tight.

"I'm wearing it tonight; it's not that small."

She was offered a napkin by Jeanie for her tears and the two of them walked back out to their friends.

The photographer was ready and waiting.

Some thought it didn't go well when they saw her crying. Mackie quelched that wrong impression by yelling out. "She said Yes!!"

Clara held up her left hand, showing off her ring.

Everyone stood up as Frank and Jeanie filled the glasses with expensive champagne. That's when the toasts started.

Paddy, true to form, jumped up and grabbed the first toast away from anyone who thought they were entitled.

"Mackie and Clara. May all your troubles be little ones and all your little ones be twins."

One by one, they stood up and gave mostly humorous toasts that were appreciated. A few were better said at bachelor parties.

It was Mr. Kelley's turn. He looked at the two of them in a very serious way and spoke.

"Clara and Mackie, I want to tell you how happy Mrs. Kelley and I are to be here tonight at this biggest milestone of your lives. When I first saw you together, I knew right away you would be married soon. Maybe not this soon, but very soon."

Clara laughed and nodded in agreement. So did Mackie.

There are few men and women that I have as much respect for as you two. I'm glad you left the room to propose to Clara. A proposal deserves to be private, quiet and spiritual. It is a sacred question and answer that is only for two people at a time.

"I know that God will bless your marriage, and we look forward to your twin little ones!"

He looked at Paddy to compliment him on his Irish toast.

"Raise your glasses to the finest people in this room and New York."

Just then, the phone rang. Mackie was startled. Mr. Kelley told him he should answer it, and he did.

"May I speak with the future Mrs. McMillan please."

"Who's calling he said playfully." He knew as he handed the phone to Clara. She looked confused and asked who it was.

"It's your boyfriend, he wants to know what you're doing here!"

She gave him a little slap and grabbed the phone as everyone started laughing again.

"Mary and Carolina, I can't believe it's you.

"Yes, I said yes. I'm getting married too, just like my two girlfriends in Montana.

"Your parents are here with us."

Carolina took the phone first. "We know, that's why we're calling you at the restaurant. We are both so happy for you."

"We, all are happy you don't have to worry about that monster anymore. That makes me so happy for you and Stephen."

"I shot him and so did Stephen. It's definitely over now," she said with a twinge of sweet revenge. Barely noticeable, but there.

"I didn't see that coming."

"I know, he tried to hurt me and Stephen, and we stopped him. Here's Mary she's grabbing the phone to probably shut me up."

"I can't believe she told you the details. I saw the whole thing. The fear and anger have come to a close."

Listen, I know you're busy, so I just want to say, "Best Wishes. We'll be talking soon. I love you guys, bye-bye."

She put the phone back and looked at the Kelleys. "Thank you for that, I really wanted the both of them to be nearby, but I'll take a long-distance call as a consolation prize. I'm so glad you came; I didn't expect you to be here."

"Why on earth not darling?"

"You know, it's not what you're used to."

"Oh heavens. Mr. Kelley and I couldn't afford a place like this when we were first married. I love it here."

She meant it. She would be back soon.

The party was coming to a close and seemed to be moving over to Paddy's Tavern. Rumors of free drinks and good times amped up the interest. "If the lovebirds are going, then we're going," was the general consensus.

Mackie went to settle up with Frank before the checks would be handed out. "I'm paying for this Frank, I may need a loan, but I'm paying for this."

"No your not. Somebody has already paid for everything, and I mean everything."

"Who?" he said while looking over to the Kelleys' table. He nodded at Mr. Kelley in thanks and respect. He was also relieved that he didn't have to pay that enormous bill. He walked over to their table and asked them to be his guest at Paddy's. Mrs. Kelley asked if they had gambling tables before laughing and accepting his invitation. Mr. Kelley looked at her, surprised.

"We'll be right behind you, I want to talk with Frank before we leave. Oh, and thanks for the dinner."

Mackie and Clara walked out rolling their eyes and smiling.

Frank came over with the bad news. It was expensive. Mr. Kelley reviewed the bill and asked why there were no markups on the champagne and flowers. The photographer wasn't on the bill either. Mrs. Kelley was talking to the photographer about approving any photos and told him that they would be paying him directly and they needed him to go with them to Paddy's Tavern. He agreed and started to pack up his camera until Mr. Kelley asked for a picture with Frank and his wife Jeanie.

He paid the bill and gave Frank and Jeanie a huge tip for everything they did on such a short notice. He promised to return to his restaurant. They became good friends and the Kelleys visited Ristorante Giancarlo many times over the years. That picture was framed and hung on the wall.

Geoffrey was waiting for them to drive them home.

"Take us to Paddy's Tavern, Geoffrey. We aren't finished for the evening."

"Yes sir. Are you sure?"

"We're sure, Geoffrey."

38

Clara and Mackie said goodbye to Paddy and the Kelleys and left to go home. They thanked their evening's benefactor again. He held her hand and floated over the sidewalk as they walked back to Clara's apartment. They were both relieved and so happy that they would be wed soon. The details would be worked out; the hard part was over, at least for Mackie.

They both had early mornings and "rushed" to bed. They changed into their pajamas and Mackie sat on his side of the bed and turned off the lamp before jumping under the crisp white sheets. Carla removed her robe and slid in next to Mackie. Tonight, she was naked.

"Let's get married this week Mackie. I don't want to have things that we can't do together. I want to touch you everywhere that I'm not allowed." Mackie moved closer and felt her skin. That's when he realized he was in bed with the most beautiful woman in the world and she was not wearing clothes. He pulled her in closer and touched places he never imagined. He liked it a lot. Clara removed his pajamas, while quietly giggling. Not because it was funny, but because she was so excited. "Who ever said the honeymoon had to be after the wedding." She thought, trying to justify what was about to happen." We're just shuffling the order a little.

The boys and girls in Montana were suffering through the same emotions and they were barely holding on themselves. After the shooting of Schmidt, they released a lot of pent-up fear and trepidation and that resurfaced as pure lust for each other. They weren't sure they could handle it.

They returned to the lodge after Carson had opened it up again. The fireplaces were roaring and slowly heating the rooms. It felt good to be back home and sitting on the soft couches in front of the fireplace with their men. Their lives were returning to normal.

Carson decided to move into the lodge. He was concerned to leave the four alone for more than a short time. He couldn't believe he was as much a hired chaperone as a caretaker. He did accept his responsibilities without reservation, after all he was a "caretaker" and that encompasses everything Kootenai.

The next month carried a much-needed reprieve from the winter. The sun shone more, and the temperatures were rising. Everything was turning green and looked new. In four months, they would be married and ready to start their lives together. Oh, and quieting their raging hormones and desires by releasing what they have been tamping down from the day they first met. Saturday July 3, 1933 couldn't come soon enough for the Harper boys and their fiancées.

Clara and Mackie were a textbook case of what can happen when two people in love are left to self-chaperon. In their case, it was like the inmates were running the prison.

They planned on a June wedding and were heading toward an unplanned April honeymoon. They were careful, but the old Irish saying, "The first baby can arrive at any time, but the next ones are usually nine months apart" was a funny warning to them. They were as careful as two young lovers that had sampled the fruit that the genie let out of the bottle.

The New York Times carried the Kelley approved photos from the engagement party as a spread article that even had two from Paddy's Tavern.

The headline in the society section was accurate

Hob Knobbing with the Regular Folks.

If it intended to depict the Kelleys as regular, down to earth and loveable millionaires, it achieved its goal.

It sure was believed by the dinner guests and partiers at Paddy's place that night. Ristorante Giancarlo was full every night and now needed reservations weeks in advance. Paddy's Tavern always had a line out the door. The fire marshal had to keep his eye on the occupancy level of Paddy and his patrons.

Mrs. Kelley became a sort of anomaly in Manhattan. Mixing easily and casually with middle class was a story that many suffering from The Great Depression appreciated. It seemed to take some of the pressure from the super wealthy to lay low and hide their lifestyles. They were not impacted by the current economy, and it angered the less fortunate whenever they saw wealth flaunting. And it gave the more fortunate the courage to visit establishments they considered "beneath them."

Prohibition ended and things were improving. Friends of the Kelleys pleaded with them to be their escorts to these places that were a bridge to different classes of people. Mr. Kelley was even queried about his new popularity with the media. He was humored by the serious questioning. It was like someone asking you about a visit to

Africa to see the "zoo" animals in their natural habitats and wondering how "dangerous" it was.

Whenever the Kelleys went out at night, the photographers and society mavens were sure to follow, hoping to discover the newest "it" place. They started going out more and really enjoyed the different scenery. Until now, they always ate at home with meals prepared by their chef and staff. Dinners with friends were always the same. If you did go out to eat, it was usually at one of the finest hotel's dining rooms. When Mrs. Whitney called to ask a favor, the Kelleys were elevated to the top levels of the society ladder. Her "favor" was to ask if they would take them out to one of those "regular" places. It's funny to watch the upper echelon trying to hitch a ride to the latest fads.

When the wedding announcement for the double wedding in Montana hit the papers, they moved up a couple more steps on that mysterious society ladder. Another bold move that the insecure would never attempt.

Mr. & Mrs. Kelley thought they needed to lose a little weight. After all, they were in so many photos and articles within the society pages. She started to notice some of her rejected photos showed a bad angle. It wasn't the angle, it was the twenty or thirty pounds that was the problem for both.

May in Montana opened up the outdoors. The sun was welcome, and the temperature reached well into the 70s. Landscapers were surveying the grounds that would be upgraded for the wedding. No plantings until June though, too risky to battle an unexpected hard frost. The Kootenai Lodge will reach its peak of perfection on July, 3.

The wedding planning was more than just for the wedding. The fourth of July was the next day and on a Sunday. Every hotel room in the area was booked for the guests that would celebrate at the lodge. Bands from the university in Missoula were practicing the latest musical fads and more traditional wedding music.

The fireworks this year would be outrageous. A thirty-minute fusillade of color and sound. Too big for the floating dock. They would use Mrs. Kelley's personal relaxation island to the south. It had a custom-built Japanese bridge that had no nails or bolts. This show of force would clear out the bears and other unsuspecting critters quickly.

All the food for the fourth was to be prepared off-site and delivered to the lodge. The kitchen staff was realieved to hear that. After the wedding, they would be exhausted. Their reduced obligation was to oversee the hors d oeuvres and deserts that were prepared in advance.

A flower covered archway with the lake behind was the outside setting for the vows. Contingency plans were in place to move the ceremony to the inside of the lodge if the finicky early July weather was uncooperative. The inside dinner tables and seats would serve as the sanctuary in case of rain. The ceremony would be on the gallery level above the massive stone fireplace. Twelve bridemaids would flank them. Six on each side on the beautiful curving log stairways rising to the deck. The world record elk would be covered with flowers and veils to not distract from the two brides.

Over 100 guests from New York would attend. Adding the Harper family's list and the local friends, over 200 would watch the joining of Montana and New York City in holy matrimony, all on the banks of Swan Lake.

39

The newly minted Mr. & Mrs. McMillan couldn't wait any longer to get married. They stood before a justice of the peace and reduced to writing their love and commitment on a single-page sheet of paper entitled: "State of New York Marriage License."

Mrs. Kelley wasn't happy with their strategy. It took them one day, and it was done. She was on the 74th day of planning and making arrangements for her two daughters' wedding.

She fantasized about them eloping, setting up their homes, and holding up their end of their grandbaby obligations. Those thoughts were vanquished when the pastry chefs and their samples and photographs were shown in by Johnson.

Clara called Carolina with the news. She was a little peeved she couldn't be with them and witness their wedding. She and Mary had thought about a triple wedding, but that was impossible. Hundreds of friends were eliminated from the invitations because of the limitations imposed by their wilderness wedding venue. She was happy to hear that the two of them would be attending. "I'll make all the arrangements; just let me know how long you two can stay."

"So, how was it?" she asked.

"What do you mean?"

"How was IT!?" Carolina teased.

"Ha, Ha, Ha. It is great my dear. The first two days were a learning experience, that's for sure."

"It only took two days?"

"Two days?" she said in disbelief.

"I thought it would take longer than two times to figure things out."

"Who said two times? It was at least ten times."

"You said two days… Oh, my goodness!" she realized the ten times were spread over two days.

"Well, it was the weekend!" Clara bragged.

Carolina was ready for her own "long weekend". So was Mary. The boys definitely were. Carson was ready too; he would soon be relieved of his chaperone duties.

It's strange how a vow said aloud in front of friends and family can change in a snap a "bad" thing into a good, right and wholesome thing. The same people praising your virtues today would be gossiping about your sins a day earlier. Is it the same as a runner leaving the blocks in a race early? Are you disqualified by society? You have cover, though, as long as a baby doesn't come along too early. That would cause people to look at their calendars and calculate your virtue score. Carolina understood that stigma better than most. She wasn't going to let that happen. Now Mary, well, that's a different story.

◇

The Harper family was enjoying this unchartered territory. Especially Daisy and Jennifer. They dreamed of their turn and what it would look and feel like. This was close to home and they were having fun helping and fantasizing and pretending it was for their own weddings.

Mr. Harper had never seen so much daydreaming coming from his daughters. Mrs. Harper was not phased. It brought back memories of her older sister's small wedding and two-day honeymoon before getting back to her farm chores. They lived in that house all their lives.

Mrs. Harper did the same thing, just in a different home. She moved in with the Harpers and enjoyed a slightly larger wedding and a three-day camping honeymoon up to the Glacier Park area. She didn't know it yet, but an ocean cruise to Europe for a month on the continent would be one of the many gifts from the Kelleys' and their friends. Even the two matching Chryslers would be gifted to them. The only caveat was that they could be borrowed during the summer months.

Mrs. Kelley wanted to discuss the wedding rings with the girls. They both had theirs and loved them. The Mrs. tried to delicately open a dialogue about possibly helping them to "upgrade" their finger hardware.

That didn't go as planned.

"No momma!" They both loved everything about their men and the rings that they wore were no different.

She knew that was a mistake and apologized. She liked that they both wanted to keep what they had. It made her feel even more happy for their weddings and success of their lives together.

Wedding gifts were arriving at the house daily. Mr. Kelley was wondering if he would need another train car for the Montana trip. He would and he knew it. He rented a extra train car with a sitting area, private bath, storage room and sleeping berths for overflow travelers. Clara and Mackie would be two of the lucky invitees. They were happy about that. They way things were "progressing," she would certainly be pregnant for the wedding and would appreciate the luxury and comfort.

Some marriages can run into trouble early on when pregnancy pops into the picture. Libidos change and sometimes men think that their new wives don't enjoy sexual relations as much. That's not an accurate statement within a healthy marriage. It's more about the soon to be mother's total attention to her new and at the same time, ancient role. Bolstered by hormones and chemical changes, they can be misconstrued as lack of affection toward her "first baby," that is, her husband.

Some husbands had the misfortune to hear things said in the birthing room that were so out of character that an attentive midwife would seek the husband on the other side of the door to console him and promise them that this happens all the time and that she wouldn't remember any of the horrible names she yelled or the descriptions of what she would do to him later if he ever tried to touch her again. Soon she would be smiling, the baby would be on her breast and the words she called her husband while in the throes of delivery would be forgotten and her healthy baby and smiling countenance would testify to her sudden memory loss.

Sometimes that helped. She might forget, but usually only time would heal those deep cuts thrust into the husband's brain.

The sheriff closed his case on Friedrich Schmidt. He was interred in an unmarked grave outside of Kalispell. Carolina had hoped they would ship the body back to Connecticut and get it out of Montana. She wanted no details about the monster. The shooting was classified as "Justified." Carolina scoffed and thought, "It wasn't justified," she said. "It was Justice."

Summer was near. The water and the temperature were gaining a degree or so a day. The boys and the girls enjoyed hiking together in the Jewel Basin area east of the lodge. Mary and Tommy hiked to a spring waterfall one Saturday. The pool of crystal-clear water at the bottom was too inviting for Mary. She took off her clothes and jumped in. Tommy looked around as if someone else could be in the area. Some people were nearby, about eight miles from them.

It was his turn. He quickly undressed and jumped in and swam to her. She was a better swimmer. He couldn't catch her. They swam hard for a few minutes until Mary stopped to rest. Tommy caught her and pulled her into him and gave her a kiss. The water was cold, but they were warm. Mary noticed something was poking her and laughed. Again, not to be mean, but because she was excited to be naked with him. Tommy let it fly over his head. He was thrilled to be hugging his future wife while skinny dipping under a waterfall in the woods of Montana. He was also glad it wasn't all shriveled up and tiny, leaving a bad first impression!

Carolina was more reserved, but not without her own close call. Her first "adventure" with Bobby wasn't what you might call romantic. They were in the back seat of the Chrysler on the side of the old logging road around the other side of the lake. It started with the usual kissing and hugging. The darkness and quiet gave them an excuse to go where neither had ventured before.

The windows were soon fogged and the next thing you knew, blouses, shirts and bras were flung into the front seats as her dress was pulled up. The remaining under garments remained in place, but not before hands were reaching into places that Bobby's dad warned him about.

Carolina was glad she felt comfortable hugging and kissing him while naked. She liked it when he kissed her breasts. They stayed hugging, kissing and touching for an hour and talked about their new lives. She had worried about how her brain would process consensual sexual activity against the rape from long ago in the Bradbury basement.

Bobby thought about that too, but really didn't think that much about it. He watched her process shooting a man to death on the lawn by the barn. Her brain completely handled it logically and cleanly. No nightmares and no problems, except for worrying about Stephen.

Sex with love would never be a problem for Carolina. It gave her great peace to not have to worry about her wedding night. She loved that Bobby was to be her husband. So did Stephen.

A week later, Mary was feeling some buyer's remorse. She talked with Carolina about it and discovered she had the same thoughts. It didn't frighten them much, but it did worry them. It was too late to back out and it would devastate the boys. They worked around it after Mary told her numerous stories of New York brides having the same reservations so close to the wedding.

This was not a negative. It was a reflection of the seriousness with which the brides took their weddings and vows. Those moments of vacillation gave them a time to deeply analyze what they were about to do. Virtually every "what if" was resuscitated and quickly put to death. This exercise was healthy and normal.

Men experience something similar, but in a more masculine role as a protector and provider. They reconsider if they can match the bride's father and his situation. The Harpers' were a textbook case of self-diminishment fueled by their brides' enormous family wealth and lifestyle. They knew that they could never approach Mr. Kelley's power and provisions.

Tommy decided this was the time to seek his guidance and wisdom. This was what he meant when he asked the boys to confide in him about the things they couldn't with anyone else. This was the time for them to ask Mr. Kelley about the things they didn't know.

"Hi Bobby, is that Tommy I hear on the other line?"

"Yes sir." He regretted falling back to calling Con, Sir. "I mean Con."

"So, what may I do for you boys?"

Tommy started, "I think we're getting cold feet." Bobby thought that was a little blunt.

"I've been waiting for this conversation. What on earth took you so long? Don't tell me. You both are concerned whether you can provide for my daughters in the manner they have become accustomed."

"Yes sir, I……"

"Don't interrupt me," Mr. Kelley knew what needed to be said and done.

"You're also worried about them becoming disappointed in the two of you and your absolutely normal and non-materialistic upbringing."

He paused for a moment. He knew they wouldn't interrupt.

"You want to be married to the same woman for the rest of your lives and the divorces and separations you hear about and read about in those stupid Hollywood magazines the girls keep around makes your mind wander."

The boys nodded their heads as if he could see them over the phone lines.

"The only thing you're not worried about is your ability to protect them." He paused, waiting for them. "Ok, you can talk now."

"Yes, sir." Mr. Kelley didn't correct them; he knew they were using that salutation out of respect and not by accident. It was the perfect name for this moment.

"It sounds like you may have gone through this before with your other daughters' husbands-to-be."

"Not really, they all come from money and grew up in the same lifestyle." He wasn't sure though; they never would have called him for advice. It wasn't arrogance, it was a fear to show weakness to the father.

"I was thinking about Mrs. Kelley after I proposed to her. I was going off to finish law school and had no extra money at all. None. I didn't even know if I could find a job at the time. She was from a wealthy family, and I couldn't for the life of me understand why she said yes to my proposal. During our rather long engagement I was constantly worried that she would come to her senses and change her mind. Even a few days before the wedding. It was a great relief that she went through marrying this regular guy when she could have had anyone she wanted."

"Thank you, Con."

"Yes, thank you, sir," Bobby said before he caught himself.

"If I didn't think you two weren't the perfect husbands' for my daughters, I would tell you in no uncertain terms and in unflattering ways. I appreciate your honesty and quite frankly, your bravery coming to me about these concerns you have. These conversations between fathers and sons to be are not common, but they should be. I hope you both keep coming to me when you need to talk about anything. I can't tell you how pleased I am that you called me about this. All I can say is that my household is behind you boys 100%. All of us, from the entire Kelley family to every person that works in this house is thrilled with you boys. And so is New York City society. My other sons in law can't compete with you in that arena. In Spanish, arena means sand, and society is more like dirt at times, maybe even quick sand!"

Tommy thought about when he punched the Vanderbilt idiot.

"I want to tell you something in absolute confidence. Will you agree?"

They both said, "Yes."

"The girls are having the same sort of reservations about you boys. It's totally different with women though. Their concerns are relational compared to a man's more basic physical concerns. I don't mean sexually physical, I mean what men have been doing since we were cavemen. At least that's the current university theory about our past. They are worried that they can't be good wives, because you and they are so different."

He continued on through the silent phone lines.

"Let me tell you something you already know about Carolina, she is more like you Bobby than your own sisters are."

He paused and then focused on Tommy.

"Tommy, Mary is exactly like you, but you can't see it. You're focusing on her surroundings and material things. Mary is the sweetest most down to earth woman I know. She is uncomplicated. I don't mean that as a backhanded compliment. She is an open book, just like her mother, and that's good news for you and your marriage. She doesn't hold grudges, and she doesn't even understand how to lie. At least not convincingly."

"Thank you, sir." I feel much better. It's just that marriage is so important to me and sacred that I out think my brain, if that makes sense."

"We all overthink important matters, but the key is to know when your decision is the right one and step away from reanalyzing it to death."

He returned to Bobby.

"Bobby, I don't know how "royalty" deal with marriage, but my experience suggests that they deal with it the same way as you and me. Don't know that for sure, because Carolina's the only royalty in my family. Look what she has been through. Look at how she raised her son. It probably constantly reminds her of her assault. She pushed through it like an army tank through brush. She came to America alone and was taken advantage by the Bradbury house. She picked herself up with the help from Clara and made the best of what she was dealt. She was immediately drawn to Mary. You don't know the old Mary. What you see now is not the old Mary. She lacked even the tiniest bit of confidence. She thought of herself as homely and not worthy of anyone let alone a man like you, Tommy. She was an absolute mess and Carolina of all the people that should have no confidence showed her how to live her life on her own terms. It was a miracle. You can see that now in my Mary. She is unrecognizable.

"They are worried that you boys are too handsome and tall and kind for them. Carolina's worried about her past and lack of family. Mary's worried that she can't live up to your expectations. The whole thing is ridiculous. We are Carolina's family now; apologies to J.S. Bach, and Mary fell back on some of her frailties about her youthful self. It's time for everyone to stop overthinking and get on with their lives."

He paused for a moment and finished.

"Not that your concerns are a bad thing; they are actually a healthy self-awareness that portends and predicts good things for your futures together."

"We have a couple of weddings coming up, boys; get back to work and quit the whining!" He laughed to lighten the last sentence. He meant every word of it, though.

The boys were relieved. Mr. Kelley was a wise man that would be a hedge against the trouble that plagued virtually every marriage in history.

Mrs. Kelley walked the girls from the edge of the cliff with a very different but savvy approach. She knew they had similar worries about long term compatibility and faithfulness. That was born from a hideous thing called doubt.

"Young people today think differently than when your father and I were your age. There were ten times more reasons that should have kept us from marrying. We just trampled over them all and when we finished, we took off our boots and threw them in the garbage along with the other nonsense that afflicts life's biggest decisions. We married for all the right reasons, and I can tell you girls are following in our footsteps. "You and they have no ulterior motives. Nothing to gain marrying you except for the love and the families you will create together. Don't think they see dollar signs when they see you. They do not, they see a beautiful woman and a perfect life with you. Try your best and you'll be amazed by what's to come. I am so excited to be able to watch your lives unfold."

The wedding was back on without any reservations. Mr. Kelley would remember this day as well as Mrs. Kelley. Each new year of their girls' happy marriages would cause them to put even greater importance onto their wise words. It would reach a plateau, because it couldn't get more absurd.

They likened it to their bear encounter on a day hike when they were bluff charged by a grizzly bear. It stopped about forty feet from them and dropped back down and slowly walked away. Each year that they retold that story, the bear got closer to them. Finally, after twenty years of recounting the tale, the griz was so close they could smell its bad odor and feel it's hot breath! That's what the Kelleys' were doing, and everybody loved both stories. Not just for the good outcomes, but also for the shear silliness of them.

40

"We're finished here Con." Mrs. Kelley looked forward to the trip out to the Lodge. "The train cars are loaded. Our friends are riding along with us. Our married girls, husbands and grandchildren will all be on board for the wedding train headed to Montana. I'm glad Clara and Mackie are traveling with us. She has been so helpful almost workmanlike in her organizational skills. She could do this for a living."

Clara would have loved to entertain that notion. It would be difficult now that she was pregnant. She wouldn't figure out about the baby until the nausea started up the day after the wedding. Mackie would never figure things out about a baby. His job would come later.

Johnson was happy to see things come to fruition. He endured hundreds of packages delivered and put in the library along with thousands of interruptions to his once mundane job. He would almost be as happy as the Kelleys were that their last two daughters were getting married. He genuinely loved all the Kelley girls, but Mary and Carolina were his unspoken favorites. He loved Tommy and Bobby too. No "funny business" with these two. They were in this deal for true love and families to be created. They were not inclined to work for Con, even though he tried to convince them. He would have formulated a job description that would let them succeed. He respected their independence.

Mr. and Mrs. Harper felt like king and queen to their princesses and princes. Mr. Harper had a rough time with Kelley's game plan that had them paying for the entire wedding. The Harper's certainly couldn't afford to even participate with this show of force and wealth. Con opened a serious conversation about this with them and asked the Harpers if they would do the same for Mr. and Mrs. Kelley if the tables were turned. Everybody knew the answer was yes. That one question ended their moaning and helped them leave it behind them.

Jennifer and Daisy were more excited than anyone. They had none of the worry and obligations of the ceremony that can fray nerves and shred emotions. They did see Mary throw a bit of a fit about her hairstyle. She would have preferred mother's stylist, Stephanie. Carolina saw it and laughed under her breath. She smoothed things over for Mary with a little love and a tinge of shame aimed at her childhood regression.

Weddings are completely different for men. To a woman, her wedding is a momentous occasion that delineates her youth from her adulthood. It is a statement to the world that she is about to get on her sleighride through life with the man she loves. It's also, among hundreds of other things, a declaration to other women to stay away from her husband.

As for a man, his wedding may or may not have been his idea. He was along for the ride and his obligations were limited to finding a ring that wouldn't embarrass his bride, getting fitted for proper attire and limiting alcohol consumption during the parties. His duties would come later and only interrupted by an occasional foreign war.

Tommy and Bobby were different than most husbands to be. They wanted to play a bigger role in the wedding. Not to inject themselves into places that they shouldn't, but to help smooth things for their brides during a most stressful time. They enjoyed the constant teasing by their Bigfork friends. Only good friends are teased with the ferocity that the boys suffered through. Unpopular people aren't bothered with teasing, no one cares enough.

Geoffrey drove the Kelleys, Johnson and the McMillans to the train station. Five sleeping cars were added to the Kelley private Pullman and over fifty friends and families started the journey to Bigfork, Montana. All had been to the lodge before, except for Clara and Mackie.

As the train gained speed and stability, Mr. Kelley walked through and greeted all his guests and family. He had five boxes of Cuban cigars sitting on his desk and waiting to be distributed by the proud papa. Mrs. Kelley outlawed them during the wedding. Outside would provide the men's VIP hangout.

The trip wasn't eventful, except for the McMillans. They couldn't believe how easy this normally difficult three-day trip would be. They even had their own private bedroom for "sleeping." Ha, enough said!

Meals were served family style. Or, as Mrs. Kelley called it, "camping style" because it was very informal. That's what everyone liked about them. They had become so informal in their lives since Carolina and the boys joined the family. Weddings aside, they enjoyed the luxury of their new relaxed lifestyle a lot. Curtesy of Carolina, Bobby and Tommy. Mary enjoyed it more than the others. It gave her a freedom like the shedding of the homely label that she self-inflicted on herself as a child. Of course there were still rules, but they were relaxed now and not as stifling. The elegance was not sacrificed.

They changed locomotives in St. Paul for the final leg to Whitefish. They took on water to replenish the tanks. No sewage tanks back then, flushing the toilets released waste onto the tracks. You don't want to stick your head out the window of a moving train when someone upstream visits the loo.

Travelers notice the vastness when crossing America. It even seems overwhelming and almost monotonous. Similar to a passenger ship crossing the Atlantic. When your train rolls up to the Great Rocky Mountains, you lose the monotonous but keep the overwhelming. If you want to seem small and insignificant, travel to the Rockies or even Manhattan for a scaled down version. The recently completed Empire State Building can make you seem small but not as insignificant as the Rockies do.

They would all be at the Kootenai Lodge or various hotel rooms in the area before dinner. A dinner party for all the guests was setup at the Bigfork Hotel. Over one hundred people would attend the 7:00 event.

The family went on to the lodge to get settled in for the week. Carolina and Mary were setting up their own marital cabins. The other four daughters, their husbands and kids peeled off to their own lakefront paradises. The weather was perfect. They prayed it would hold.

The boys wouldn't be spending time with their brides after the evening's dinner party. Last night in the lodge would be the last time they could be a little "naughty" with their girls until after the vows were said and done. Then they would become extremely "naughty," but allowed by society and its sometimes smothering morals.

Like most of the soon-to-be-married, the days leading up to the wedding night and being alone together were torturous. A boiler of emotions and pent-up desires were dangerously close to igniting from spontaneous combustion. It's like the friction of two delinquent mortgages on a property that mysteriously burst into flames, only to be extinguished and saved by hefty insurance policies. The insurance policy here was not seeing each other until the wedding day. Both sets of parents would make sure nothing caught fire before Saturday night.

Carson and Johnson had a lot of work to do and jumped right in. They seemed to like the friendship that developed over the years. A cowboy and an Irish/Scottish butler had more in common than not. Both single, no kids, just nice families that would have to suffice. They both chose serving others and had no regrets.

Clara would stay at the Bigfork Hotel with Mackie. She loved the little town on Flathead Lake. It was a big lake. Larger than the popular Lake Tahoe in California. Larger than any lake west of the Mississippi River. Its waters came from the north flowing out of Glacier National Park.

On Wednesday, the red Jammers, as they were called, would be filled with the wedding guests as they traveled the "Going to the Sun Road" to the top of the world. It had just opened for visitors for the season. Forty feet of snow was cleared from the newly constructed paved road that would allow the White Motor Company's red tour busses to get to work. Yellowstone had yellow versions of the same bus. The entire top would open up for tourists to view the incredible peaks and year around snow-covered vistas.

Thursday, the Flathead Recreation Ranch on the lake was reserved for horseback riding. It would later become Averill's Flathead Lake Lodge and was a required stop for the Kootenai Lodge visitors in the forties and fifties. After the war, Les Averill took care of the unskilled riders from the big city.

A picnic on Friday afternoon gave the attendees a chance to visit the lodge and meet with the other guests. The boys were allowed to attend for an hour before being sent back home. The girls stayed in Mary's cabin and looked at their beaus from afar. Carolina found her binoculars in the drawer and the two of them took turns looking at and fantasizing about their new husbands.

Stephen was hiding out at the Harpers and helping around the farm. Manual labor was not his forte. They were kind enough to relieve him of his duties so he could practice his violin. He came with his new dad to the picnic. They loved each other and that was such a relief to Carolina. It would have been a deal breaker if not.

The boys headed back to the farm after their allotted time. The girls snuck out and waved and blew kisses to them as they left in the truck. Stephen gagged, complete with placing his finger down his throat.

"Here they are!" Mr. Kelley bragged. "The two spinsters!"

"Don't ever say that again, Mr. Cornelius Kelley." she used the mad name for her husband.

"Why not, after tomorrow it would be a lie."

The girls were enjoying every moment of the spotlight they were in. Even Mary. That would have been unthinkable the first week Carolina moved into the house. Mr. Kelley never said it out loud, but thought Mary would not be getting married if it were not for Carolina.

Carolina had a blue and white gingham sun dress on. It was the perfect dress to make her happy. It was a reminder of her meager beginnings and a beacon to her new future. A matching bonnet was the perfect accoutrement. She was so beautiful. Stunning in the most simplistic clothing.

Mary wore a Hawaiian style shoulderless dress that was a beautiful turquoise print and draped to the top of her knees. Mary of all people was wearing a sexy little dress in public. The Mr. and Mrs. noticed immediately, and then both looked over at Carolina with their hands in prayer. It was the international signal of thanks and gratitude. Mary's matching hat was a standout.

"Money well spent, girls," Mr. Kelley thought. "Money well spent."

Tonight, the family would get together in the massive bar room. The main hall was filled with tables and chairs, a bandstand was built, and the place setting were "set in place." Off limits until the wedding.

The boys were asked to deliver some decorations to the lodge at five. They hoped to see the girls, if only from a distance. Mrs. Harper made them clean up and put on nicer clothes.

"Why mom, we're just dropping off decorations." They didn't know they were invited to the cocktail party. Mr. and Mrs. Harper were too of course, and they would leave five minutes after the boys so as not to give away the surprise.

They arrived at the lodge just as the two girls were running out to see them. They were wearing their skimpy sundresses, hats and all. They always said their girls looked good in blue jeans and flannel. Not this good, was the consensus.

Bobby looked around before kissing Carolina. He thought he might be in trouble. Tommy didn't care. He looked straight at Mary and went in for the kill. Con and Francis were spying like the Harper girls were as they watched their brothers fawning over girls for the first time.

"Surprise, you're invited to the cocktail party, boys!"

This was sort of the calm before the storm. Just the Kelleys and the Harpers and all the kids. "I am so glad, baby; I can't stand being away from you anymore." Bobby was truly lovesick and homesick for the lodge. "One more day," he sighed.

Tommy felt the same way. He couldn't wait until the wedding was over and they were alone in their cabins. "One more day," he laughed.

Sinning is always easier than holiness. That's what premarital sex was called, sinning. They boys and girls were somewhere in the middle and probably leaning more toward the sinning side of things. Not much, just a little off center. Nothing a good marriage couldn't fix.

These were the times they would look back to all their lives. These were the memories that counted the most. Whenever Carolina and Bobby had a spat, he would change the subject and with a wave of his hand, say to her, "Remember how hard it was to not touch each other before we were married? I'm so glad I can touch you right now and kiss you." And that's what he would do. Spat over.

Tommy had a similar strategy. He would recall how the two couples went to their cabins after the reception in the lodge. Their "friends" chained the doors so they couldn't get in. They both almost crashed into each other while racing back to the party for the keys.

"Bobby, Tommy," their male friends yelled. "You gotta drink water, you have to stay hydrated if you hope to survive the girls attacks on you tonight!" Even Mrs. Harper chuckled at that.

They snatched the keys and ran back so fast they had no breath left. The brides were standing on the porch laughing so hard, they almost fainted along with their winded grooms.

"Remember that?" he asked. She conceded. "I'll race you to the bed!"

It's life's little moments that stitch together a lifetime of memories.

A little champagne was served, and various cocktails were consumed. It was a nice family get together. Stories about the brides and grooms were told by almost every family member. The girls had the most stories about growing up and the boys were mostly about hunting. The oldest Harper girls had all the dirt on their brothers, and they could have planted a garden with all that soil. Nothing, bad, just stupid brother stuff. Jennifer recalled Bobby get invited to the Sadie Hawkins dance by three different high school girls for the same night. He had never been on a date, so he couldn't say no. He pleaded with her to get him out of the jam he was in. Somehow, she did.

The night came to a close and everyone left for their proper bed. Mary and Carolina stayed up and talked. They said goodnight and then looked at each other with puppy eyes. Carolina and Mary spent the last night of their single lives next to each other in the same bed, like they had so many times over the years. They were usually sad, frightened or confused, and they needed to get through them together. Tonight's was pure joy and happiness. It was a fitting close to their youth and the continuation of their eternal friendship. Tomorrow, they would each have husbands to lay next to, fatally interfering with their old habit.

41

The sun rose at around 4:00 am and woke Stephen. He grabbed his "fancy violin," as he jokingly called it and headed to the dock. The air was as still as he had ever seen it. The lake was dead calm. Sailors hate dead calm; young outdoor violinists live for it.

The sky was clear, and the early morning was cool. Stephen walked to the end of the dock and remembering the trout that hit him in the head, moved back a few feet.

He tuned his Strad and tightened the old, curved bow and then laid it across the middle strings and pulled gently to release the beautiful sound that was its sole purpose for two hundred years.

He played his *Montana Concerto* to the bald eagle sitting across the lake, staring back at him. The gentle sound brought the hummingbirds that were attracted by anything red. He saw the color red on the note he was playing. "No, they can't," he thought.

He finished his hour-long concert and started to pray for his family and for his new dad. He wished this could have happened when he was younger. He knew he was cheated out of a real father by the man he shot to death in the spring. Bobby somehow made up for all of that. They were both pretty different. Bobby was a farmer/rancher. Stephen was an intellectual genius and musician. The only thing that mattered to Bobby was the reality that Stephen was a hard worker. A harder worker than anyone he knew. And he respected him more than any man he would ever know.

Stephen was rejuvenated now and jumped up to head to his room. He was ready for the big day. As he turned around, he noticed a small audience of wedding guests were applauding him. It was 6:00 am.

The army of servers, party planners and florists were soon dancing around the lawn and reception hall. The flowers just kept coming. Conrad Florist was as busy as the bees that pollinated their blossoms. By the time the wedding started, there would be no flowers available from any florist for fifty miles.

The flower-covered arch was set up on the lawn in front of the 225 chairs that were facing Swan Lake. It was 8:00 am. The weather was holding and perfect. Carolina said it was Stephen's dawn violin recital that distracted and tamed Mother Nature that day. She sensed it was more divine than that, though.

A breakfast spread was set up to feed the guests and workers before the festivities began. It was cleared out almost as fast as it was put out.

The inside decorations and flowers were mostly setup the night before. Now, the outside had their turn at a makeover. Flowers were placed everywhere you could imagine. Orchids were hung under the branches of the massive Burch tree on the edge of the lake. Legend had it as the largest Burch in the state. There were many legends surrounding the Kootenai Lodge.

The musicians were starting to file in and settled into the log building by the spring-fed pond. It was the oldest building at the Kootenai. Built in the mid-1800s. That's an old building in Montana. It's a young state and lacks the past centuries of eastern states and commonwealths. Even the Rockies are younger than the Appalachians and the Great Smokey Mountains.

"Everything was on schedule and according to plan." Mrs. Kelley announced to Con. That's about the time every mother of the bride, the bride, and the groom whisper the same words. "I'll be glad when this is over."

As 4:00 approached, the rented red Jammers from Glacier Park were picking up guests from Bigfork and bringing them to the wedding. Only one had to wait for the stragglers.

The ushers escorted the guests to the correct side and seats to watch the ceremony that would begin in fifteen minutes. It was a 5:00 ceremony.

The brides were set and ready. Not much drama at all. Even Mary's hair was approved and good to go. They had tried on their gowns so many times before, they felt they weren't new anymore. They played "Wedding" more than once during the weeks leading up to this day.

The boys wore their brand-new western-style cowboy suits and adjusted their new Stetsons. Stephen surprised the family and guests with his own western cowboy suit, complete with Stetson hat. That was his idea out of respect for Bobby's "culture," as he put it. Johnson helped him pull that off. They all checked their new cowboy boots and bolos and headed to the deck to await the start along with Mr. Kelley, who coincidentally had on a cowboy suit and hat. That brought good cheer and laughter as soon as anyone realized it was him. A lot of double-takes occurred. It was perfect.

The Girls were in the entertainment cabin in front of the Burch tree. It was their staging area. Carolina couldn't help noticing that the roulette wheel was facing them. Her marriage would not be a gamble.

They could see the string quartet through the multipaned windows. Stephen joined them and made it a quintet. He directed them playing the beautiful Vivaldi wedding preamble. All the subsequent music would be Bach. He didn't stay for the next songs; he had ceremony obligations along with Mr. Kelley. First, though, he handed his baby to Johnson for safekeeping. He always had to worry about the Strad, and he didn't want to.

As Stephen walked to the deck, the quartet began playing. The boys, Stephen and Mr. Kelley, took their places. Bobby and Tommy walked self-consciously to the flowered arch and waited while facing the lake and the minister. They were not allowed to turn around and look. Brides' orders. They promised.

Carolina and Mary walked across the lawn to the lodge and met their escorts. Stephen would walk his mother and Mr. Kelley would walk Mary. The four cowboys were ready for the two Montana cowgirls to be escorted.

Stephen saw his mother and held his breath. She really was a real princess, he thought. Princess Carolina Augusta Wilhemine Bach. Mr. Kelley had the same reaction to both his daughters. They certainly were real princesses, even if Mary didn't hold a title. The whole princess thing made him chuckle.

They slowly walked them together up to the boys. Tommy turned around and broke his last promise before getting married. Bobby followed. They still did not believe this would ever happen. How could anything so beautiful be marrying them? The girls had the same thoughts about them. They were unbelievably handsome on their wedding day, and their cowboy look was as perfect as the weather above.

Mary had to hold back laughter when she saw her dad. Carolina couldn't. Soon everyone in the immediate family was laughing like they used to around the dining table in the city.

"I'll explain later," Mary told the minister. The photographers were swarming around them. The New York Times would have to wait for the photos to make it back to them. A full, two-page spread would be slotted for this wedding.

Stephen kissed his mom and shook Bobby's hand and started to walk back in his best cowboy impression. He stopped and waited for Bumpa. He was kissing and hugging and shaking hands. He even shook the minister's hand before he realized he wasn't getting married.

When the final "You may kiss the bride" was heard, two new couples were married in Holy Matrimony. A signature on the certificates made it official. Two new Mrs. Harpers joined the family, and two Mr. Harpers joined theirs. Stephen thought about his last name. Should he change it? "To Bach, maybe."

Photos were taken in all of the scouted locations around the lodge and the lake, river and creek. The barn was not left out. Carolina wanted one of the "hootch vaults," that was shut down by Mrs. Kelley.

Charlie Russell showed up a little late. He drove in from Great Falls and brought a gift for the lodge. It was an unfinished painting entitled "The Kootenai Lodge." It was a painting of the sweat lodge tents that the Kootenai Tribe used many decades ago. He promised to finish it soon.

The concrete in the patio was adorned years ago with his unplanned stick drawings. He added his artwork by using a Burch stick that was dragged through the newly poured concrete. Charlie was the most famous Montana artist. He painted virtually everything in the state capital and every important public and private place in the state. His bronze sculptures were found throughout the lodge and cabins. His bronze likeness would be included in the U.S. Capitol Statuary Hall as one of two of Montana's most famous citizens.

The photographers gave the wedding party a break. The newlyweds headed back to their marital cabins without a chaperon in sight. It seemed strange. Carolina and Bobby changed clothes in the same room and couldn't resist looking, no, staring, at their spouses' physiques. They behaved themselves. "We have a wedding party to attend!"

Now, Tommy and Mary, well, let's just say they were already under the covers and consummating their wedding in a very physical way. They were due back at the lodge in a few minutes. Luckily, Tommy was new at this sort of thing. They arrived right on time.

Carolina saw Mary coming in and could tell something was different about her. She was flushed and relaxed. "Oh my gosh," she thought. "Why am I not surprised."

She slid over next to her and quietly asked, "Well, how was it?"

"Fine, a lovely wedding."

"How was IT?" she asked exactly how she and Mary grilled Clara.

"Can you tell?" she looked worried. "Definitely, but I'm your sister."

She leaned in and whispered, "And like Clara, it may take ten times or so; my boy Tommy was in a hurry!"

They both laughed way too loud at that. They didn't want Tommy to look over and see them laughing.

She whispered, "At least he seems to be amply endowed." That caused another Kelley girl outburst.

"Stop, stop, stop it," they smiled.

Stephen came over, and that silenced that discussion.

"Hi, Mr. Harper, and hi, Mrs. Harper." He kissed his momma and hugged her tight. He hugged Mary and kissed her cheek, too.

They decided it best if they separated for a while and visited their guests.

Stephen took over the Ampico piano rolls on the Steinway and cued up a suitable Brahms piece. He noticed a pretty girl looking at him. "That's something new."

He was offered a glass of Champagne and accepted it. He only took a few sips during the toasts.

Mr. Kelley was happy and relieved that he didn't need the Pinkerton detectives to protect Carolina. That would have put a damper on everything. He still couldn't believe she shot him. "That's my girl, no fear!" She would have disputed that assumption.

The cocktails from the bar would be paused as everyone found their tables in the main hall. It was stunning. The western style chandelier lights were lowered and diffused a warm glow over the room. The quartet took their places on the stage as Stephen walked over to join them. He had made the arrangements for the music and selected the compositions. Bach himself would have been as proud as a god-fearing Lutheran from the late 1600's could be. It was almost entirely his great grandfather's compositions.

The quartet read from sheet music and Stephen led them from memory. He played his Stradivarius just like Bach, he hoped.

The young girl that had been watching him was now staring at him while sitting in a chair next to the stage. Stephen saw her and smiled.

She returned an enormous smile back at him. "What do I do now," he thought.

He violated his rules about concentration when in a recital. He almost lost his place because of this pretty distraction. "Concentrate." He thought.

She clapped too enthusiastically after every piece. She seemed to know them and when the proper time to clap was, unlike half the people listening. Her music acumen intrigued him. "Concentrate."

"Was this what the boys felt like when they met the girls?" he questioned. "Concentrate!"

He was glad the dinner was about to be served and was able to put down his violin. He set it in his case and turned around to find her standing behind him. He was startled at first.

"May I see your violin?" she politely asked. "My name is Ann."

"My name is…"

"I know who you are, Stephen." No, she doesn't, he thought, nobody knows I'm a Bach relative except the family.

"May I?" she asked before playing his violin. She studied violin but she always wanted to be an attorney. She knew she would never be a successful violinist, but her father's intellect ran through her blood. He was an attorney before a senator.

"I'd love to hear you play," he politely said back to her, knowing it would be bad.

Hesitantly, she started playing Bach's concerto for Violin in A Minor. He loved anything in a minor key, and this was a major favorite of his. He never played it; he heard it on the phonograph. It was written in 1717 and certainly Bach would have played this concerto on this very instrument she was gracing. It may have been the first time in two hundred years that his violin heard this played, albeit clumsily.

"I'm sorry." She stopped playing and handed the violin back to Stephen. "That's the finest violin I have ever played. Tell me about it."

"Long story, I'll tell you about it later. Where's your table?"

"In the back corner."

"Is that your mother?"

"No, she's over by the side door in the lavender dress."

"Maybe we can talk later?"

"I would love that."

Stephen watched her walk away and missed his chance to sit at her table.

He found her mother again by the door and walked over. "My name is Stephen, and I would like to sit next to your daughter this evening. If it's alright with you, I would like you to ask her for permission."

He watched her walk over to the table to talk with Ann. Her back was facing him as her mother asked her from across the table. He was now standing one foot away, behind her chair and out of view.

"Mom don't tease me. He didn't really ask to sit with me. Mom, tell the truth. Did he really ask to sit next to me."

Stephen tapped her shoulder. "Indeed, I did, Ann."

She closed her eyes and tried to make it all go away. She had never been so humiliated in her life. But like any native Montana, she got back on her horse and touched his arm almost for safety and spoke.

"I—am—so—embarrassed!" she whispered into his ear as he bent down and leaned closer to hear. She nearly touched his cheek with her lips.

"That's good, because I'm afraid of girls." He laughed. "I'm waiting for an answer to my plea."

"Yes, yes, please do."

"I'll return shortly, I need to tell my mother that I'll be sitting here for a while." He walked up to the front to find her.

"What a nice young man," her mother said to her father.

"Who is he?" her father asked.

"Stephen Kelley I think. A bridesmaid told me he was Cornelius Kelley's grandson."

"Does he know who you are?"

"I don't think so, we've never met before."

She was the daughter of the United States Senator Burton K. Wheeler. Although he was born in Massachusetts, he moved to Montana quite by accident when his luggage was "stolen" on the way to Seattle. The story was that he lost it in a poker game. He was elected senator in 1922 and was a sitting senator from Montana.

"Good, he came to sit with you without knowing the perks."

Stephen came over and sat down. Space was made on her right side. He was sitting very close to her and looked at her father for approval.

He stood up and introduced himself. I am Stephen Augusta. My mother is Carolina. One by one they acknowledged each other. When it came to Mr. Wheeler, he paused. "Are you Senator Wheeler?"

"I am, sir."

"I very much enjoyed the *Time Magazine* Cover Story about you. I was very young, but I still remember reading it. Do you know Bumpa, I mean, Mr. Kelley?"

"Yes, he's the largest employer in the State of Montana."

Stephen looked embarrassed. "Now I know how you feel right now, Ann."

That did it. Stephen was preapproved to court his daughter.

As family and friends spotted Stephen in the back corner, they came over to say hello. Soon the table in the back was the place to be. Stephen loved introducing a state senator almost as much as the senator enjoyed the attention. He also enjoyed introducing Ann Wheeler as his new friend almost as much as she did.

"Whose Stephen's new friend?" Bobby asked Mrs. Kelley.

"She's our state senator Burton Wheeler's daughter."

"I better look into this, I'm his dad now."

The party went off without a hitch. The three chefs and the staff were magnificent. Big tips would be doled out to this crew on Monday.

The dance band started to play the latest fads and fancies. The dancing was an interesting blend of east and west. It was a battle between cowboys and Manhattans.

Stephen was respectfully dancing with Ann and after a couple of rounds on the floor, decided he needed to infuse this party with his fiddle playing. He talked things over with the band leader and they had enough direction to kick it up a notch. Stephen grabbed his Strad to use it like the old-time fiddle playing he heard on the radio late at night. Bach would have been amused he hoped.

The cowboy style polkas and the new swing style were introduced to the guests by their hosts; the new Mr. and Mrs. Harpers'. The bar was heavily used by this crowd, they were on vacation and fewer obligations.

Mr. Kelley looked around for his wife. He didn't see her. He thought about the roulette wheel in the entertainment cabin next door and walked over. There she was running the illegal gaming operation.

"Should I invite the minister and the senator?"

"The minister's okay, Burton's a crook."

He walked over to her and smelled alcohol. "Oh my, my delicate little wife is drunk!"

"I *shirtainly* am not."

"Oh yes you are my love. How many glasses of Champagne did you have?"

"A few, it's really quite *refressing*."

He ran to get his daughters' help. She needed to be in bed. He would apologize for her absence due to exhaustion.

Stephen and Ann were enamored with each other. Her over the top embarrassing exuberance paved the way for him to be less fearful of girls. He was telling the truth about being afraid of girls, but he was doing a good job overcoming them; the boys took notice. So did momma.

Ann's excitement when her mother told her about Stephen's request to sit with her reduced the early stages of courting to one night instead of a dozen or maybe more. With Stephen at the helm, it could have plugged along forever, as is common with young and inexperienced men.

The party was coming to a close, and the guests were expected back for the barbeque planned on the lawn for the Fourth.

The Jammers were brought around and that cleared everyone out at about the same time.

Stephen asked Ann if she could stay and play the violin together.

"Boy, I don't know. I mean I want to, it's just that my dad won't like that. How would I get home?"

"I can drive you. You're just in Bigfork, right?"

"Yes."

"Can't win if you don't bet, Nana always says."

They walked over to the Wheeler's table and Stephen made his pitch. "We won't be out late sir, it's still early."

He leaned over to Mrs. Wheeler for advice on these matters of love.

"She's almost twenty and she is in college." She was on Ann's side. "We know the family. Why not Burty?"

She pulled out the old "Burty" on him. He was in a losing election on this one.

"Go ahead, if it's okay with our hosts."

"Good point, I better make sure it's okay with my mom and dad."

He enjoyed saying that: "My mom and dad."

He started with his mother. She would be easier and a step in the right direction. Conquer and divide.

"Momma, can Ann stay a while longer to play the violin with me?"

"Bobby, will you come over here for a minute?"

Conquer and divide failed.

"Do you think Stephen can stay a little later with Ann and then drive her back to Bigfork?"

"I don't know. I haven't had the "talk" with him yet."

"Oh, heaven's Stephen whined. I know more about the birds and bees than you do. At least until tomorrow."

"He does have a point, Bobby."

"Yes, go ahead. She seems really nice. I'm gonna check on you guys in a little while, so behave."

"Yeah right, you're gonna check on me on your wedding night. Sure dad."

"Get out of here," he said as he lovingly waived Stephen away as if swatting a nuisance fly. Have fun."

Stephen gave Ann the thumbs up, and she grinned.

"My parents said I could if you agree."

"We have, please bring her back by midnight."

"1:00, Daddy, please."

"Okay."

The party emptied out and the only ones left were the people cleaning and staging things for tomorrow's party.

"Let's go out and sit on the dock and play."

"Really?"

"It's my favorite place on earth when it's dark and calm."

They went to retrieve his violin and the one that Bumpa sent after his Strad was stolen. He tuned them by the light in the lodge and walked out together to the end of the dock. He held her hand so she wouldn't stumble. He thought that was a clever idea.

Sit here next to me. Ann sat down on the smooth wooden dock and moved closer than he expected.

"You go first she said."

"Okay," he leaned over and kissed her lips.

That wasn't what she meant, but she could live with it.

"I meant you should be the first to play."

"I knew that." No, he didn't.

And that's how it started. At his favorite place to play music. Now he was sitting next to and kissing a beautiful young lady. He would remember this evening forever. He loved everything about her. Her smell, her laugh, her eyes, and all the other "stuff" that attract a young man to a young woman.

He started to play. It was so quiet that Ann moved even closer to him to hear. As the volume and notes increased, she was drawn into his world of lights and sound. He looked up at the Milky Way and she followed his eyes to see it for herself. She laid her head on his lap and looked at the universe that was behind the back and forth of his moving bow. She would never forget this night either.

A young man's first love is indescribable. His body is bombarded with feelings that he has never experienced. With it comes a feeling of despair, knowing that it will soon all go away when she returns to her life in Helena. It casts a heavy pall over his hopes and dreams and newfound emotions.

It's not easier for a young lady to understand her first love. It makes her tremble and also somber. Just like Stephen, she knew the odds were stacked high and against them for this to last. He would soon be in his own world, and she would be in hers. Letters may help, but absence of touch and talk and sight was a romance killer. The old saying, "absence makes the heart grow fonder," was misleading and a cruel lie. Absence opens up opportunities for new liaisons that tend to destroy a first love.

They were both quiet and almost sad. Stephen got up and reached his hand out to help her up. They walked back hand in hand and sat on the deck. He took her around to the couch in the corner and after carefully putting the violins down, took off his jacket and put it over her shoulders. It was getting cold.

They sat facing each other from the side and looked at each other's face. He could do that for hours. Ann could too. Ann sensed his mood and tried to make it better. Not just for him, but for her too.

"Listen, I know tomorrow will be our last day together for a long time. I'm leaving study at Columbia in August and you'll be 3,000 miles away."

"No, I won't."

"What do you mean, where will you be?"

"Julliard School of Music. It's the old Institute of Musical Art. About two and a half miles from Columbia. It's up in Morningside, right."

Like a lot of lovesick young men, he made that up on the spot. Sure, Julliard wanted him, but he wasn't so sure about wanting them. Now he was. He would secure his spot Monday morning.

"You are not!"

"I swear it."

The solemn mood turned to jubilation for both. Ann leaned in and kissed his lips and didn't pull back for quite a while.

"I am the happiest girl alive, Stephen, I mean it. I really want to see what happens between us. I hope you feel the same."

Stephen felt even more so. He was a little worried he could be waitlisted, but Bumpa could help move things along at Julliard.

He drove her home and stopped on the empty street along Electric Avenue before dropping her off.

They hugged and kissed for another ten minutes. Ann broke it off and said she better get to the hotel. "My dad will be waiting up."

He was, and Stephen was glad he dropped her off before his deadline. He walked her up to room and gave her a peck on the cheek, nothing more, just to be careful.

The weather for the Fourth of July party was glorious. The two sets of newlyweds were still in bed. They had clothes on. Not because the novelty wore off, mind you, but because it was very cold early that morning.

Carolina couldn't wait to see Mary, and Bobby couldn't wait to see Tommy. There would be a lot a smiles and thinly veiled sexual remarks thrown around before breakfast. It happens with every newlywed. You just have to tease them, now that they are part of the club. "How many times?" was the inside joke as they tallied their results against Clara and Mackie's. The boys would have been mortified if they knew what was going on.

Stephen came walking up and if he thought he could escape some teasing, he had a lower IQ than was thought. He didn't and it wasn't.

Bobby and Carolina were careful not to tease him. Tommy did a little and then read the room and stopped. Stephen was happy he did, he had a lot to worry about with Julliard.

Breakfast was faster than normal. Everything had to be washed and put away. The caterers were on their way and every minute counted.

Decorations were being installed on almost every place you could attach something red, white and blue. The wedding flowers were recycled and put on each table and flat spot around the lodge. The front walled patio was transformed into a fairy tale. The red geraniums that were planted everywhere were donating splashes of color to the white wedding flowers. The Conrad girls did a great job.

The bus with the marching band from the University of Montana was on its way up from Missoula and traveling around Flathead Lake. As it came over the hill in Polson, the ones who had never been to the Flathead were stunned by the massive lake that was hidden behind the mountains until this very moment. It is difficult to describe the immense beauty.

Everyone was dressed and ready for the guests. The receiving line would not be necessary again as the same guests for the wedding were returning for the Independence Day party.

Stephen was hanging around the drive out in front. Carolina was about to ask him what he was doing and then suddenly figured it out. He was waiting for his girl. She left him alone with his excitement and agony. She'd been there before.

Johnson was running around but had things under control. Carson checked on the generator, just in case, and looked in on the pump house too. "All was well with the well" was his funny line and it was repeated every time after checking it. Mr. Kelley was always kind after hearing it a hundred times and he let him see a little laugh.

Stephen greeted the cars as they arrived. He hoped people would think he was posted there for that purpose.

And then he saw her. Her father drove a Marmon Sixteen. A rare and luxurious autocar. Stephen recognized it from Manhattan. "You don't see Marmons out here senator. It's a beauty." He gained a few more bonus points with that comment.

"How are you Mrs. Wheeler?" He opened the doors and helped them out. The car attendant took over from there.

"Hi Ann, I'm so happy to see you," she nodded and smiled. Her parents were amused by the show of nonchalance. No cowboy outfit today, he was dressed in a tweed jacket and tie over a crisp white shirt.

"May I escort you in?" he asked.

"Thank you, Stephen," Mrs. Wheeler responded. "How was your evening with Ann last night?"

"Very nice, thank you."

They walked through the patio that was covered in patriotic paraphernalia and the repurposed red and white flowers and into the lodge and out to the deck.

"May I show Ann around the grounds?"

"If she wants to, yes."

She wanted to. She wanted to be alone with him as much as he did with her. He grabbed her hand and walked her proudly through the lodge out to the drive in front and headed toward Johnson Creek.

But first, he stopped at the underground vault.

"What's this?"

"You'll see."

He walked her down the steps to the vault that both Mary and Carolina brought the boys so that Carson couldn't find them. He thought it was only his idea to take a girl down there.

"It's Bumpa's liquor vault."

"It sure is dark in here. Someone could steal a kiss, and no one would know." Little did he know it would be her stealing the kisses. She planted a big one on his lips and they stayed standing while hugging and kissing for ten minutes.

"I dreamt of you last night, Stephen," she thought she did but couldn't really remember.

"Me too." Stephen slept like a rock and couldn't recall any dreams.

They both laughed when it was clear they were both lying.

They were blatant lies. They both were so exhausted from being love-struck that a deep sleep was not to be denied.

He took her back up the stairs and stopped on the stone bridge over Johnson Creek. He showed her where Swan Lake, Swan River and Johnson creek all ran together. It was Will Roger's and his favorite spot at the Kootenai Lodge.

Next, they crossed over the polo fields. He explained that a few years back the Argentine team played an exhibition match on the pitch. "That's why it's so flat."

They came up to the barn and he walked her in to see Copper and the Herefords and hogs. "I don't feel safe here she said."

"What?" Stephen didn't understand.

"Someone might try and kiss me here without my permission."

"That won't happen. May I have your permission?"

He didn't wait for an answer.

They headed back to the party before it became too obvious what was going on. They got back to the deck and were pelted with questions from the adults on the deck. They looked at each other and realized how obvious things looked.

The marching band came onto the grounds playing Souza marches. The guests all looked around as they marched in formation on the outside of the lodge to the lawn on the lake.

They stopped and when the signal was given, they began playing the Star-Spangled Banner. It earned the official status as the national anthem by an act of Congress in 1931. Many didn't know the lyrics yet, but they recognized the tune.

The party had officially begun. The weather was crystal clear and that was good. The Fourth always brought back memories of Carolina's lightning strike. She was so happy she could hear clearly again. Every year the trauma she suffered moved to the back of her memory, pushed a little deeper.

Today would be a less rigid and formal agenda. The fireworks weren't scheduled until 10:30. The late summer sunset in Montana was nice for just about any day in the state, except for the Fourth and its fireworks. Lawn games, and swimming were de rigueur at the lodge on the fourth. Races to the floating diving board pontoon, canoeing and even fly fishing. Mr. Kelley hired local guides to give lessons to his guests. A dozen fishing casting poles were ready for the kids to give it their best. Badminton and croquet on the perfectly mown lawn was always a treat. The court was next to the children's playground, complete with the permanently installed jungle gyms and small hand pumping carousel.

Stephen and Ann sat and enjoyed lemonade while watching all the activities. She challenged him to a swimming duel. What could he say? They changed into their swimming costumes and met at the dock.

Ann was standing next to Mary and Tommy. He looked over at Ann and froze with his mouth open. Mary put her hand over it and snapped him out of it. He was looking at his girl in a bathing costume and was stunned by her shape and curves. It just kept getting better with Ann. Her blonde hair was covered by a cap and looked silly to him. He would pull it off after he won the swimming contest.

He lost. She was too good for him. He made a mental note to practice over the summer. The cap stayed on.

They climbed the ladder to the diving board, and he found himself diverting his eyes as he climbed behind her. He quickly changed the order, and she was following him now and diverting her eyes. He could barely control himself. He had to get back on shore.

They swam to the beach and got out. He grabbed her a towel and wished he could dry her off with it. He knew that would be impossible.

"Let's get changed and play croquet. I challenge you to that game, Madam."

"You're on, loser boy!"

Bobby and Carolina felt so relaxed now that the wedding was over. This was the second day of their marriage. They snuck over to their cabin more than once. Ah, to be young again!

Tommy and Mary were missing in action too. That allowed them to surge ahead in the "three girl wedding competition."

The party winded down and the Jammers delivered their passengers back to the hotel to refresh and change into warmer clothes. 10:30 at night in Montana can be chilly. They would be returned to the lodge for after dinner snacks, deserts and cocktails before the fireworks show. By Tuesday, most would on their way back to their homes and the festivities would be only memories.

Stephen and Ann weren't interested in anything but themselves and their last few hours together until the Fall. This would be the time to learn who it was they were attaching themselves to. This was the time to hold back the romantic and discuss the reality of their place in each other's hearts.

Stephen asked Ann to follow him to the dock in front of the Russell Cabin. They sat on the bench overlooking the lake and Mrs. Kelley's "Relaxation Island." It was a perfect spot to watch the fireworks that would be coming.

"Ann," Stephen started slowly. "I've never had a girlfriend before." He paused. "That's what you are right, my girlfriend?" she nodded and whispered, "Yes." He was more confident now. "I'm holding some secrets that you need to know about me and my mother."

Ann looked confused. "What do you mean, Stephen?"

"My mother had a very difficult childhood. In Germany and especially in New York City. She is an orphan. We don't even know who her mother or father was." He didn't want to tell her about her rape by his own father. The father he shot in the head and killed. It was needed to be said, but maybe it should wait until later.

"No," he thought. "The time is now."

"Ann, my father is dead."

"I'm so sorry Stephen," she said while taking his right hand in hers.

"You shouldn't be," he looked at her and then said it. "He raped my mother when she was just a teenager. Your age, Ann. Your age."

"Are you telling me this now because you think it will change how I feel about you and your mother?" She raised her eyebrows. It made her feel like she was being treated as if a child.

"I don't know. I feel you should know."

She looked into his eyes and saw the pain he was hiding. His trembling hand couldn't quiet it. "Stephen, if we somehow conquer courtship and survive the next steps, you'll know if it upsets me. But, right now, the only emotion I have is sadness for your mother and for you too. That's will never change. I am not a callous person; you'll see over time that I am logical and kind."

"There's more." He was trying to figure out how to tell her that he killed him, it would be a long story. "He went on the run and jumped on a ship to Germany to escape the charges my mom filed against him. We thought we'd never see him again." He gave her a kiss on her cheek, not to give himself courage, but to remember his last kiss if she was repulsed by what he was going to tell her.

"He returned a few months ago and found out where we were living. He was tracking her down to give her a gift that he thought would make her break her engagement with Bobby so we would live happily ever after. He was crazy."

"Where is he now?" Ann was worried about this crazy animal trying to hurt his mother and Stephen.

"I'll get to that." He bit his lip and began to speak. "The gift he had was my violin. It was stolen from me while visiting Yale School of Music. A new associate professor stole it. It was very valuable and rare. We didn't even know it. My mom brought it with her from Germany as a young child. He saw it when he visited our house in New York and recognized the maker."

"Why was he at your house?"

"He was a guest of Friedrich Kreisler and brought him to dinner and to listen to me play."

"You played for Kreisler?" This story was unbelievable to Ann.

"Yes, and that's when this Assistant Professor Beamish examined my violin and the original music in its case. He acted like it was nice, but nothing special. Kreisler knew better.

Before leaving, he invited me to Yale to audition for the school. I didn't like the guy, but I accepted. I asked my soon-to-be dad to go with me because something was off about him. He brought along Tommy."

"But how could he steal it without you knowing?"

"He was clever. After my audition we left it in the rehearsal hall and went to eat lunch nearby. He told us to order and said he had to run back because he forgot to lock up. School was on break and the campus was deserted. We finished lunch and had to make our train back to the city. He delayed us so that we had to run to catch it. We grabbed our coats and my violin and boarded. The next day we left for Montana on Dad's private train car. That's when I noticed it was stolen. I opened the case and found a cheap student violin in its place."

"How did the rapist get it?" she carefully chose that name for him.

"Thank you for not calling him my father." He hated that name, father.

"The professor was such an obvious suspect that he had to hide it when the Pinkerton Agency was put on the case by Grandpa Kelley. They roughed him up a bit and that caused him to search for a scapegoat to turn it in. That scapegoat was my mom's attacker. He inherited a house, car and money from his uncle and came back from Germany to claim it. He was still a scoundrel and looked the part. When the professor found him in a pizza joint, they made a deal for him to turn it in to the police. He thought that would get the Pinkerton men to stop beating him up for information."

"You know this is almost unbelievable, don't you?"

"I'm not finished, it gets stranger." He stopped and looked at her to make sure this wasn't too much for a second date. He couldn't tell. "He finds out about the value of the stolen violin from a newspaper article and decides to keep the money and the violin. The professor learns that it wasn't turned in when another visit by the detectives ends up in another serious beating. He finds him and ends up at his inherited house to demand the violin back. That's what Pinkerton thinks. This guy Schmidt, that's his name, gets the gun from him and shoots him. Not before the professor described me and my mom to him, and he figured out it was his rape victim from years ago."

"What kind of violin would cause someone to murder for it?"

"It's a Stradivarius."

Now Ann was starting to wonder about Stephen's crazy story.

"Did you get it back?"

"Yes, that was the "gift" that he thought my mom would accept along with having him in our lives."

"What a nut case!" Ann couldn't believe it.

"Anyways he found us and drove out to Bigfork to find my mom and give her the violin that would be his redemption for raping her. He also knew I was *her* son, which made me *his* son."

He paused again to make sure she was okay.

"He came to the Harper farm. Mary, my mom and I were the only ones there. He grabbed me from behind the barn and put a gun to my head and made me drop my rifle. We were guarding the place. He yelled for my mom to come out."

"What did she do?"

"She came out. He didn't know it but, she had a revolver under her sweater. When he told her to open the trunk of his inherited car to see the gift that he brought her. The gift that would cause her to love him and call off her engagement."

"What a nutjob."

"I know. So, my mom gets the violin and since he was holding me and couldn't see her, she puts the gun under the violin case and points it forward with her finger on the trigger and walks toward him. She smiled at him like she was happy. I convince him to take the gun off me and he did. That's when my mom shot him. He fell back injured. I grabbed the rifle I had when he jumped me and pointed it at him while he was on the ground. He went for his gun lying next to him. I decided then and there to kill him. I wanted to be the killer of this monster, the monster who raped my mom. I didn't want her to deal with killing someone, no matter how awful he was."

He stopped again before his next sentence.

"That's when I shot him to death. That's when I killed my own father."

He could see she was having a hard time processing this crazy story, so he stopped talking and held her. He didn't want to let go; he didn't want her to be frightened of him. She said nothing. Finally, she spoke.

"Oh, Stephen, are you okay? I can't believe you and your mom had to suffer again from him. You must have been terrified. You and your mom are so courageous; that's the only word for it: courageous." She hugged him tight and kissed his cheek. "Thank you for telling me this. I know it was hard for you; I could see it in your eyes."

"I'm just glad he's dead and this is over. I am mentally healthy and over it. I never think about it anymore. He's gone for good and that's good. He's never going to hurt my mom again. That gives me peace."

"Okay, you're still here talking with me and not running off," he quipped.

"Right," she gave him a sideways glance.

"There's more."

Now she started to worry. Did he save the worst for last?

"The violin is a rare Stradivarius."

"I know about Stradivarius, Stephen."

"Not this one," he looked at her and smiled. "This is the Strad that was given to Bach in 1712. It is the rarest violin in the world for two reasons. It was owned by J.S. Bach, and it was made during what is called the Golden Years at the famous Italian shop. It is from the most perfect period for making violins. When you played the concerto for me, I wondered if you were the second person to play it on his violin. I wondered if no one else had ever played it again until you did. When

I heard you play, I was so happy that you were the one bowing our family violin. It's a part of my heritage and you played it like great grandfather himself."

"Did your great-grandfather play?"

"Yes, and he composed the violin concerto you played last night in the dark on the dock of Swan Lake!"

"I don't think so; it was composed by Bach in 1717." She couldn't figure out what he was talking about.

"I know," he said, "He's my great-grandfather a couple of times past. I am the last surviving Bach."

"I know it's a great violin, better than any instrument I've ever played, but what makes you think it was Bach's and that you're his last surviving relative? This is a crazy story."

The Pinkerton Agency discovered its provenance while investigating the theft. They have copies of documents that prove it. The last known owner was in the mid-1800s. Her name is Carolina Augusta Wilhelmine Bach, and she is my mother's grandmother. My mom's name is Carolina Augusta Wilhemine. She never knew her full name. She may have been an illegitimate baby. That would explain the lineage break. "She was most likely born in Leipzig."

"Where Bach lived and died."

"Yes, and my mom lived just outside of Leipzig on a small farm as a servant girl. She was an orphan."

He took a breath and continued. "Here's the interesting part; it appears my mother has royal bloodlines. My mother is royalty."

"This is the wildest story I have ever heard. I'm waiting for you to stop and tell me it was all made up, that it was a story you read in a dime novel."

She paused, almost as if she was giving him room to confess to his story.

"As far as I know, it's all true. The Pinkerton Agency is not known for mistakes."

Ann was getting a little chilled and started to move closer to Stephen.

"Boom!" She almost jumped in his lap. The fireworks had begun, and Ann took advantage of the opportunity to hold him even closer. Stephen responded, happy that she still liked him. She did, and it was more than just liking.

The party ended at 11:30. It was an exhausting week for the hosts and the guests. Stephen exchanged phone numbers and addresses with his girlfriend. Kissed her and said goodbye to her and her family. Mr. Wheeler noticed the kiss. It was the correct kiss for the moment, and he approved.

42

That summer of 1933 was the last time the family was all together. The family traditions carried on, but it never had the splendor of the almost thirty years when all the girls were frolicking in their private Montana playground. Its memories for the girls were of fairy tale caliber. They knew it could never be replicated and that caused them to bow to their parents for giving it to them.

Stephen went off to Julliard and lived with the Kelleys in the big empty house. Mrs. Kelley loved Ann and made sure she came to dinner every weekend. She earned her degree in law, but she never used it much. She had too many children to take care of. She married Stephen a year after graduation. Stephen became the concertmaster of the New York Philharmonic and recorded many records, mostly playing Bach. Ann had her brood of six blond-haired children. Five girls and one son. Johann he was named, and he was now the last of Bach's surviving children. He loved to play the violin. Stephen saw his promise and helped to move it along.

Clara and Mackie had their first child in February after they were married. He arrived a little early like the first born are *want* to do when passionate lovers jump the gun. He was promoted to Captain and that made it easier to schedule his work hours to comply with his desire to care for his four children in a more "hands on" way that was not customary for fathers then. Clara's nursing skills were not wasted. The four McMillan boys played hard and rough and often required her professional medical attention.

Mary and Tommy waited to have kids. Two years to be exact. They had two boys and two girls. Tommy and Bobby started a business together and built homes and commercial buildings throughout the Flathead Valley. They were very successful. Mary was involved in her church and charities. She was a generous woman, just like her mother.

Carolina and Bobby had their two boys and two girls right away. It turns out Carolina and Bobby won the "newlywed bedroom competition." They all, like Mary and Tommy, lived at the Kootenai Lodge and raised the kids there. All eight kids loved playing together and made a lot of noise while having fun.

Mr. and Mrs. Kelley had so many grandchildren that they couldn't keep track. Every Christmas, the train would be sent out to Montana to bring them all back to New York and to the "big house." That's what Bumpa Kelley called it at Christmas. He joked that they were prisoners to all the kids and commotion.

Mr. Kelly died in 1955 surrounded by his daughters and Stephen. It was a peaceful ending to an amazing life. Mrs. Kelley lived another ten years, kept alive by her grandkids and their mischief.

Each daughter received a $10 million inheritance. Johnson was left a million dollars. He had retired and was back in Ireland. The shock almost killed him. Even Stephen was gifted $5 million. There was plenty more left over. Mrs. Kelley bought a lot of artwork once she had control of the purse strings. When she died, she bequeathed most of it to the usual museums in New York.

The Kootenai Lodge was finally sold. The asking price included the Russell painting over the fireplace. It was valued at $25,000 dollars, too much for the new buyer. It was kept by Stephen after the purchase price was reduced. The unsigned, unfinished Charlie Russel painting that was hung over the fireplace and below the gigantic elk mount was sold at auction fifty years later for $7 million.

Clara and Mackie were surprised to learn they were left a million dollars. The kids were grown now, so they packed up and moved to Montana. He was able to take an early retirement.

Christmas was shifted to Montana, and the remaining family got together every year, even after Mrs. Kelley passed on, along with the private rail car. Planes made it so much easier.

Whenever a family member returned to Montana, it always profoundly affected them. They couldn't pin it down because there were so many memories to roll through. Everyone had their own recollections and histories, and that made them all different. The one universal emotion is obvious when you come home to Montana. Left behind are the stresses and problems of the modern world and the speed it travels. You sleep throughout the night and, wake up later than usual and completely rested. The quiet of the Kootenai Lodge was stunning.

The history and the story of The Kootenai Lodge will live on in the upcoming sequel entitled --- Kootenai: The Restoration.

About the Author

JK Worth is a passionate storyteller who splits time between the majestic landscapes of Montana and the open waters of the Gulf of Mexico and the Atlantic Ocean. JK now enjoys life aboard the yacht, "Big Sky," cruising between Orange Beach, Alabama, the Florida Keys, and the Bahama Islands. With a deep appreciation for adventure and a rich imagination. JK channels these experiences into compelling narratives that captivate readers.

Inspiration strikes in the most unexpected places, and you can expect a boat themed novel in the future. Whether on land or sea, JK remains dedicated to crafting stories that explore the complexities of human nature.

JK Worth can be reached at: jkworthauthor@gmail.com and would love to hear from you.

JK's X account is: jk_worth